ABSOLUTION

LP LOVELL

STEVIE J. COLE

WARNING

The purpose of this story is to take you out of your comfort zone. There may be topics in this book you find repulsive or morally wrong-that is the intent. The main character comes from a religious cult, so please remember the religion within these pages is not a "real" religion. There are elements in this book some may term BDSM, but this is NOT BDSM. There is no respect, no safe word, there is no limit, please keep this in mind as we have a deep respect for people who practice that lifestyle. There are elements of abuse, violence, and explicit sex. If you are not okay with possibly being dragged out of your comfort zone, you may not want to read this book.

When you turn the page, you will be thrown into the mind of a psychopath. At times things may seem incoherent, and you will most likely feel overwhelmed...and that was the plan. Oh, and yes, the italics is Evie's chapters, that is her little demonic voice that talks to her.

PROLOGUE

The door to the kitchen creaks open, but I don't bother to turn around. "Evelyn," my father's voice is angry. "What have you done? You sinner!"

I turn up the temperature to the eye, watching the oil in the iron skillet pop and bubble. I'm not going to acknowledge him. *Evelyn, it's his fault too.* My inner voice whispers. *He wouldn't protect you. He's the one who said Zachariah is righteous.* Squeezing my eyes shut, I shake my head and will my little demon to quiet as my fingers grip the handle.

"Evelyn!" I turn to face him just in time to catch a backhand over my lips. Blood pours into my mouth. "Have you not learned your place? Nineteen years, and you're still a defiant little whore just like your mother was." His eyes burn with anger and resentment as he glares at me, his jaw twitching while he shakes the sting from his hand. *It's wrong, Evelyn. This is all wrong. Liars. Sinners. Blasphemers.* Shut up! *Do what's right. You need forgiveness.* Father grabs the nape of my neck and I flinch. "How can people follow me as their leader if my own daughter doesn't learn her place? You are a disgrace to the work of God, disgusting and wretched. You make men sin, and God hates you for it."

Without thought, I take the heavy skillet and swing it around. There's a loud crack when the pan meets the side of his face, and he falls back, his body making a loud thud when it hits the tile floor. Shock ripples through me as I watch the deep red liquid ooze from the gash in his forehead. I fall to my knees next to my father, the pan still in my hands. *He let Zachariah hurt you.* Lifting the skillet above my head, I use as much force as my weak frame can gather to hit him again. Blood splatters over the white tile. *He beat you.* I bash his skull again with the heavy pan. *He's made you a monster in the eyes of God.* It's no longer me that's bashing his head with the pan over and over. It's this demon that's been trying to claw its way out of me every day since I can remember. And for a moment everything fades to black. I can feel my arms dealing out blow after blow. I hear the gruesome cracking of bone, the wet sound of the skillet hitting his mangled face, but I'm disconnected.

Breathless, chest heaving, face coated in a mixture of tears and blood, I come back to the moment. I toss the pan to the side and scramble across the floor on my hands and knees as far away as I can get from the massacre in front me. I go to wipe my face but realize my hands are covered in blood. My heart is in my throat in a quivering lump. *Look what you've done, Evelyn. What a mess you've made all over the clean kitchen floor.*

"Forgive me for what I've done. Take away these sins..." I choke on a sob because murder is a sin, but I feel no guilt. "Forgive me for..." *Nothing. F*orgive you for nothing because this man allowed you to be hurt again and again. *Evelyn, he did that to cleanse you.*

My mind swirls through a kaleidoscope of memories, the reel violently stopping on one in particular.

I'm crying because Zachariah told me he'd kill me if I told anyone, but I'd rather die than keep taking his form of punishment. Pain is punishment, but what Zachariah does to me is far more than pain. Father glares at me. "You've sinned, Evelyn." He shakes his head in disapproval. "On your hands and knees." I tremble, but do as I'm told and submit to his demand as we've all been taught. I hear the old hinges of his closet door groan and I know what he's getting. This is not what I expected, I expected he would protect me, but I know better than to question him because that is yet another sin that I'll need to be cleansed from.

I BLOCK out the pain as the leather rips into my back. I ignore the shameful names my father calls me as he delves out my atonement. I've learned to accept this. I've been taught that this pain brings you closer to righteousness, that with each scar we are healed. We are imperfect, and our sins should marr our bodies as not to marr our souls. I think of my sins as he beats me and by the time he is through, I feel cleansed. I feel that my body is now broken so that my soul can heal, and I wonder if this is what it's like for the others my father calls blasphemers. I wonder if people who do nothing more than confess their sins can ever feel absolved, because surely there must be pain to be forgiven.

"Evelyn?"

I glance up to find my sister, Hannah, holding on to the door frame, her face white, her gaze locked on Father's lifeless body.

You're both saved now, Evelyn. Run. I swallow. I stand. My legs wobble from the fear still coursing through me. "We need to go, Hannah. God told me we should go."

1

EVIE

FOUR YEARS LATER

The large wooden door to the cathedral creaks open and I stumble into the darkness. I trace my fingertips over the wooden pews, guiding my way until I come to the altar and fall to my knees.

"Forgive me," I breathe, my voice catching in the back of my throat. My desperate whispers echo into the pitched ceilings and I wait for an answer I know will never come. "Forgive me Father for what I am about to do…" I bow my head and my chest tightens.

Confessing your sins, asking for forgiveness, I've still not grasped this concept. It never feels as though I'm forgiven. How can something as simple as asking for forgiveness absolve you from your sins? What penance is there if there is no pain? Clenching my fists, I rest my head against the step and listen to myself breathe. In. Out. In…

"Please take my beauty and use it as you will…" *Beauty is wicked, Evelyn.* The memory surfaces of my father beating me because a man called me beautiful. My nails claw at the carpet as I unwillingly become lost in that memory.

"Don't flinch!" he shouts at me. "Don't cry! You thank God for allowing you to be cleansed of your sin. You learn to love this pain because it is the only thing that keeps you clean!" The belt bites at my skin again and I hold my breath, forcing my back to remain rigid so it won't bow away from the pain. "Beauty is a mark of the devil, and despite that I've prayed over you for eighteen years, the devil still lives inside you. Just like he did your mother." Another loud crack sounds as the leather lands over my shoulder. "Pray, Evelyn," he says with such anger I fear he may beat me to death this time. "Pray where I can hear you."

I squeeze my eyes shut and exhale. "Dear Lord, please forgive me for my beauty--" CRACK. The sudden pain stops me mid sentence, but I hurry to continue my prayer. "Please, I don't want to be a temptation. I don't want to be a sinner."

"You are sin Evelyn. Not a sinner. You are the sin and you're going to have to pray much harder than that to be freed of your chains." WHACK.

"Forgive me!" I shout, pleading. "Forgive me for being sin, for being a creation of the devil. Forgive me for the sin I force upon others, I beg you--" CRACK. My fists clench around the wooden footboard of my bed. Tears roll down my cheeks and I want to weep, I want to sob, but I know if I do it will only make it worse. You need worse to be cleansed. *I suck back the tears. "Forgive me. Forgive me. Forgive me."*

The bells in the old cathedral toll, the deep boom tearing me from that nightmare. My heart sits in the back of my throat, pounding and forcing a thin sheen of sweat over my entire body. "Forgive me. Amen," I choke as I take in the silence surrounding me.

I push away from the altar and make my way down the aisle. The heavy door groans as I pull it open, and the ice-cold wind whips my hair around my face. Cinching my coat, I step onto the sidewalk and I am quickly swallowed by the bustling Manhatten crowds.

Several men walk past me, eyeing my body. Their eyes skate up my bare legs and I tug at the hem of my skirt. *If I weren't pretty, they'd leave me alone.* At one time, I prayed that God would take my beauty away from me, but I have learned to embrace it and see it as a tool. You see, beauty and sex are the most powerful weapons a woman can wield, and they can bring any man to his knees in a matter of seconds, leaving him begging and at your very mercy. And I want them at my mercy.

It's a short walk to Matthew's apartment, but I'm nearly frozen by the time I reach his building. I knock on the door and wait. A month ago, I was nothing but a whore to Matthew. After the first time I fucked him for money, I followed him for several weeks, watching him take home a different whore every night.

But I changed that.

I've spent the last few months pursuing him, making him want me, making him feel like he needs me. *Making him love me.* It's a lie. I am the last thing he needs. I am death dressed as his deepest desire: a weak woman. But I am not weak.

The door opens, and there stands Matthew, beer in hand and smiling. "Hey Matthew," I coo in a breathy, sex-laced tone as I step inside, closing the door behind me.

He grabs my hips and tugs my body to his as a sickening groan presses through his lips. His filthy little hands move to my ass and squeeze. "You're so hot." His mouth lays against my neck, his hot breath blowing over my skin when he whispers, "You smell like something I want to eat."

I swallow the acid burning up my throat, and I force myself to giggle. Honestly, I have it ingrained inside my soul to cringe when a man touches me. But sex is a means to an end. Something to make them vulnerable. And I learn all of their vulnerabilities.

He walks me back through the hallway to the bed, his hands groping clumsily at my body, clinging to my curves. I drop my purse to the floor when the back of my legs hit the mattress, and I fall onto the bed, batting my eyelashes at him as I curl one side of my lips into a seductive grin.

He bites at his bottom lip and rips his shirt over his head. I force my eyes to trail over his body. His stomach is hard, carved, his arms a perfect example of what a man should look like. It's a shame he's such a piece of shit. I drag my gaze down to his crotch, and there, it freezes. Men want to feel like they are being worshiped. I make him think I want him. I make him feel as though I want his filthy, dirty hands all over me.

"What I'm going to do to you..." he growls as he shoves my skirt up around my hips and yanks my thongs off, throwing them to the side of the room.

What I'm going to do to you.

What I want to do is make him beg for forgiveness as I slit his throat, but I've found over the years blood makes everything too messy. You learn the person, you learn ways they could die that no one will ever question, and this man right here--*forgive me Father*-- this man right here will OD with or without me. I know he has a drug problem. The first time I broke into his apartment, I found a plethora of high-end drugs spread out over the coffee table. All of his family and friends will just assume it's an overdose and bury him six feet under. Just as I'm thinking this, Matt pushes my thighs apart, and buries his face between my legs. I close my eyes and fight off the feeling of sin crawling all over me like insects. His mouth is wet and warm and filthy. I don't let myself enjoy this, but I play the part. I moan, I grab his hair and lace it between my fingers. I grind my hips over him, riding his face as I tell him to fuck me. I call out his name. I make him think he is a god, when he's nothing more than a wretched sinner.

Suddenly, his mouth is off of me, and he slides up next to me in the bed, pushing his pants down and freeing his hard dick.

I lean over him and place my lips inches from his. "Wait," I whisper as I grab his cock and squeeze. I want to squeeze it until the circulation cuts off, until the head of his dick engorges and goes numb, but I don't. I just imagine that scenario while I work my fist up and down his shaft.

"Wait? My dick's about to explode, Evelyn."

"Uh-uh." I reach for my purse at the foot of the bed and grab the pill bottle, dumping out a handful of tiny blue pills into my palm. I glance over them and quickly spot the one with an 'A' carved on it. I take that one, place it on the tip of my tongue, and swallow. I hold out my hand, smiling because I just took an Aspirin, but that's not what he's about to take.

He lifts an eyebrow and his gaze rises to mine. "What is it?"

"Poison," I laugh. "Oh, come on Matthew, it's roll. Don't tell me you don't do it? I know you do." Most men would know not to trust a whore, but then again, I'm not most whores...

"Fuck me, where have you been all my life, huh?" He laughs, pleased, and takes a single pill, places it on the tip of his tongue, then swallows. "Beautiful and dirty and knows how to have fun."

"Oh, just waiting on you, sweetheart. Just waiting on you…"

I take the rubber from the side table, tearing the foil with my teeth and rolling it down his hard-on. I straddle him and push myself down around his twitching erection. Fucking him like this makes me feel so dirty, but it is worth the end product. I will pray time and time again to be forgiven because surely God understands a man is at his weakest when he's buried inside a woman. I keep my eyes trained on Matthew's, watching intently as I ride him, slow at first, then faster and harder.

I stare down at him. I need one more thing from him before he dies. I need complete control of him. "Tell me you love me." His brow furrows, and I stop moving.

"What?" he asks.

"Tell me you love me."

"I mean..." he laughs, "what, are we role playing now?"

Heat spreads over my face. I don't have time for this. "Just do it. Tell me," I say, slowly grinding over his sick little dick.

"I love you, Evelyn," he says with an edge of sarcasm.

That demon inside of me wails because he doesn't. He is lying. He pretends he loves me, just like he pretended he loved the girl before me, and like he would pretend to love whoever came after me if this wasn't his last night on this earth. All men lie. He would never save me or protect me. I am a vessel for him to use and toss away, but no Matthew, no. Tonight I toss you away!

Ten minutes in, sweat is dripping between my breasts, and his breathing deepens. He grabs at the neck of my dress, pushing the material underneath my breasts. His eyes flutter, then pulse open. *He's fighting it, Evelyn.* He holds them wide open before they slam shut against his will. Tiny beads of sweat form on his forehead and roll down his temples. He keeps licking his lips, and I know it's because his mouth has gone dry. His hands drop from my chest to the bed, and I ride him harder.

"Look at me," I say, and his eyes groggily open. "Look at me."

"I don't…" his words slur, his eyes rolling around in his head like water circling a drain. "What did you. That. I…I don't …feel…"

I grind over him fast, hard, angry. I'm so angry because I'm *not* the sin. He is. And I'm taking this little piece of wrong out of the world. I'm doing good. His judgment has come and he is guilty. *And the wages of sin is death.*

I stop fucking him, straddling his stomach as I stare down at him. His face twists and morphs, and now all I can see beneath me is Zachariah. His dark hair, his blue eyes. The person who broke me time and time again. The man who made me his sin. The reason I murdered my father. The person who forced me and my little sister to run away. The person who forced God to choose me to carry out his will by killing men like him. Everytime I kill a man all I can see is Zachariah's face because I want nothing more than to kill him, and with each man like him, I do. I kill a tiny, miniscule piece of that evil that lives inside of me.

"This is what you deserve, Zachariah. You did this to yourself."

I watch Matthew gasp for breath, and life is a precious, precious thing, but watching evil as it's sucked out of this world like a vortex is a beautiful thing. He's no longer fighting death, he's embracing it. His eyes are closed and his chest is rising in ragged swells. I lay my head to his chest and listen to the sluggish sound of his heart fighting for each beat. I move off his stomach, lying next to him and grinning as I trace my finger over the indentation of his pecs. "Men like you deserve far worse than this, but if I took pleasure in this, well, that would be a sin wouldn't it?"

I lay there for another minute or so until the uneven thumping silences and his chest stops rising. I climb off the bed, pushing my skirt back down and straightening out my hair. His eyes finally fix on the ceiling in a glassy stare, his lips slightly parted. I take a few pills and scatter them on the bed. When the police come, they'll think it's a bad batch of drugs he got into. And in a way, it was...

I take a washcloth from the bathroom, pull the condom off, and wipe myself off of him, stuffing the damp rag into my purse. On my way out of his apartment, my eyes land on a Bible in the center of his bookshelf. I walk over, pull it from the shelf, and clutch it beneath my arms as I leave.

2

EZRA

T he belt makes a resounding crack when it meets her skin, and she screams, her back bowing. Her naked body is pressed flat against the heavy wood of the cross, and every time she flinches away from the pain, the leather restraints bite into her wrists.

"Take it, Maria!" I shout at her, cracking the belt against the back of her thigh this time. She screams and writhes desperately, submitting to her body's natural reaction.

What I do is psychological manipulation more than anything. I have to override her survival instinct. I have to make her want me, want to please me, want to take the pain. *But,* I still want her fear--her screams, her tears. I do not want her submission. Why? Because submission does not make me money. It's her fear my clients pay top-dollar for.

There's a market for everything, and the world is full of sick people. I just happen to be a man who exploits their fucked-up fantasies. It's all about supply and demand.

I can barely remember a time when I haven't needed this, thrived on it, wanted it.

Seamus, my father for all intents and purposes, said that everyone has their place in this world. There are those with power and those who serve the ones with power. And in order for me to evolve into what he wanted, he put me in a position of power, and I became sick with it. As I beat Maria, I think back to the first time I ever took a belt to a whore.

He places a belt in my hand and I stare at it as he points at the wooden door. "You are going to walk into that room. In there is a girl, restrained."

I swallow heavily.

"You're gonna to take that belt and hit her with it." He smiles, inhaling on his cigar.

I glance at it again, the light reflecting off the polished black leather. "Why?" I ask.

"You have a lot to learn son." A thick cloud of smoke puffs from his lips as he laughs. "Men like power. There are those who have it, and those who serve it. She..." He points once more at the door. "Is here to serve, and that service means fulfilling sick little fuckers' desires. You understand?"

"Why do I have to hit her?"

"Because she needs to be trained." His lips twist into a smirk as he strokes a hand over his short grey beard. He bends down and brings his face close to mine. "She needs to be broken. She needs to reach the pain barrier and be pushed over it. They never know how much pain they can take until they're pushed." He grabs my chin, forcing me to look into his hard eyes. "She will cry, and you will keep hitting her. You're too soft, Ezra. This is a test. Do not fail. Break. Her."

I want to please him. I do not want to fail, so I nod and turn away from him, pushing the door open. There, in the middle of the room, is a four poster bed. The girl is standing at the end of it, her back to me, both her wrists bound and tied to the two posts of the bed so that her arms are pulled up and out. Her red hair cascades around her shoulders, her naked body is pale, her skin perfect, completely unmarred. She keeps her head down because she's been told to. My eyes trace the curve of her back, her round arse, and I can't help the erection that starts pressing against my jeans. Her shoulders rise and fall rapidly with her accelerating breaths. She's terrified. I learned a long time ago that sympathy is weakness, and as I watch fear eat away at her I know I should feel something for her, but I don't. I feel nothing.

I feel nothing because she's a whore, this is her job. I will beat her and she will get paid for it. The feeling of nothingness is replaced by disgust, and I step up behind her, running the belt through my fingers.

I swing my arm back. The belt sails through the air with a satisfying whistle before it connects, cracking against her perfect skin. Her back bows and she yells, her knees buckling. A brilliant pink line blossoms across her back. I swing again and again, and then again. I keep hitting her, anger coursing through my body because she is a whore, a filthy whore, and she deserves this. She wants this. She will take this, because I hold the belt, I hold the power, and she...she is here to serve, to give pleasure, to be used. The more I hit her the more the scene morphs. She is no longer a girl I have never met, she is my mother, my dirty, good for nothing whore of a mother.

Pink skin turns red. Blood runs down her back, over her arse, until it trickles down the backs of her thighs. And the blood only spurs me on. I hit her until my arm is too tired to lift it anymore, and I fall to my knees on the floor.

The door swings open and Seamus walks in. He looks at the scene before him, his eyes tracing over the girls ruined body. She's uncon-

scious, hanging limply in the restraints. I'm breathing heavily and shaking as a thin sheen of sweat covers my brow.

He looks at me, his face a mask of indifference. "Lesson number one, you never ruin your merchandise, because without merchandise, you have no client, no money." He nods at the girl. "High end clients like to beat girls, but they don't want to see scars where another has already done it. Powerful men covet that which others cannot have. They will pay for that which looks innocent."

I learned my lesson. Never mark the girls.

Maria's beautiful sobs yank me back to the present. Her body hangs limp in the cuffs, and I clench my fist around the belt.

"Stand up!" I shout. I deliberately leave the cuffs loose so the girls are forced to hold themselves up. This is not about the pain, this is about *enduring* the pain, fighting the instinct to let the pain consume. Her legs tremble as she struggles to stand on them.

"Pain is in the mind, Maria! Endure it. Fight it." CRACK. "Master it." I watch her hands wrap around the chains of the cuffs as she steals herself. I smile at her perseverance and hit her again. She doesn't flinch away from it this time. She embraces it.

I drop the belt to the ground and approach her, staring at the angry red marks covering her back. Those rising welts are beautiful. Her body heaves with sobs as she leans her forehead against the cross. I wrap an arm around her waist.

"Good, Maria." I glide my hand up to her tit, pinching her nipple as I nip her shoulder. She shivers, but otherwise makes no move. I sweep my hand up to her neck, slowly winding my fingers around her throat, applying only a small amount of pressure. Her breath hitches, her pulse quickening under my fingers. I slide my free hand down her toned stomach and between her legs. "Spread," I say with a growl. She does so without hesitation, and I slam two fingers inside her wet pussy. A strangled gasp leaves her lips as she clenches around me. "See, you're wet, Maria. You secretly want to be beaten, to be forced to endure this." She groans as I pull my fingers out and thrust back inside. "You want to be owned."

I fuck her with my hand, all the time tightening my hold on her throat. I feel her panic for a moment when my hold becomes tight enough to restrict her air. "Embrace. It." I demand.

Her body shakes, her pussy gripping my fingers as she gasps for air. "Don't fight," I tighten my grip further and she relaxes, submitting to my hold. "Good." I rub my thumb over her clit, and her body tightens. Her head falls back the second I squeeze her throat with enough force to choke her. Her back arches, forcing her arse against my cock. Moaning breathlessly, she comes hard. When her body goes limp, I release her and step away. I pull a tissue from my pocket and wipe my fingers clean as I study the way she hangs in the restraints. Her head is rolled to one side and resting against her arm. It's beautiful when they give into it. I leave her in the room, breathless and beaten, still hanging from the cross. One of my guys will show her out.

When I step out of the room, I find Jonty right outside the door, his enormous frame leant against the wall, smoking a cigarette. Dave, my doberman sits at his feet, waiting patiently. Jonty is my best friend, my brother in many ways.

We grew up together, both of us raised to be ruthlessly efficient, to prioritise the business and the family at all times. I flourished in a world where brutality and cold calculation were valued, but Jonty has always fought with his own morals. Jonty runs the club with me, but he gets attached to the girls, see's them as people.

They are business assets, nothing more.

"What's up?" I ask.

He inhales a lungful of smoke and holds it for a second before he speaks. "Soph's dead, Ez." He rubs the back of his neck, keeping his gaze fixed on the floor.

"How?"

His eyes lock with mine. "Zee."

"Motherfucker!" I walk past him, heading to the office.

Jonty follows me down the hallway and shuts the office door behind us. Dave assumes his position, laying down under my desk. I clench my fist as I brace myself against the desk. I'm trying really damn hard not to lose my shit. I need to keep calm. I need to think.

"How?" my voice snaps.

"Cindy found her body down by the river outside of their flats. She called the cops, then called me. She said Soph had been badly beaten, covered in cuts. Probably bled out the way Cindy made it sound."

"And you know it was definitely him?"

"She said Soph never came back after her appointment." He shrugs and swallows heavily. "You know how it is. Sometimes they take it too far."

We handle two operations outside of the club itself. We run whores from the club that work the street. We protect them and they cut us in. Simple. Then we run elite 'escorts', expensive whores, trained whores that cater to the less civilised clientele. Sophie was one of the elite, and she was one of my best girls. *The* best. That girl had no limit, no threshold. She could take everything and then some. She's booked up solid for the next three months, putting me out of pocket by over sixty grand. And Zee is going to pay for it one way or another.

"You find him and you bring him to me!"

Jonty stares at me for a second. "Ez, he's a client..."

"He just cost me fucking money. You bring him to me, Jonty if you have to shoot his knee caps off to do it."

A small smile pulls at his lips and he leaves the room.

———

ZEE SITS ACROSS FROM ME, his ankle propped on his knee and his arms folded across his chest as though he hasn't got a care in the world. I'm keeping a firm hold on my temper, but his lack of concern for his own wellbeing in my presence pisses me off.

"I should put a fucking bullet in your head," I say with a slight growl, stubbing out my cigarette in the ashtray.

"What do you want me to say, Ez?" Zee shrugs and a twisted smile forms over his lips. "She wouldn't scream."

"Fuck!" I push up from my desk and pace. This is a shitstorm, and I'm going to get the blow back. Whores is one thing, but *dead* whores... that's a damn headache, not to mention a blow to my profits.

"We're done," I tell him.

"No, Ezra," he laughs, "*we* are not done."

I pull my suit jacket open, making sure he sees the Colt 45 holstered to my chest. "We. Are. Done. Now get out." He still doesn't move and I pull the gun, releasing the safety and pointing it at his head.

"Oh, you don't want to do that." He's too calm. People have different reactions when a gun is pointed at their head, some panic, some beg, and a few will even get angry, but they are never calm. "You see," he says, his thing lips curling into a smile. "You kill me and your entire world goes to shit."

I lower the gun an inch, glaring at him. "You have two minutes, and then I shoot you."

"Victor Moorcroft," he says with a smirk. I freeze, my pulse rising.

Victor Moorcroft, the British politician who was shot outside his home in London. By me. He was dirty, his pockets overflowing with mob money, family money. Money we paid to ensure that certain bills would pass, and laws not apply to us. He wasn't the first to turn dirty, and he sure as shit won't be the last. Moorcroft was the first high profile politician we worked with, and he made the mistake of thinking that his position gave him more power than the family. No one has more power than the mob. Seamus took me in and raised me as his own when I had no one else, and that is why I didn't question it when he chose me to take Moorcroft down. I did what had to be done, and then I was forced to run. Seamus has my absolute loyalty, which means I would do it again in a heartbeat, but equally, I don't fancy spending the rest of my life behind bars. How does this little shit know anything about Moorcroft?

"Bullshit," I say.

Zee sighs, pushing his hand into his pocket, and pulling out a small MP3 player. He hits play and my own voice fills the room.

"Moorcroft is dead." There's a pause and then a loud exhale.

"Confirmed kill?" Seamus' course Irish accent comes over the recording.

"Yeah."

"Good." I hear a drawer open and close. *"I don't know what Moorcroft put in place, but he will have something. He's not stupid. Here's a passport, and your plane ticket. Go to New York. Run the club, and lay low until I tell ya otherwise. I don't need ya gettin' arrested."*

Zee presses the button and the recording cuts off. My finger twitches on the trigger. I remember having that conversation in Seamus' office, so either Seamus sold me out, or someone planted a wire. Seamus would never sell me out. I know he wouldn't.

"You kill me and I have people ready to send this straight to MI5." Zee grins. *Shit!*

"What do you want?" I say through gritted teeth.

His smile widens and I want to slice it to his ears. "Well..." He clasps his hands together in front of him. "You know I work in the sex business."

I know he sells girls from Mexico. I don't necessarily agree with it, but it's not as though I expect my clients to be the most upstanding individuals. I've wondered before why he would pay such high prices for my girls when he has his own, but then I guess rape must get boring after a while.

Zee's beady eyes narrow. "As you've probably guessed I have an acquaintances who informed me of Seamus' little operation. That's why I started using your girls. I wanted to see for myself exactly what you're doing. And I have to say," his eyebrows arch, "you don't disappoint. I've fucked your girls, Ezra. I've beat them until they should be ruined, and yes, they scream and they cry, but low and behold, the next week, there they are. Subservient, willing." His eyes flash with excitement. "Do you know what someone would pay for a slave like that?"

"My girls are whores. They are *paid* and they *choose* to do this. They are not slaves," I growl. That is my line. None of these girls are here against their will. They are paid well. What their motivations are for being here are--I don't care. It's not my problem.

"But they could be slaves," he purrs. "Millions. They are worth millions."

"They are not for sale."

"So train my girls." He shrugs. "No one produces girls quite like you do. They're so resilient, yet so very fragile." He closes his eyes, shaking his head. "It's an art form, it really is. Come into business with me. I'll make you more money than the mob ever has."

"Yeah, spare me your professional courtesy. I'm not for sale either. So either turn me in or get out of my office."

"I don't want to turn you in, Ezra. You're much more useful to me here than behind bars. This," he waves the device at me, "is simply insurance, to ensure you don't kill me. You'll forgive me for not trusting your reputation, but you are a business man, and I'm sure you can see the merit of working with me." He claps his hands together. "Anyway, I'm going to leave you to think about this little opportunity."

"I don't need to think about it." I raise the gun again.

He narrows his eyes. "I like you, Ezra, but do not push me. I can, and will, take everything from you if I have to." His face slips back into a smile. "I'll be in touch." He stands and leaves, my gun fixed on the back of his head the entire time.

"Fuck!" I launch a bottle of whiskey off my desk, smashing it against the wall. Jonty is still standing beside the door with a scowl etched onto his face. "Get me Seamus on the phone."

3

EVIE

It's half past eight by the time I reach my apartment. My cheeks are on fire from the heavy winter wind whipping between the buildings, and my fingers have grown numb from the cold. I clumsily fumble with my keys as I round the corner, stopping dead in my tracks when I see two police officers standing outside my apartment door. My heart holds back several beats before going into a full-on sprint. I tell my feet to move, but they betray me and remain firmly planted on the floor. *They've come for you, Evelyn.* Flashbacks of all the men I've rid this world of dance through my mind. These police will never understand that what I did was justified. My hands shake from fear, causing my keys to jingle. The noise catches their attention and they turn around. I swallow. I tell myself to breathe. I force myself to smile because I look innocent. I do.

You look like a whore. Like a dirty little sinner. They will see that, Evelyn.

I inhale just as one officer flashes his badge. "I'm Lieutenant Prescott. This is officer Keith. Are you Evelyn Wright?"

I try to judge the expression on his face because it's not anger. It's not one of accusation. And my heart sinks to the pit of my sinful little stomach. Swallowing, I wet my dry mouth so I can form words. "Yes," I whisper.

"We need you to come down to the station with us."

"Why?" All I hear is the loud pounding of my heart.

"Is your sister Hannah Wright?"

I nod slowly, and his expressionless face becomes full of sympathy. "I'm sorry, Miss Wright" he steps closer to me and places a hand on my shoulder, "but we believe Hannah is dead." It feels like a rusted knife has been jabbed into my chest. I can't breathe. I can't move. "I'm so sorry," he says, his hand still on my shoulder. "Due to circumstances surrounding the death, we need you to come and identify the body."

A coldness jolts down my spine and my body shakes. I nod and the officer moves his hand to the middle of my back, guiding me back onto the street.

I know she is dead. I feel it.

***********BREAK***********

I never believed they really had family members come into a morgue to identify a body. I thought that was only used for dramatic effect in crime shows and movies. But here I stand, staring at that black, zip-up bag. Officer Prescott stands beside me, one hand on my shoulder as the coroner unzips the bag. Her skin is grey and wet, her dark hair matted to her head, her glassy eyes fixed toward the heavens. I only look for a moment before my eyes slam shut. Bile rises in my throat and I swallow time and time again to force it away.

I step toward the metal table. The officer follows behind me, afraid I'm going to hit the concrete floor at any moment. Little does he know I've probably seen more dead bodies than he has, but this...this effects me in ways none of those other bodies could. This lifeless mound of flesh is my sister's. Those lips have shared secrets with me, those arms have comforted me. She is the only other person who understands the hell I've lived through. She lived through it, she escaped it with me, and now she is gone. The only person I have ever loved. The only person who cares-- cared for me. Tears swim in my eyes as another lump of acid burns up my throat. I stare at her, everything blurring as memories flood my mind.

Hannah clings to me, her entire frame shaking as she cries.

"It's okay," I whisper.

"He's going to hurt me." Her fingers dig into my arm and I wince.

"It will be okay. You have to let him hurt you so you can be forgiven."

His footsteps are right outside of the closet, and we both freeze. We know we must be beaten to be freed from our sins, but we still fear the pain, the punishment.

"Please don't let him hurt me, Evelyn. Please." She cries, burying her face into my neck, her wet tears rolling down my throat.

The door yanks open and Zachariah stands with a long rod in his hand. "Hannah, come."

She holds so tight to me I can't breathe.

I look at him, swallowing before I speak. "Let me take her punishment." I feel her grip on me tighten. "Zachariah. Punish me. Let me bear her sins."

A deep smile twists over his face as he reaches for me and jerks me to my feet with Hannah still clinging to my side. "As you wish," he says. And the punishment I receive for that is nearly unbearable, and to punish Hannah, he makes her watch.

I step closer and notice gash marks along Hannah's collarbone. Tiny cuts, long cuts, criss-cross patterns. I can't ignore the bloody mess they're trying to keep covered. Before anyone can stop me, I grab onto the bag, ripping the zipper open farther. The officer grabs me, the coroner rushes to zip the bag closed, but they are too late. I lean over my knees, bile spewing from my mouth and splattering onto the officers shiny black shoes.

I close my eyes. I scream. I attempt to shake that image from my mind, but I'm afraid it has been forever etched into my memory. I don't know that I will ever be able to think of my sister again without seeing her mutilated body, every inch of her covered in knife wounds. My heart sinks to the pit of my stomach. Part of me feels responsible. I was the first one to realize posing as a whore gave me easy access to filthy men. I was the one who killed the first man and realized that I could rid the world of sinners, that I could protect other women from men like Zachariah. And I told her. I prayed with her about it. I went with her the first time she killed a man. She wanted to help me do this work. Had I never told her, she wouldn't be dead right now.

No, Evelyn. It was a job that had to be done. Her purpose was fulfilled, and you must carry on until you fulfill your purpose.

She was all I had.

*****break******

"Forgive me for the thoughts I cannot control..." my voice catches in the back of my throat. All I want to do is crawl into one of the wooden pews and cry. I want to mourn the loss of my sister. I have no one to confide in, no one to trust. I have no one to help me carry out this work now. *Evelyn, you have work to do. Nothing can come between you and the work you must do.* I lay down on the steps of the alter, scratching my nails over the rough carpet. My mind becomes a cyclical pattern of guilt and despair and fear. "Forgive Hannah." The image of her mutilated body pops to mind, and I only hope that the beating she took before she drew her last breath was enough to cleanse her from her sins. "...enable me to forgive those who have treated me poorly in the past..."

I notice I'm sweating and inhale, pushing myself up from the floor. I don't want to forgive them which means I am lying. Lying is a sin.

"…help me be an instrument..." I open my eyes, my hands still clasped tightly together. "Please let me find the man who hurt my sister so I can kill him. Amen."

I leave the church, taking the subway to the side of town club Sin is on. That club was where my sister worked. She found the men she killed there, but the person she wanted to kill more than anyone else was her pimp, Ezra James. She said he was the devil.

I shift my legs and the cold fiberglass seat touches my skin. I sit, losing myself in my grief until the train screeches to a stop at the next exit. Grabbing my belongings, I rush out of the doors and hurry up the stairs, the chill in the wind biting at my bare skin when I exit the station. Garbage litters the sidewalk. Everywhere I look I see broken beer bottles, used condoms, needles. There's a homeless man slumped against a doorway to an abandoned shop, dead or drunk, I don't know, but no one pays him any attention as they go about their evening. Turning the corner, I focus my attention on the neon light flashing "Sin" into the dark sky. It's like a beacon.

"Fucking whore!" I hear a man growl from the alleyway, then I hear a loud bang followed by a shrill scream. "You are worthless. Fifty bucks and you can't even get my goddamn dick hard." A loud smack bounces from the brickwork. I turn to my left and see a man looming over a woman who is on her knees in front of him. She's holding her face where he hit her. *Kill him! He could have done the same thing to Hannah. He would do the same thing to you, Evelyn.* I walk away, my heels clicking over the pavement as I will that voice to quiet. *Kill him. Kill that worthless little sinner. Take his life.*

I shake my head as I whisper to that little demon, "It's not planned. It's a sin." It must be planned, or it's a sin.

It was a sin to allow your sister to defile her body like that. You are a walking sin right now, lok at your short skirt! Kill him.

But I must plan this out. It has to be precise. He has to be forgiven. I must have control...

The shouting continues to boom down the alleyway and I stop, leaning against the tinted window of Sin. I can feel the bass from inside rumble through the pane, and I attempt to focus on that, but the moment I see the woman run past me, her lip bleeding and her eye swelling, my control slips. That demon screeches, clawing its way up my chest. The man follows shortly behind her and his gaze drags over my body, coating me in a slimy film of sin. He opens the door to the club, and the song "Highway to Hell" pours out from inside. And I know what I must do.

My heart clangs against my ribs as I follow him inside. It's dark and crowded. The entire place reeks of sweat and sex. The dance floor is littered with sinners, and I scan each face for that man from the alleyway. I find him at the bar slamming back a drink. Swallowing, I press my shoulders back and sway my hips as I approach the counter. I squeeze myself between him and the overweight man beside him. The man glances down at me, a smirk playing over his disgusting, thin lips. "Aren't you a pretty little thing?" he slurs before guzzling half a mug of beer.

I bat my eyelashes and fuck him with my eyes as I bite down on my bottom lip. I pop the top to the poison ring on my right hand before I swipe his drink.

"May I?" I purr, and he nods.

I take a quick swig, and tilt my hand over the top of his glass. My eyes remain locked on his to ensure he doesn't notice the white powder now dissolving in his drink. I will kill him because he's a bad man. I will kill him because he sins. And since this wasn't planned, I will beg for forgiveness later. I need this to mourn Hannah, and he needs to see how wicked beauty really is.

4

EZRA

We walk back to the club, Jonty whistling "Knocking on Heaven's Door" the entire time. He's a big bastard, six and a half feet tall, with a long scar across one cheek, a reminder that the Russian mafia are nasty little bastards. Some people cross the street in a bid to get away from us as we walk toward them, whilst others all but press themselves into the side of buildings as we pass. Jonty and I seem to have developed a reputation around here.

A woman stands beneath one of the street lamps, puffing on a cigarette. My gaze skims over her long, bare legs exposed by leather hot pants. Smoke billows around her face, and her blonde hair hangs down her back in waves. She turns at our approach and flashes Jonty a sensual smile. Mel. She's one of my best earners on the streets, but she's also fucking Jonty. He's a scary bastard, but women...they can't get enough of him. Must be the dark and dangerous thing. She takes one step forward before I stop her.

"Get back to work, Mel." I snap the order at her without stopping. She scowls at me, but doesn't argue.

"Harsh," Jonty quips.

"You using her pussy doesn't earn me money, but that guy..." I point to the scummy man making his way across the street to her, a perverse grin on his face. "When he puts his dick in her, I make money. You see how that works?"

"Whatever," Jonty grumbles. "You're a cock block, Ez."

"I just hope you triple bag that shit, mate."

"Look, just because you surround yourself with pussy, yet somehow have this unholy restraint, don't judge the rest of us mere mortals."

"They're hookers, Jonty."

He grins. "*Hot* hookers."

"No one wants to fuck ugly girls."

"Amen to that." He chuckles, and then goes back to whistling.

We're almost right outside Sin when I hear a muffled noise from the alleyway to our left. We both glance into the dark side street. I listen for it again. There's a low groan and a 'fuck yeah', followed by 'suck me'.

Damn whores doing their shit on the street. How many times do I have to tell them? Take the clients upstairs or to the bloody hotel across the road. They're gonna have the cops on my arse. I signal Jonty to wait for me, and he rolls his eyes, pulling out a cigarette and leaning against the wall at the mouth of the alley.

A low moan comes from behind the dumpster. I round it, expecting to see SJ fucking the shit out of some guy because never has a girl been more suited to spreading her legs for a living. I'm constantly bollocking her for blowing some John in the toilets at the club, or in an alleyway.

The dim street light casts enough light that I can tell this girl isn't SJ, but whoever she is, she's on her knees in front of a guy I recognise as one of the Johns. His head is thrown back against the wall, his hands in her hair. He thrusts into her face and she moans as if she's loving every second of it. Anyone else would walk away, but sex is how I make my living and this shit is bad for business. His groans suddenly silence and his hands tighten in her hair as he hisses, "What the fuck?"

He yanks her away and shoves her to the side. She falls, sprawling out across the pavement, laughing under her breath. I guess she bites. He staggers a few steps before leaning against the wall. She stands up and watches as the guy slowly slumps down the wall. Her heels echo off the walls as she makes her way toward him and drops to a crouch, her black dress riding up her toned thighs. She whispers something into his ear and his eyes pop wide, before his labored breaths stop, and a deafening silence rings through the dirty alleyway.

"Damn, that must have been some blow job," I say, clapping my hands.

She gasps, standing and whirling around to face me. Her eyes are wide, and for a second I'm pretty sure she's going to bolt, but instead she pushes her shoulders back, steeling herself.

"He took something. He's just passed out." She lies easily, and I almost want to laugh because if she's going to lie she really should work on her acting skills. She attempts to brush past me, her high heels clicking against the concrete.

Sighing, I reach out, wrapping a hand around her small arm. "Firstly, he's dead." I glance at the body on the ground before looking at her. Now that I can see her properly I see just how beautiful she is. Stunning. If I died with those lips wrapped around my dick, I'd die a happy man. She looks like a porcelain doll with dark hair and pale skin, and eyes so big and blue they almost don't look real. The show stopper though is those lips, which even after just blowing some guy are still flawlessly painted in slut red lipstick. Here eyes lock with mine, watching me check her out.

She's completely calm, unphased. If a guy just overdosed and dropped dead at her feet, she should be phased, which means she was expecting it. I shouldn't find that shit hot. I should find it disturbing, but my rock hard dick is proof of just how fucked up I am. She tries to move past me again, and I sigh as I grab her jaw, pulling her face towards mine. I catch the light glint from a small silver cru-cifix hung around her delicate neck, and I smirk. "Sec-ondly, you're on my turf sweetheart, and dead or not, if you're blowing him it means my girls aren't. So indi-rectly, you're taking money out of my pocket."

"Some guys don't want to pay for it. And last time I checked this alley was the property of New York City, not whoever the hell you are." Her voice is shaking. She's trying to mask her fear, and it makes me smile.

I jerk her forward, yanking her body against mine. "A whore that doesn't charge? Well now that's just tragic, sweetheart. I know men who would pay a pretty penny for you." She glares at me, her eyes spitting fire. I do love a fighter. "As for New York City...I own these streets. I run these streets. You want to test me on that?" I let go of her and step back, spreading my arms wide. "Be my guest."

"Are you threatening me?"

I laugh and move back into her personal space, leaning down to whisper in her ear. "I don't threaten. Ever. If you knew who I was little girl, you would have run the second you saw me." Her breath hitches and her body goes rigid. Skimming my nose along her throat, I inhale the scent of her perfume. "Now, you just killed one of my clients, who incidentally, really did like to pay. This pisses me off--"

"I didn't kill him, go check his pulse," she interrupts me.

I keep a good hold around her waist, smirking as I pull the gun from the back of my jeans. "Really?" I aim at the slumped body and empty the clip into him. She thrashes in my hold, screaming, but her cries are drowned out by the gunshots echoing off the walls of the alleyway. "Now he's dead." I wink at her.

That confident air she carried a few seconds ago vanishes. Her face goes white, her lips trembling. "Please, let me go..." she begs.

I cock an eyebrow at her and laugh. "Oh, *now* you want to go."

She starts screaming again, looking around desperately for help that will never come. Damn, the woman sounds like a banshee. I place the barrel of the gun under her chin, pushing until she tilts her head back, and slams her lips shut.

"That's *really* fucking annoying," I say through gritted teeth. "Now, if you scream, no one will come. Same as no one came when I put six bullets in your friend there." She's shaking, gasping for air likes she's hyperventilating. "I told you, I own these streets and everyone on them, so do me a favour and shut up."

Those doll like features make her look so innocent, and even though she's clearly a whore, I really want to fuck every last shred of innocence out of her.

I drag my fingers over her trembling lips. Now her lipstick is smudged all over her face. I pull her body closer to mine, then grab onto the back of her neck, digging my fingers into her warm skin. She whimpers as her eyes slam shut.

"Now you and I need to have a little chat." She shakes her head silently, trying to rip free of my grip. I sigh and again tighten my grip on her. "We can do this the easy way or the hard way." I drag my eyes over those long legs of hers showcased by her short, tight dress. "I'm sure my customers would appreciate the view if I have to throw you over my shoulder."

She drops her gaze to the ground, and her shoulders sag in defeat. I let go of her neck, and pull out my phone to call the cleaners. "Pick up. The alley beside Sin." I hang up, and put the phone back in my pocket. I grab a couple of bags full of rubbish and throw them over the body to hide it before leading her back into the club.

I PUSH THE DOOR SHUT. When I turn around, I catch Dave trying to shove his nose up her skirt. She's frozen, not moving a muscle, her eyes locked on the dog.

"Sit." I gesture to the seat and she obliges whilst chewing her bottom lip. Dave sits down next to her and proceeds to stare at her like a creeper.

"Why am I here?" She glances nervously at him. "What do you want?"

I laugh. "What do you think I want, sweetheart?"

Her gaze falls to her lap and she nervously picks at her nails. She looks like she's going to cry at any moment. My dick twitches at the thought of breaking her, making her cry for me. And it shouldn't because she's a whore.

I lean back in my chair, allowing my eyes to roam over her petite yet curvy frame. "You're a whore," I state. She narrows her eyes, but doesn't argue with me. "A whore who kills her clients...*my* clients more specifically."

"I didn't kill him," she whispers, and her eyes slowly rise to meet mine. "You shot him."

I chuckle. "You and I both know he was already dead." I tilt my head to the side and study her. "Honestly, I don't care. Just don't do it again. That shit's a ball ache to clean up." I lean back in my chair and prop my ankle on my knee, watching her. She looks like a lamb ready for slaughter.

She frowns, her full lips pursing together. "Why did you bring me here then?"

"I'm willing to offer you a deal, but," I smile wryly,"and this is a very big but...I need to know that you aren't some kamikaze whore out to chop off dicks and shit. It's bad for business," I shrug a shoulder. I don't think I even care if she is. There's something about her. Hell, maybe I'm just trying to justify the fact that she makes my dick hard.

She flinches and glances down at her lap with wide eyes. I follow her gaze to where Dave's head is now resting on her bare thigh. Her fingers grip the arm of the chair hard enough to turn her knuckles white.

"Really?" Some guard dog he is. The second a pretty girl walks through the door and he's all over it. "Dave," I call him. She relaxes as soon as he drags himself away.

"I run Sin." I wave dismissively around the room. "And the hookers you see around here, they work for me in a capacity. They cut me in, and I in turn protect them. All the clients around here know the consequences of crossing the line. Me." I smile easily.

"Who are you?"

"Ezra. And you are?"

She lifts her gaze to mine. "Evelyn," she breathes.

I drum my fingers over the desk. "Tell me, *Evie--*"

"Evelyn..." she corrects quickly.

I fight the smile trying to make its way onto my face. "See, that makes you sound like my grandmother, God rest her soul. And well..." I drag my eyes over every single curve of her body, letting them rest on her perky tits. "You, sweetheart, are nothing like grandma."

Her eyes go straight back down to her lap and she blushes like the sweet, innocent little thing she appears to be, but we both know better, and I can't work her out.

"Are you offering me a job?" she asks, a slight tremor in her voice.

Her eyes meet mine again and her lips part, flashing perfect white teeth. Everything about her makes me want to take the belt to her until she begs and cries. The timid tone of her voice makes me want to draw blood, to watch it run down her perfect curves. My cock stiffens painfully and I shift in my seat.

"I think I might have a job for you..." I lean back in the chair, and her eyes follow my every move. I know this is a bad idea. This girl is unpredictable, a risk if ever I saw one. Realistically, I can't trust her with clients, but I want to watch her skin flush crimson. I want to see how beautiful she looks when she cries. She's terrified of me, and I want her fear, every last scrap of it. I want her to scream and cry as the monster I am takes everything from her. I clear my throat and do something stupid. "It's five grand a night, no questions asked, no limitations."

Those fuck-me-bright blue eyes of hers narrow on me and there's a long silent pause. She bites her lip and nods slowly. "Okay." She has no idea what she's just agreed to.

I arch an eyebrow. "So you're not even slightly curious as to what you'd actually have to do for five grand a night?"

"No." She smiles, those red lips of hers just begging to suck my dick.

"There are three stages you must pass in order to work. Call it an interview if you like." I lean forward slightly. "You want the job? Phase one starts right now." I stand and walk to the door, pulling it open. Never have I been so excited at the thought of taking the belt to a girl.

She rises. Inhaling, she walks towards me, her shoulders hunched, her eyes aimed at the floor. She looks like she's being marched to the gallows, and in some ways, she is. Damn, some of my clients would pay a fortune for her. I turn and walk down the hallway, the sound of her heels clicking behind me. I go through the same routine I always do. I unlock the door and close it behind her, waiting in the darkness for a moment, allowing her anticipation to build before I flip on the lights.

I watch for her reaction as the enormous wooden cross against the far wall illuminates. Her eyes pop wide for a second but she quickly recovers. She glances away from me, reaching for the silver cross at her neck. Curious, a religious whore.

"Sweating like a whore in church, sweetheart?" I laugh.

"I'd hardly call this a church," she mumbles.

"Ah, but there is a cross."

She swallows and I hear her breath hitch slightly. She's uncomfortable. Well, this could be interesting. "Strip."

She drops her gaze to the floor, her shoulders stiffening. "Do you want me to have sex with you? Is that phase one?"

I snort. "I don't fuck whores." I don't want to fuck her. I want to hurt her *and then* fuck her, whore or not.

Her jaw clenches and she closes her eyes as she reaches behind her, slowly unzipping her dress. The material falls around her ankles and she removes her bra and underwear, standing in nothing but her patent leather red heels. "Should I take my shoes off as well?" she asks.

"No." I keep my voice level, calm, controlled. I keep my distance. This is strategic. Everything is done for a reason. I never touch them until they're tied up.

My eyes trace over the curve of her waist, the flare of her hip, her perfect arse leading to long legs that drop into those fuck me heels. And her skin, her beautiful skin is so pale she almost looks unreal. I narrow my eyes on a scar, running in a perfect line down her spine and disappearing beneath her thick hair. I step forward and scoop her hair to the side. She flinches when my fingers brush her skin, but she makes no other movements. She doesn't even look at me. Now that her hair is pushed to the side, I see that the scar reaches the base of her neck, and there's another line spanning her shoulder blades. *A cross.* She has a cross carved into her skin. The black hair, the pale skin...if it were anywhere else I would think this was some weird religious emo shit. But, well, you can't carve your own back And that scar is a deal breaker. There is one thing I promise my clients, and that is perfection. Anything less will tarnish my reputation of supplying elite merchandise. In a strange way, the scar adds to her mystery, but I can't use her. I should tell her that, let her walk away, but I don't. I don't say a word, because I want this. This is no longer business because I just made it personal. I close my eyes and inhale her sweet scent.

"Go to the cross," I tell her. "Stand in front of it, face the wall. And do *not* look at me."

She nods silently and does as instructed. I watch her arse as she walks away from me and I smile. Her gaze remains fixed on the wall when she stops in front of the cross. Excitement mounts in my chest as I step up behind her, standing close enough to feel the heat from her body. Her breaths are staggered, her shoulders tight.

"Are you scared of me, Evie?" I smile.

Her head slowly twists to the side, her eyes glancing back at me. "No," she whispers, holding her gaze with mine. I should punish her for looking at me, but I don't because I like what I see in her wide eyes. Fear. It's evident in the subtle tremble of her voice, in her erratic breaths. And damn, how much harder can my dick get?

She gasps as I press my body against hers, and slam her against the heavy wood of the cross. "You will be, little killer," I promise against her ear. I skim my fingers over the skin at her waist as I move toward her shoulder and then trail down her arm. Her breathing accelerates, and I can see her pulse beating rapidly at her throat. I wrap my fingers around her wrist and pull it up, raising her arm and securing it within the leather cuff. I repeat the process with her other wrist, and loosen the cuffs, leaving her to stand easily. Sweeping the hair off her neck, I gently brush my lips over her exposed skin. "I have a feeling you're going to be a strong one," I whisper against her ear. These are the words I tell every single one of them. Why? Because it makes them want to be strong. It makes them want to please me. And why would they want to please a guy they don't even know? Because I'm good at what I do. With only a few strategically placed touches, I can make her feel connected to me. Really, it's a gift.

The thought of watching her skin turn pink, of listening to her cry and beg causes my cock to press against my fly. I grab her hips and yank her arse back against my erection. "Do not turn around. Do not try to look at me again," I say. She keeps her eyes fixed on the wall, steeling herself, pretending she's not afraid even though I can practically hear her thrumming heartbeat. That sound is like music to my ears, but I don't want brave faces. I want tears. I want screams.

I grab a handful of her hair and yank her head back. "I'm going to hurt you, sweetheart." I skim my teeth over the soft skin of her throat. "You will beg me to stop, but I won't." I twist her hair and knot it into a messy bun, and she trembles violently at that touch. I place a soft kiss against her jaw, trailing my finger over her scarred back before I turn away.

I unbuckle my belt and drag it through the loops. "You will cry for me, Evie," I say quietly before swinging the belt at her back. The second the leather makes contact with her skin I almost groan. This isn't BDSM or any of that prissy shit. There are no rules, no safe words. I do not want her willing submission. I want to drag it from her, screaming and crying. I want ultimate power over her, and while she's here in this room with me, I want to own her, body and soul.

As the belt bites Evie's back, she doesn't flinch, she doesn't make a sound. I strike her harder, and again she doesn't move a muscle. I clench my jaw as I strike her with more force, right on the border of drawing blood. Nothing. The part of me that craves power roars at me to break her even if I have to bleed her dry to do it.

5

EVIE

"You will beg me to stop, but I won't," he growls against my neck. His coarsely sophisticated British accent makes the threat somewhat beautiful. I try to breathe, I try to control the urge I have to scream. The sudden silence makes my frantic heart pound harder and panic sets in. Out of instinct, I yank against the restraints, and the tough leather cuts into my skin.

I remind myself why I am doing this, and when I do, I see her.

Hannah is dressed in an expensive looking red dress. She has on new jewelry. She smiles at me, her eyes flashing. "Actually, I got a promotion."

What kind of promotion can a prostitute get? I swallow at the thought.

"Evelyn, I'll make five thousand dollars a night. A night! And the men I will have access to..." She smirks. "Sinners."

This man is the same man who gave Hannah that five grand a night deal--the same five grand a night deal he's offering me. And that deal is what lead to her death.

"You will cry for me, Evie," he whispers, and then I hear the loud smack of leather against my back just before I feel the shock. The pain radiates up my back, causing my eyes to water. The slap of the belt echoes in my ears again and I brace myself against the splintering pain. He strikes me with such brutality. I'm scared that he will break me, that he will kill me, but the sinner in me relishes in each horrific blow. I close my eyes and as the next lash lands over my backside, I smile because it's been forever since I've been forgiven of my sins like this. *Forgive me for my sins.* And in the pain, I feel my release. Prayer does not touch what pain does. I feel as though all the sins over the past four years wash away from me. I find freedom with each strike, with each sharp bite of his belt. I can't stop myself from tossing my head back and smiling at the beautiful forgiveness stinging its way through my body. This man is granting me things I have longed for, and I feel connected to him in a way I shouldn't.

There's another crack of the belt, and aside from that, the only noise I hear is the even sounds of his heavy breaths. Although my body flinches away with each strike, I need more. I have many sins I need release from and this man...this man will grant me the penance I've sought for years. I stand taller, spreading my legs wider apart as I prepare for him to hit me once again. I want him to hit me, I need him to hit me. I was raised to believe pain equates to forgiveness and, as deranged as it may sound, I do believe this more than anything I've believed in my life. It is the one part of my religion that makes complete sense to me. You do something wrong, you are punished. Punishment teaches you to obey, and, when it doesn't, you at least are paying for what you've done. I think of the day I killed my father. I replay the image of his bloodied body lying in the kitchen floor, and I will Ezra to beat me harder.

The metal buckle clinks when Ezra drops it to the floor. My back is on fire, and the muscles in my arms ache from the tight restraints. I press my forehead against the cool wall and bask in the atonement just granted to me.

The heat of his body scorches through me as he steps closer and yanks my hair out of the knot. Jerking my head back, he presses his body against mine. The cotton material of his shirt feels like sandpaper over my abused skin, and I'm tempted to thank him for granting me absolution. His warm, heavy breath blows over the back of my neck.

"Do you like that, sweetheart?" he asks. "Does it make you wet?" His lips caress the side of my neck, sending chill bumps over my skin. He tugs my hair even harder than the last time, forcing my head to the side before his teeth sink into my neck.

That sensation makes my pulse pound in my throat. For the past four years, I have always been in control with a man, but this...I have no control over this. I am at his mercy, and he just purged me of my sins. I am white as snow, pure and innocent and chained to a cross in front of him. My breaths are too ragged, my mouth too dry to answer him. He takes me by the hips and drags my body against his. I can't focus on anything aside from his hard dick pushing against me through his pants.

He fumbles with the restraints on my left hand and violently jerks the buckle, like he's angry. As soon as the restraint opens, my hand falls to my side. Pins and needles tingle over my fingertips as the blood rushes back to them. Ezra steps toward me. His black eyes gleam as one by one his fingers wrap around my throat, and with one swift movement, he rips me from the cross. Even though my right hand is still cuffed and suspended above my head, he slams me against the wall. The cold wall feels like a bed of nails against my tender back, and I choke on a gasp.

His body rubs over mine, his fingers twitching over my throat. In this moment, when his hand is wrapped around my neck, his eyes locked on mine, I drink in each precise detail of his face. The clean shaven lines of his facial hair are meticulous, making his high cheekbones pop. His dark blond hair is styled in a way that looks messy. His lips have a perfect dip in the middle that I shamefully want to run my tongue along. The broad muscles in his shoulders and chest strain against his shirt. This man is breathtaking, like he's surrounded by God's glory, but then, when I look into his eyes, I know he's of the devil because all I see is depravity and squalor. His eyes scream sin and hell, and I close my eyes. This man is everything I despise. I'm terrified of him because he could easily end my life right here, and since Hannah is dead and gone, no one would even miss me. Slowly, I open my eyes. There's a beat of silence before he growls and tightens his grip around my throat.

"You're supposed to break, little killer. What is it going to take to make you cry? Do I need to make you bleed?" His lips pull up in a small smile and his eyes flash dangerously at the thought.

My heart sits in my throat, sweat coats my body. I will not grant him my tears. I save those. I do not cry for any man, and I most certainly will not cry for this one. There's a tense moment of silence. The hard beat of my pulse bangs through my ears as his fingers tense. I envision my lifeless body as he throws me into the Hudson River.

"Fuck!" With one final squeeze, he releases my throat, and drops to his knee's in front of me. He forces my leg over his shoulder, and then his warm, sinful mouth is on me. All over me. I flinch away, but his hands pin me in place, refusing to let go. I'm pressed against the wall with nowhere to go. This is wrong. This is sin because it feels good. And things that feel good are unholy. He groans against me, blowing his hot breath against my pussy before thrusting his tongue inside of me. My legs threaten to buckle from the warmth of him on me--in me. Pain, I want the pain. I do not want this. Just as I close my eyes to fight the feeling of lust he's stirring inside me, the warmth disappears. He's gone.

My leg drops to the ground, and my eyes remain closed because I cannot look at him. I hear his heavy footsteps as he storms across the room. The hinges to the door creak..

"Phase two. Friday. Ten o'clock." His deep voice echoes from the walls.

And the door slams shut.

I wait several seconds before opening my eyes. Ezra has left me naked, beaten, with one arm cuffed to this cross because he knows I need to be punished. And for that I am grateful.

THE CARPET BURNS my knees when I fall in front of the altar. My heart is still racing even though it's been hours since his hands were on me.

Closing my eyes, I look for the words I need to pray, but I'm at a loss. Instead of holy thoughts, all I can think of is him. Ezra. He is beautiful, stoic, perfect, but beauty is the work of the devil. I see that now. The image of his thick tongue flicking over my clit fogs my mind, blood pools between my thighs and parts of me throb, parts of me that I shouldn't feel while on my knees in a church...*because he's the devil.* I want to cry and I dig my nails into the stair, trying to ground myself.

He's a means to end, Evelyn. A test. That is all he is.

I choke on a sob as I lean my head against the stair. "Grant me peace. Forgive me for the thoughts I have."

Sweet'art--his thick British accent rustles through my mind, sending chill bumps sweeping over my flesh. *Use him, Evelyn. Seduce him. Bring him to his knees and he will bring you to the man who killed your sister. He is the heartbeat of all the sick men in this city. Use him.*

Rising from the altar, I stare up at the stained glass window. I take in the beauty of the dark blues and purples surrounding the cross before I turn and walk toward the exit. As soon as I reach the sidewalk, the smell of exhaust wraps around me. When I turn the corner I notice a tall, wide man staring at me, and I pick up my pace. The farther I walk, the stronger the unsettling feeling that someone is following me grows. I glance over my shoulder, and that tall, wide man is walking closely behind me, whistling the chorus to "Knocking on Heaven's Door". A chill sweeps down my spine. The faster I walk, the louder he whistles. When I'm not in control, men make me nervous, and I can just imagine this man plotting to drag me into an alley and have his filthy little way with me right before he slits my throat and tosses me in a dumpster. *Please keep me safe.* I'm almost jogging, my heart drumming into my throat when I come to my building. Just as I reach to unlock the entrance, the whistling stops.

I sprint up the stairs, unlock my door, slam it shut, and lock it.

As soon as I catch my breath, I go to my room and I pull out my devotional, flipping to the last page. I run my finger along all the men's names that have been crossed out. They are dead and gone. Twirling the pen in my hand, I wonder what the name of the man who hurt Hannah is. I want nothing more than to write his name in this book, but for now I draw a blank space. At least that way I know I'm looking for him.

Write Ezra's name.

"No." I shake my head and close the book, tossing it to the foot of the bed as I lay down.

Evelyn...Evelyn.

"Go away!" I shout.

You know you have to kill him too.

I swallow, shaking my head as I bury my face in my pillow, covering my ears.

He is sin and he'll make you his sinner if you don't. You must kill him.

"I don't want to. Because of what he did tonight, I've been forgiven."

Sin for sin. He may have released you from some sins, but he's bound you to others, Evelyn. Kill him or you'll never set foot in heaven.

And I know I'll have to, but only after I find the man who killed my sister.

6

EZRA

I brace my hands on my desk, my chest heaving. The muscles in my shoulders ache from hitting her so hard, but I could have hit her harder. I wanted blood. She flipped a switch in me that I try very hard to keep under control. And why? Because she wouldn't scream, wouldn't cry and beg me to stop like every other girl has I've ever taken a belt too. I know how messed up it is. I know I should feel bad or something, but I don't, and honestly, guilt is such a pointless emotion anyway. Only a pussy lacks the self-control to not do something they'll later feel guilty for. I hit Evie because I wanted to, because it made my dick hard. End of.

I groan as I think of how her skin turned that beautiful scarlet. She embraced it, her body gravitating toward the lashes as though she needed it. Her fear of me completely contradicts the lack of fear she has for the belt. To fear pain is natural and to lack that, to override basic survival instinct, well, that just makes me want her even more.

She's perfect. I've never wanted to sink my dick in a woman so bad. So much so that I broke my biggest rule: Do not fuck the whores. I just needed to taste her, and so I snapped. In fifteen years I've never snapped. Not once. And this woman had me on my knees for her, tasting her pussy within fifteen minutes of her taking her clothes off.

She calls to my depravity, makes me want to possess her, to ruin her, because something about her tells me she can't be broken. Or perhaps she's already ruined, damaged beyond reparation. After all, you can't break what's already broken.

I really hope she comes on Friday, and that's sick and twisted, because she won't pass. No matter how good my girls are they will still cry out, sob, scream when beaten. Clients pay good money for those screams, it's what gets their dicks hard. Evie won't scream. And even though she's beautiful, she's scarred which means she's no good. I have a reputation for producing premium merchandise, and as beautiful as she is, she is flawed. My cock twitches, and I squeeze my eyes shut trying to push the image of the cross on Evie's back out of my mind.

I need to see Jen.

I met Jen in a club a couple of years ago. She's a good fuck, and I swear she could suck a golf ball through a garden hose. We fuck, that's it. It's a mutual agreement that works. Sometimes I pick up girls for a night, but Jen fulfils my needs in ways that would have most girls running and screaming. *Evie wouldn't run.*

———

JEN JUST STORMED out after I blew my load and told her to leave. I'm not in the mood for her bullshit tonight. Our agreement is clear, but well, she's a woman, and they like to push the boundaries.

Grabbing a glass of whisky, I turn on yesterday's game. Dave hops up on the sofa next to me. I bought him as a guard dog, but he thinks he's a damn poodle half the time. I prop my feet on the coffee table and rest my hand on his back.

I'm halfway through the first quarter when my phone rings, dancing across the coffee table. I pick it up, glancing at the unknown number.

"Yeah," I answer.

"Ezra, how are you?"

I frown, pausing the game. "Who is this?"

"That's no way to greet your new business partner." *Fucking Zee.*

"My answer is still no." I spoke to Seamus and he's looking for the rat. It's the only explanation. He suggested I shoot the little prick, and then lay low for a while just in case he's legit, but I'm not running, certainly not over this little turd. I want to know how Zee got his contact, how he managed to infiltrate the family, and who is holding that recording for him. Better yet, I need something on him. If someone grabs you by the balls you grab back and squeeze harder. Jonty can hack anything, get almost any information imaginable, but he can't find shit on Zee.

Zee sighs. "I'm losing patience, Ezra."

"So, turn me in."

"I don't want to turn you in!" he screams, and I pull the phone away from my ear. "I told you, I need you," he snaps, an edge of hysteria in his voice.

"So you have fuck all leverage then." I smirk. "Not the sharpest tool in the shed are you?"

He growls, actually growls down the phone at me. "Okay, I tried to be nice." And then he hangs up.

That's it? The guy is insane. Insane and blackmailing me. I'm shit out of options here, so I call the only person who might be able to help me, someone with more power and money than God. Alexei, the Russian Mafia boss. Alexei is a crazy bastard with the biggest balls of anyone I know. He has a hand in everything from whores to illegal fights to weapons dealing. Basically, he is the guy to know, and the guy you do not want to piss off under any circumstances. Eight years ago, I saved his life, took out one of his own guys who was about to shoot him in the back. We've been friends ever since, and he's a handy friend to have.

The phone rings, and Alexei picks up shouting in Russian, "*No whores in the house. I'll cut your dick off and feed it to you with a silver spoon.*" He clears his throat. "Ezra!"

"Hey, Alex."

"It is good to hear your voice my friend. What do you need? No dick in spoon I hope."

I laugh. "No. I need a favour. I have a little problem..."

The angry red welts from Ezra's belt have turned a deep purple, some of them framed in a blueish-black line. I smile as I stare at my reflection in the mirror. I am forgiven. Ezra granted me penance, and the burden has been lifted from me.

I grab the black belt laid at the foot of my bed and thread it through my fingers. I bought it because it's just like the one Ezra beat me with. The sight of it makes my stomach clench in a delicious way. Even though it's almost been a week since Ezra beat me, it's all I can think about. The things he stirred within me...Even though I feel ashamed, I also feel a strong desire to have him near me.

I waited two days before I followed him. And now I've been following him long enough that I know his routine. I know what kind of coffee he drinks--latte, extra shot of espresso, no cream. They say eyes are the windows to the soul, well, the windows of apartment 3C are the eyes to Ezra's life. I know that he loves Chinese food, and that he smokes too much. He also drinks too much. Every day he wakes up at noon and takes a shower, and after he's toweled off he sprays one squirt of Chanel Blue over his bare chest.

I grab my newly purchased bottle of Chanel Blue from my nightstand and spritz my wrists. The clean scent surrounds me. Closing my eyes, I drag up the memory of his chest pressed against my bare back. I just want a tiny piece of him. It's obvious to me that my preoccupation with Ezra has gone too far. I always follow the men I kill, learning every last detail of their life. But it is never like this. I am chasing him because I want him to want me. I shouldn't. I should be after him to find the man who killed Hannah, and I am, but I'm also after him because he is a god and the devil all at the same time. The internal conflict he's causing me is like a catastrophic tsunami threatening to swallow me whole at any moment. Those black eyes of his flash through my mind, sending chills down my spine. *"You will cry for me, Evie."* The elegance of his accent made that statement seem more like a beautiful promise than a threat.

He's like a devil. A devil who can grant me forgiveness, and for some reason I feel forgiveness at the hands of a demon must be more sacred than any forgiveness found at the steps of an altar. It is a contradiction. Just like I am. Just like Ezra is.

I attempt to shake the thoughts of him from my head, but I fail. Miserably. He's become an obsession, and I have to stop that because my obsession right now should be finding the man who killed my sister. And once I've found him, I must kill Ezra to honor Hannah. It's what she would want. But the more I think about him, the more I need to see him.

EZRA

"When did Zee take her?" I shout, storming down the pavement, Dave trotting beside me. Jonty and I are on our way to deal with a client who hit one of my girls, and now I hear Zee is taking them. I can kill Vinnie, but Zee...I can't touch him. Shit!

"This morning. She was finishing up with a client and coming out of the motel. A couple of the girls saw Zee take her and recognised him."

"That little prick." I knew he was going to do something, but this...this is a fucking war. He thinks he can take my girls?

"Put the girls on lockdown. They work in the club and at the motel only. Put security outside our rooms in the motel, and tell the other girls to stay in their apartment building. They do not leave until I say so." I pay for the girls to live in a high security building because with the clients they have, you never know when one might get a little obsessive. Case in point, Zee. "Fucking shit!"

Jonty taps out texts on his phone, firing off instructions to the relevant people. "You want me to handle Vinny?" he asks.

I clench my fist. "No."

Vinny is about to see exactly what I do to people who damage my fucking merchandise. I push the door open to the grimy little café. The smell of grease and shit coffee assaults me. There are only a handful of tables in here, and I spot the guy I'm looking for immediately. When his eyes land on me, he tries to hunch over, pretending he can hide from me.

There are two guys sat at another table. I vaguely recognise them as junkies who sometimes come into the bar. One has his back to me, but the other looks up, locking his gaze on me. I stare him down and jerk my head to the side, signaling him to the door. His eyes drop quickly, and he nudges his friend. My reputation around here is far reaching and never questioned. They stand and leave without a word.

I walk over to Vinny's table and drop into the seat opposite him. Jonty grunts as he sits beside me, hefting his weight into the small chair.

I slide Vinny's plate of chips in front of me, and I watch him swallow. "Vinny," I say calmly, then pop a chip into my mouth. He glares at me while I chew. He knows what's coming, but sometimes in a man's last minutes he becomes defiant.

"I told you before, Ez, you pay for a girl, you expect her to take a bit of rough. If I wanted to tiptoe around a woman's feelings I'd fuck my wife."

I remain unmoving, impassive and clasp my hands together on the table in front of me. "I told you before that the next time you leave a bruise on one of my girls, I'll do a lot more than break your jaw." Now I'm aware that this may sound hypocritical coming from me, but SJ is not five grand a night, and she is not trained to handle that shit. Plus, no one wants to fuck a girl with a smashed up face. I'm all about profit margins. To the average Joe Bloggs using one of my average whores, the rules are simple, never hit the girls, or you will have me to deal with. To break my rules is to directly disrespect me, and I really don't like being disrespected.

"Come on, Ez," he laughs nervously.

I pluck another chip from the plate and shove it inside my mouth. "Do you think I'm soft, Vinny?"

"No," he says warily. *Wise.*

"Do you think I'm a guy that just says things for shits and giggles?" He shakes his head, but doesn't answer. "I'm a fair guy, Vinny. I give people a chance to rectify their mistakes." I glance at Jonty and shrug. "I don't know, maybe I'm too nice?"

Jonty laughs and shakes his head. "Sure. Nice. That is exactly the word I'd use to describe you."

Grinning, I reach across the table, grab Vinny by the hair, and slam him face first into the table. The crunch his nose makes and the blood that splatters across the table makes me grin. Vinny screams, grabbing the edge of the table and trying to push away from me.

"Do I strike you as nice Vinny?" I push his face into the table, smearing blood all over the place. He cries like a little girl and struggles against my hold.

"Please," he begs, his voice a faint mumble.

I stand up and lean across the table to whisper in his ear. "You disrespected me, Vinny. I warned you."

Jonty raises an eyebrow when I glance at him. He takes a butter knife, and slides it across the table to me. It skitters across the surface before bumping against my hand. I straighten up, wrapping my fingers around the cool metal of the knife as my grip tightens in his hair. He whimpers as I yank his head up off the table.

"Please," he mumbles. Blood tracks down his face and throat. He's whimpering like a damn dog, his fingers desperately clawing at my wrist in an attempt to break free of my hold. I smile, because for all his front, it's these last seconds that count. When you watch someone's life drain from their eyes, you see the panic, the fear. It's then that a man shows his true colours, and you either die a sniveling pants- pissing-mess, or with dignity.

I use my body weight to jab the knife straight into the side of his thick neck. His eyes pop wide. His mouth gapes open and closed like a fish out of water. When I yank the blunt blade out, blood spurts across the room, spraying the wall a few feet away. Vinny panics and grabs at his neck in an attempt to stop the bleeding, but I've just ruptured his jugular, nothing will stop the blood continuing to pump through his fingers. I watch the red liquid trickle down his forearms and I'm satisfied. When I release his hair, Jonty's hand shoots out, yanking the bowl of chips away before Vinny's mangled face hits the table.

I take a napkin and clean the blood from my hands as I watch him flail on the table. Jonty never moves, just sits there eating Vinny's chips.

Vinny's cheek is pressed to the table, his face white, eyes wide with fear. These are his last seconds. I crouch down next to him, and I smile. "See, I am nice Vinny. I *almost* killed you quickly." He gasps two short, staggered breaths, and then he falls still. I throw the crumpled napkin down beside him and turn for the door.

"Get this shit cleaned up, and then find Lydia!" I say.

I'm going to go on the war path.

9

EVIE

I park outside of Ezra's apartment complex, turn the ignition off, and wait. I wait for him to come home because I need to see him.

He steps out of his car and bypasses the stairs. A redheaded woman in a too-tight white dress saunters up to him. I watch as he grabs her by the waist and pins her against a parked car on the side of the road. He kisses her the way men kiss women in movies, and then grabs onto her arm and drags her up the stairs. My heart drums in my chest because I am jealous. I can just imagine she's giggling. She's wearing white. She's playing innocent, although the sway in her hips and the fact that I don't see an underwear line tells me she's anything but. I count in my head the one-hundred and twenty seconds it usually takes until Ezra's lights flip on. *One-hundred twenty one, one-hundred twenty-two, one-hundred twenty-three...*I swallow because I imagine he has her pinned against the wall in that stairwell with his hand up that short, slutty dress of hers. Finally, the living room light turns on, followed by the light in the bedroom. I can't help but wonder what he fucks like. And I shouldn't. But I do.

Before I realize what I'm actually doing, I find myself scurrying along the sidewalk to the adjacent building. Here I stand, staring up at the window on the side of his apartment. Shadows bounce across the brick facing of the opposite complex, and I have to see what they are doing. I hurry to the fire escape. It's old and rickety, and most likely not up to code, but it's proven to hold up every other night this week. I grab onto the rusted railing and up I go, my heels clanging and catching on the broken stairs several times before I reach the second landing. I'm covered in shadows, and I press my back against the cold wall, keeping completely still so as not to be seen.

The girl is on her knees, his dick in her mouth, her hands gripping his hips. I watch his hands grab onto the back of her head and now she's not sucking him because he is brutally fucking her mouth. For some reason, and I don't know why, but I wish that was me with his dick in my mouth, and that makes me feel dirty because I never *want* to do anything with a man. *But he grants you absolution, Evelyn.* He does and that would make it okay for me to fuck him and enjoy it. He could beat my lustful sin out of me while he fucks me.

Ezra takes the woman's red hair, wrapping it around his wrist as he yanks her up from in front of him. He grabs her dress and hikes it up with such need-- the need for release, and it makes me envious because I want him to need me the way he needs her. He is making this woman his sinner, but I want this man to be *my* sin.

When he slams her against the window, I actually hear the thud, and it echoes down the alleyway. I want that to be my bare back pressed against the cold window. My pulse hammers in my ears, shouting what a wanton slut I am for allowing this man to force such sinful thoughts into my mind, and I shout back for it to shut-up. I can only imagine that this throbbing between my legs and the tingly feeling buzzing over my skin would be ten-thousand times more pleasant if I were actually the one he had pinned against that window. I could have him fuck me, and then go at my back with his belt, and then I would be absolved for this wretched desire crawling over me like insects.

That little redheaded slut is slapping at his chest, clawing at him. He leans into her neck, fisting her hair as he probably whispers something utterly wicked into her ear. I bet he's telling her she will cry for him, and all I can remember is the way his hot mouth felt over me, how he replaced the pain with something so pleasant that made me feel the need to be beat all over again. And then he pulls her from the window, and for a brief second, he stares out of it. For a split-second I fear he's sees me, but if he does, he would never be able to recognize me. Eventually they move away from the window, and I make my way back down the fire escape, flushed, and dare I say, jealous of that Jezebel in the too-tight white dress.

Envy. Lust. Those are both sins, and they are waging like a rampant fire inside my body--my body, which is supposed to be a temple, but tonight it's a chasm that I fear if I'm not careful will open up into the mouth of hell. I clasp my keys in my damp palm, listening to the soft click-clack of my heels as the pound over the pavement. I walk past Ezra's car, and instead of crossing the street right here, I keep going. My eyes hone in on the shiny black paint of her BMW. My palm twitches as I stand next to it. *Slut.* I take the key and place it against the paint. The screech of the key I'm dragging over the metal provides me a sick form of amusement. Jezebel will not like this at all. But I don't like her at all, so it's a fair trade.

I don't take time to admire my artwork. I go to my car and drive home. I say my prayers and climb into bed, and here I lay, unable to get the images of Ezra fucking that woman out of my head. It's like a porno reel on replay in my mind, and that makes me feel filthy. I close my eyes...and then...I wake up, my clit throbbing, my hand pressing over my panties in ways no good girl should touch herself. He's infested my dreams, tainted my unconscious mind with his sins. I feel sweat bead along my brow as I yank my trembling hand away from my body. I swallow and immediately shove the covers off, dropping to my knees beside the bed to pray.

"Please forgive me for my impure thoughts, for the things I've allowed to seep into my soul. Please take away my want of unholy things. Amen."

The throbbing between my thighs won't stop and all I want to do is touch myself while thinking of that man, of the way his large hands felt on me. The release he provided me. Tomorrow is Friday, and it can't come soon enough.

10

EZRA

There's a soft knock at the door and Dave jumps up, growling.

"Come in!" I shout.

The door cracks and a tiny figure steps into the office. Her black hair falls in waves around her shoulders. Evie.

Dave sits down in front of her, continuing to growl low in his throat. Her eyes lock on him and she nervously presses herself against the wall.

"Dave!" I snap, and he turns away, grumbling as he lies back down.

She watches me for a second, those wide blue eyes meeting mine. There's something so beautifully tragic about her, that false innocence that draws me in.

I like to know everything about my girls, because preparation is everything in business. At least that's what I'm te'
myself. I had Jonty follow her. I now know where sh'
where she goes to church, but that's it. I can fin'

on her, no social security number, no birth certificate, she's a ghost and even for a whore, that's suspicious.

She shrugs out of her coat. And my gaze is immediately drawn to the tight black dress clinging to every single curve of her body. Just looking at her is making the front of my jeans tight. I lean back to give my dick some room and shift uncomfortably.

"You came," I say, resting my elbows on the arms of the chair and clasping my hands in front of me.

"You told me to come back..." she glances anxiously at Dave and clears her throat. "Phase two, remember?" I remain silent and stare at her. Her cheeks flush pink, and that makes my cock twitch.

"I remember." I smirk. "I just didn't *expect* you to come back. Most don't." *You shouldn't have.*

Her eyes drop to her lap and I think I can see a subtle smile on her lips. "I'm not most girls," she whispers. *No, she's not.*

I stand, and Dave goes to get up, but I signal for him to stay.

"Follow me," I tell Evie, leaving the room. I walk down the same hallway to the same room, and again she follows me, the quiet tapping of her heels seemingly deafening.

This time she doesn't flinch when I walk into the room and switch the light on. She doesn't give anything away. Her face remains completely impassive. With most girls, the second time is usually worse. They've experienced the first session so they assume that whatever is about to happen must be worse than that. It's phase two. It has to get harder. They fear the unknown. Not Evie though, she looks calm, as though she's come to terms with whatever awaits her. She surprises and fascinates me at every turn.

"Strip," I tell her.

She removes her clothes without hesitation, and I'm almost disappointed. Part of me wants her defiance so I can tear those fucking clothes off of her. Her submission is not nearly as exciting as her fight would be. She unzips the dress and it drops to the floor, leaving her standing in a white lace thong and bra. My eyes trail down her legs to her red heels, and I'm forced to adjust my cock for what feels like the hundredth time.

"Kneel."

She does so willingly, lifting her head to watch as I circle her. "Why did you come back, little killer?" I grasp her chin and jerk her face up.

"You told me to."

I smile. She's a killer, a fighter. She didn't come back here because I told her to. She came back here because she wants to be here. I'm just not sure *why* she wants to be here. I move to the chest of drawers and pull out the flogger. I hate this shit because it seems so theatrical, but given what I'm about to ask her to do, a belt won't do. I run the leather tassles across my palm as I approach her, and her gaze is set on my movements, curiosity in her expression as I hold the handle out to her. She takes it from my hand and examines it.

"You are going to use this." Her eyes pop wide when I say that. They always think they are going to hit me. I laugh as her eyes drift from the flogger to me, and I shake my head. "You are going to hurt *yourself*, Evie." I hear her swallow.

Her eyes lock on mine, and for a brief moment, I think she's going to cry. And I hope she does.

"Why do *I* have to do it? What's the point?" she asks as she fingers the leather strands.

"You do not ask questions. You are to be obedient, *submissive.*" I spit that word, because I hate it. "But, I will tell you because I like you, sweetheart. The point is discipline. If you can hurt yourself, and I mean, *really* hurt yourself, you can endure anything they might inflict upon you, and trust me, what they will do to you..." I don't know why I'm saying any of this to her, or why I'm pretending that she's still interviewing for the job. She's not training to be an elite whore. She's here because I want her here. No other reason.

She nods her head in acceptance. Those blue eyes of hers remain trained on me, her face without expression as she holds the flogger out, whipping it over her shoulder. The loud smack of the leather as it slaps over her skin echoes around the room. She doesn't flinch, she doesn't move, and her eyes never leave mine.

"Again," I say.

Another loud lash rings out followed by another, then another. There are no tears, no screams. She is completely stoic, and it is making me hard as cement. She stops, dropping the flogger to her side, and I shake my head, smiling. "I didn't tell you to stop."

Her eyes narrow and I can see resentment burning behind them. I crouch in front of her, taking her chin in my hand. "Harder..." I whisper.

She jerks her chin from my grasp and raises the whip, slapping it over her back again and again. I lose count of how many lashes she gives herself. But no matter how many times the leather strikes her, she doesn't break.

"Enough."

The black leather tassles splay across the floor when her arm falls to her side. She hands me the flogger and peers up at me through her thick, dark lashes. Her white teeth rake over those blood-red lips of hers. "I want you to do it," she whispers as her eyes drop to the floor. "Please." She doesn't give me enough time to respond, she simply turns around and waits. My gaze skims over her pale skin, tracing over the raised, red welts she inflicted on herself. That wasn't enough for her?

I tighten my grip on the wooden handle, warring with myself. She doesn't get to make demands here, but fucking hell, the fact that she wants it, that she likes it...Damn, do I want to make her cry. The problem is she won't cry. She has no fear, no threshold of pain, and damn if that doesn't make my cock twitch, I don't know what on this earth will. It makes me want to fuck her until she screams, and I'm not sure I trust myself not to beat her bloody in pursuit of those elusive tears.

I swing the flogger back, bringing it down across her shoulder blades. The leather bites at her skin and I clench my jaw. I hit her again and again, and the harder I hit her, the more relaxed she becomes. My cock's getting harder by the second. I growl and hit her with enough force to draw blood. That lash causes her back to bow ever so slightly, and I swear I hear her moan. This isn't punishment for her, it's pleasure.

I release the flogger and it hits the ground. I can't take this bullshit any longer. With a few quick strides, I close the distance between us. Standing in front of her, I grab her hair and yank her head back. Her face is now level with my cock as she stares up at me with wide eyes.

"Do you like it when I hurt you, little killer?" Her eyes drop, her cheeks flushing. I stroke my free hand over her cheek. "Don't be ashamed, sweetheart. It's fucking beautiful," I whisper.

Her trembling hands lift to my waist, and she timidly pulls at my belt buckle. She's so unsure, so innocent. Her eyes meet mine for a split second before quickly lowering again, and her hands fall back into her lap. I brush my thumb across her bottom lip before slipping it into her mouth; her warm, wet mouth. Her tongue flicks across my fingertip, and that simple action has my cock jumping up and down like a puppy waiting to be petted. When she moans around my thumb, I hiss out a breath. Shit. I don't fuck whores, but it's just her mouth right? And she's not like any whore I've ever met.

I rip my thumb from her mouth and yank my belt open, shoving both my trousers and boxers down. A small frown line marrs her forehead. My other hand is still in her hair, and my hold tightens, slowly pulling her to me until her face is only an inch from my cock. Her short, hot breaths blow over my dick, and I can't wait for the heat of her mouth.

"Take it," I growl. I have to restrain myself from shoving my cock down her throat and fucking her face until she gags. I want to watch the tears pour down her face as she literally chokes on my dick.

She timidly lifts her hand and wraps her delicate fingers around the base. I groan at the small contact, and then, her lips are on me, her tongue tentatively flicking across my bellend. My fingers tense in her hair as she explores me further. Her mouth sinks down around me, and I watch as my cock disappears behind her red lips. Now my entire dick is in her warm, tight little mouth. My body is strung so fucking tight, my balls ready to explode down her throat. Her eyes flash open and meet mine. Even with my dick in her mouth she looks innocent. She drags her tongue over my length, moaning slightly. And I lose it.

I grip her hair and thrust my hips forward until I touch the back of her throat. I fuck her mercilessly, chasing release. I throw my head back and groan because nothing has ever felt as good as her mouth does right now.

"Fuck, Evie!" I thrust harder, faster. My balls tighten, my muscles tense, and then I come deep in her throat. To her credit, she swallows, then drags her tongue over me to lick me clean. My cock pops out of her mouth, and there she sits staring at me silently. I'm shaking, my breathing ragged. Her mouth is fucking magic.

After I've come back to my senses, I pull my boxers and trousers up, then quickly fasten my belt.

What did I just do? I turn and walk away from her, dragging a hand through my hair. Shit. First, I wanted to hit her, then I ate her pussy, and now she's sucking my cock. I don't fuck whores. I don't hit girls unless they're going to work for me. *What is wrong with me?* This girl makes me lose control, and I never lose control. Everything I do is a conscious choice. What is it about her? She's turning me into one of the sex crazed idiots I make so much money from.

When I turn back around, Evie's still knelt, and still very naked with her eyes fixed on the floor.

"Get dressed," I tell her, angry with myself for losing my shit.

She doesn't look at me when she stands to grab her clothes. She quickly dresses, keeping her eyes on the floor. "Phase three is when?" she asks as she smooths the hem of her dress down.

"There is no phase three." I pull a cigarette from the pack in my pocket, remaining silent as I place it between my lips."You didn't pass phase two." I flip the lid to the lighter and hold it to the cigarette, inhaling the thick smoke before I flip it closed with a heavy snap.

Her eyebrows pinch together and her eyes narrow angrily at me. "Why? What didn't I pass?"

I smirk and take another drag of the cigarette as I slowly step towards her, closing the space between us. "You don't flinch. You don't fear pain."

"I thought that's what you wanted," she whispers.

I take her chin between my thumb and forefinger. "Me personally, yes. My clients...." I lean in closer, dragging my nose across her throat, inhaling the scent of her one last time. "They want you to scream and cry. They want you to beg them to stop." I kiss her neck gently before pulling back to meet her eyes again. "They do not want you to like it. They want you to fear it."

"I...I can scream. I can cry if that's what they want." She nods her head as though trying to convince herself. "I can pretend, whatever you want." Her jaw clenches and she glares at me.

The thought of her pretending to cry makes me angry. I drop my hand from her face. Tears are merely a reaction to fear, and fear is not seen, it's felt. "Even if you could fake it, you're scarred. I can't charge thousands of dollars a night for flawed merchandise, sweetheart." My eyes flick over her perfect face. "No matter how beautiful you are."

"Why did you ask me to come back then? If being scarred means I'm flawed, why did you bring me back here? You just wanted to hurt me?" She's shaking, her nostrils flaring as she glares at me.

I laugh, inhaling another drag from my smoke as I thread a handful of her hair between my fingers. "Exactly that." I blow a steady stream of smoke in her face as I pull her against my chest. "I've never wanted to take a belt to anyone as much as I do you, little killer," I whisper, my lips brushing against hers as I speak.

Her breath hitches and her eyes widen. She attempts to push away from me, but I wrap my hand around the back of her neck, locking her in place. "You make me want to hurt you, to make you cry while I fuck you. But I don't fuck whores." Releasing her, I drag my eyes over her body. "Shame." I turn my back to her and head to the door. "Don't come back here, Evie."

"Please..." she begs.

I should keep walking and never see her again, but that innocence in her voice halts me.

"Give me another chance. Please, Ezra."

I turn and face her. "Why?" A small frown line marrs her forehead. "Why?!" I shout.

"I...I need this job."

I narrow my eyes at her, studying her face. "Get. Another. Job."

"No!" she shouts too quickly. "I can't...I need *this* job. I need the money."

I didn't get to where I am by being an idiot. I can read people like a book. "You're lying." I should just throw her out, forget about her, but curiosity has me rooted to the spot waiting for her answer, yet she remains silent. I'm out of patience. I close the gap between us and slam my hand around her throat, yanking her toward me as I press my fingers into her soft skin. "I don't deal well with bullshit, sweetheart," I breathe against her ear. "Don't fucking test me."

She gasps as she struggles in my grip. "I..." Her pulse thrums against my fingers, and she squeezes her eyes shut. "I like it," she chokes out.

"What do you like, little killer? I loosen my grip as I press my cheek against hers, my lips at her ear. "Say it."

"I like it when you hurt me," she whispers, her voice breaking. I can't help but groan as the raw urge to fuck her up on every level rises to the surface.

I adjust my grip, grabbing her jaw and pulling her close to me. My gaze drops to her full, parted red lips, and I brush my lips against hers. Her rapid breaths falter before she slams her lips against mine. The second her tongue sweeps across my lips, I'm done.

11

EVIE

His lips are on mine, the rough stubble of his face scratching against my skin. He tastes like sin and heaven at the same time. My skin heats from that contradiction. This feeling buzzing through me must be what Eve felt as she plucked the bright, red apple from the tree; as she contemplated sinking her teeth into it's tempting flesh. The taste of sin, the taste of something forbidden--it's unlike anything else in this world. And Ezra is sin, yet he is forgiveness, and I know that if I eat of his flesh I will burn in hell. *You shouldn't like this, Evelyn.* But I do. I shouldn't, but I can't help it. And so I sink my teeth into the forbidden fruit. I claw at the back of Ezra's neck, scratching my nails through his thick hair as my mouth crushes over his. I press my body against his. I moan into his mouth. He may say I'm damaged, but he wants me. He wants me and I will seduce him. I will make him sin, I will make him my sinner. I will let him lead me to the devil, and then, I will kill him.

My heart bangs against my ribs, and my demon wails inside my head. *Evelyn, you are not doing this to use him. You are doing this because you want him to use you, you wretched little sinner.*

No! I need to find the man who killed my sister, slit his throat, and watch every last drop of blood bleed from his pathetic body, and the only way I can do that is by keeping Ezra close to me. That is why I am pulling him harder against me, *that* is why my hands are roaming over his hard muscles. He must know who killed my sister. He must have some idea, and I need Ezra to love me. I need him to fall to his knees in front of me. Sex is power, but love is damning, and I need him to love me so that he will do anything for me, even if it means betraying his own self.

His fingers dig into my jaw with a bruising grip, taking me, owning me. His tongue invades my mouth without apology before his teeth sink into my bottom lip, biting down hard enough to draw blood. And right when I'm knocking on the devil's door he shoves me away.

I stagger back, clutching my aching jaw.

Ezra glares at me through his dark, soulless eyes as he scrubs a hand over his mouth. He is a sinner. A filthy, depraved sinner, and yet, I can see him judging me. He turns and walks out without another word. The door slams shut with a bang that echoes around the silent room. I stare at that door and my chest heaves. My fingers curl into fists and tear into my skin. I'm angry, confused. After several minutes, I realize he is not coming back, so I decide to leave. When I round the corner, I see Ezra bracing himself in the doorway to his office. His judgemental glare bores into me as I disappear down the stairs.

My mind is a jumbled mess the entire way home. I want to cry. I want to scream, but I can't because there are people around me on the subway. As soon as I get inside my apartment, I slam the door, and scream because I can still taste his dick in my mouth.

My back is on fire and so is my soul. I'm ashamed that I let him do that to me, that I want to be that redhead in the too tight white dress. I wanted to feel his filth, his sin crawling over every last inch of my skin, and then I wanted him to beat that sin right out of me. And that is a sin. That is such an *evil* sin. I enjoyed how he felt in my mouth, the way his fingers tangled in my hair with pleasure. He is the devil in all his brutal, raw beauty that leads the innocent into temptation. *Evelyn, he is the head of the snake. Cut off the head and the body shall die.* That demon screams inside me and I can't block it out. *Use him to find the wicked, then kill him.* And I will kill him.

I go to my bedroom, immediatly stripping down to my underwear. I glare across the room into my mirror. My lipstick is smudged across my face, my hair disheveled, and the image of him thrusting his cock into my mouth loops in my head. I close my eyes, and all I can see is him. Those dark eyes, his broad shoulders. *The devil, Evelyn.* I fall to my knees, burying my face in the sheets. He's infested my mind, muddled my judgment because although I know everything about him is wrong, I long for it to be right. If he is wicked, I want to be a sinner--*Evelyn, you will burn in hell.* And sometimes I wish I could. My entire life has been spent seeking absolution from sins although I know I will never be completely pure. Ezra called me a whore, and that made me feel dirty. I want him to think I'm pure. I feel tears well in my eyes, but I fight them because I will not cry for him. Ever.

Pulling my devotional out from beneath the mattress, I sit back on my knees. I take the pen and flip to the back page of the book. My chest heaves as I angrily scrawl the name Ezra James over the paper. I stare at his name, even his name looks beautiful, and I hate him for it.

"Ezra James," I whisper his name like a prayer before I close my book.

EZRA WANTED ME. I know he did, and so it only makes sense that I follow him. But over the past two days, I've realized he wants that redhead more. I've watched him fuck her. Time and time again. I've seen the pink flush staining her chest when she leaves his apartment breathless and lost within a blissful fog of forgiveness. I need him to want me like he does her, and that's why I'm standing in the middle of her apartment right now.

This place smells like roses and magnolias. Flowery, pretty, feminine. It's decorated with vintage vogue posters and daisies in vases. She is one of those prissy girls that spreads her legs for any man who will have her. Her life has probably been perfect. And I hate her because I am not like that. I make my way to a bedroom and push open the door. The sheets are crumpled in the center of the bed, clothes strewn about on the floor. Pulling in a breath, I flop back onto the mattress and close my eyes, imagining what it must be like to lay here after Ezra has beaten me, fucked me, and made me his. *Evelyn, sinful thoughts make you weak.* My eyes pop open and I push myself up, continuing to browse through her bedroom. There's a picture of Ezra on her dresser. No smile, cigarette in hand, those tar-black eyes of his empty and lost. I take the picture and drop it into my purse as I open the door to her restroom.

On the counter is a bottle of Coco Mademoiselle. I pick it up and spritz some on my wrist. I take her brush and run it through my hair while staring at my reflection the mirror. I turn around and open her closet door. At the very front of her closet hangs that too-tight white dress. My heart thumps in my chest as a smile works its way over my lips. I snatch the dress from the hanger. I will make him want me in ways he's never wanted a woman.

Ezra wants sin draped in innocence. He wants a woman who will cry, he wants a woman who loves pain, he needs someone as depraved as he is. This redhead is nothing more than a slut, a vessel he can use to feed the sins of the flesh. What he needs is a devil cloaked as an angel, wicked and pure. And that is what I will be to him in this too-tight white dress.

12

EZRA

I have fucked Jen so many times this week that my dick should have dropped off by now. No matter how many times I beat her and fuck her, it's not enough because she breaks too easily. Her tears are meaningless. All I can think about is Evie, about breaking her and taking her in every possible way. And she shouldn't even be a thought in my mind. I have Zee so far up my arse I can practically taste him, and with no means of outsmarting him, he's slowly backing me into a corner, which is only pissing me off. Evie is the perfect release.

I open my laptop to look for the CCTV footage from last Saturday night. I search through until I see the image of Evie stepping up to the cross. I click play and watch as I wield the belt. The leather hits her back and, from this angle, I can see her lips part and her eyes drift shut as though she's on the brink of coming. It's beautiful, and my cock turns rock hard.

Without hesitation, I yank my belt open and shove my hand inside my jeans, wrapping my fingers around my erection. I fist my dick, pumping hard. I watch as I hit her harder and harder. With each blow her jaw slackens further, her head tilts back as she gravitates towards the bite of the belt. I imagine bending her over and yanking her hair back as I slam balls deep inside her. I imagine her begging me to stop whilst moaning in pleasure as I reach her limit, the point where pain and euphoria blend so perfectly.

I stroke myself over and over, and I watch the video of me beating her the entire time. She's perfect, unbreakable. I grit my teeth as my balls tighten and my muscles stiffen. I imagine her screaming my name, her pussy clamping around me, and I come with a guttural groan.

I can't remember the last time I came that hard by my own hand. This woman is screwing with my head.

I'm breathing hard, my dick still hanging out when my phone rings. I grab a tissue, wiping the spunk off my hand before I pick up.

"Yeah," I answer.

"Ezra," Alexei purrs.

I'm instantly alert. "Did you find anything?" Alexei has more spies, rats and dirty politicians in his pocket than anyone. I need something on Zee. Jonty has used every means available to try and find Lydia after Zee took her, and nothing. It's like she's disappeared off the face of the earth.

"Mmm, he sells pussy, yes?" he asks.

"Yeah, sex slaves."

"Moorcroft was taking cut."

"Sneaky bastard." If Moorcroft was taking a cut it means he was probably helping Zee get girls into the country. Which means, if Moorcroft is dead, then we just fucked Zee's European trade. We took from him, and now he wants what is ours, girls who take a beating. After all, it's not every day that you find a politician corrupt enough to let you import and sell slaves, even *with* the money. But if Zee was dealing with Moorcroft, the minute he exposes me, he also exposes himself. "Do you have evidence?" I ask.

He laughs. "Of course. Bank transfers, shipping orders, the usual."

"Okay, now I just need to find out who he has on the inside." Nothing makes me angrier than betrayal. We may be criminals, but we have loyalty. Rats are the lowest of the low.

I hear Alexei spit and curse in Russian about someone's mother. "Leave it with me. I find the rat." The phone cuts off and I find myself staring at the blank touch screen. I actually feel sorry for the fucker, because when Alexei finds a rat, well, let's just say I once witnessed something involving a firework, some duct tape, and an arsehole.

As soon as I hang up, I dial Seamus. The problem is that whatever I do with Zee, it doesn't just affect me. If I'm implicated then Seamus is too.

"Ezra, how are ya, son?" He asks, his raspy Irish accent so familiar.

"Not good. Zee took one of the girls." I pinch the bridge of my nose. "But I think Alexei just helped me get a good grip on his balls."

"Good." He laughs. "You put that little shit in his place."

"Any news on your rat?"

"I'll find him," he promises.

"Careful. I think Alexei might beat you to it. You know how he feels about rats."

"Jesus Christ. All I need is that mad bastard over here. If he sets off another bomb in the house, I swear..." he trails off.

"Has Zee shown any sign of actually turning you in?" Seamus asks.

I sigh, dragging a hand through my hair. "He needs me, and he can't have me if I'm locked up now can he? That recording is his insurance policy to keep him alive. He's trying to push me by other means."

"Well then, ya best push back son. Remind him of who you are, who we are. I'll work on his source," he grumbles and hangs up.

Push back. He's right. Zee needs a reminder of who he's dealing with.

AN HOUR later Jonty knocks on the door before walking in with a scowl on his face.

"He's taken Candy."

"Motherfucker!" I take a deep breath, trying to rationally think through the haze of rage. I stand up and take the decanter of scotch, pouring Jonty a glass and then one for myself. I neck the amber liquid in one gulp, relishing the burn it creates on it's way down. This has gone too far. The *one* thing I offer these girls is protection. One girl going missing can be passed as a one off, but two? Even if Zee doesn't take all of them from me, he's making me look weak, and they'll leave of their own accord if I can't protect them.

"You have him followed," I say. " I want to know where he lives, where he goes. He takes a shit I want to know about it. You find out where he is taking my fucking girls!" I know it's not Jonty's fault, he's just getting the brunt of my anger right now. Zee is shafting me up the arsehole and he thinks there's nothing I can do about it, but he's wrong if he thinks I won't push back.

13

EVIE

Stop *thinking about him. Stop it!* But I can't. I can't stop thinking about the way he tastes like whiskey. I can't stop thinking about how hard his chest felt pressed against me, how uncontrolled, yet controlled it was to have him beat me, scourge me. His eyes flickered when I asked him to hurt me, and I reveled in it. He is a man drunk with power and pride, lust and greed...I struggle to free my mind of Ezra as I fight to remember what my purpose was to begin with. I swallow, nodding silently to myself when Hannah's mutilated body pops to mind. I must keep focused. Ezra is a name on my list, a man I must use. A man I must not care for, or love, or want, or need. I stare at his name, tracing my fingers over each letter.

You make me want to hurt you, to make you cry while I fuck you. He said that. He meant that.

He is my temptation.

I fall back onto the bed holding the notebook above me. I continue to stare at his name, muttering it over and over until it no longer even sounds like a word. *Temptation.* I drop the book to the floor, and close my eyes. All I can see is Ezra's face, his full lips. All I can remember is the way he felt behind me, grinding against me. I can hear the crack of the belt, the way his breathing grew shallow and passionate. And then, all I can see is that redhead pressed against the glass, his hands roaming over every inch of her slutty body like she was a god and he was her worshiper. He is brutal, but something in his ruthlessness is beautiful. Something that should seem so violent, so wrong--seems so rewarding and divine in its own right. Ezra is like a storm, violent and turbulent, and as long as you aren't the one swept up in his winds, it's tragically beautiful. The destruction and power, the chaotic control...it's something you almost have to respect.

*The way he looks at me like I am something he wants to devour, the fact that he could have killed me, but didn't...*My hand trails between my breast, chill bumps sweeping over my skin. *The way he speaks to me like he needs to possess me...*My hand creeps lower, skimming over my stomach. *His hot breaths on my neck, my throat...*My hips tilt up as I push my underwear down. *The way my name sounds rolling from his lips in such a desperate whisper, an edge of restraint hidden in his growl.* My finger sinks between my thighs and my legs squeeze together in a bid to create more pressure. I rub my other hand back over my stomach, up to my breasts, and I pretend it's Ezra's hand feeling over me. My thumb brushes over my throbbing clit and my back arches. *His face...*I sink one finger in. *His mouth...* Two fingers, now up to the knuckles and my legs fall apart. I pretend Ezra is standing in front of me, watching, his eyes locked on places they shouldn't be. *His voice*: *"You will cry for me, Evie."* I pretend to be that redhead, tossing my head back and moaning while he violates me. I imagine his hand gripping my neck, threatening to take away my ability to breathe. I hear him calling me his innocent little whore and I come, the aftershocks of sin rippling through me like a tremor, parts of my soul splitting open and pieces crumbling into an abyss. I lay, breathless, my hand still held between my shaking thighs. What wicked things that man makes me do.

Wicked and filthy and shameful.

I glance down at my fingers covered in my own sin. The waves of pleasure subside and shame washes over me like a rogue wave. I lie on my bed undone by my own hands and the thought of Ezra James. He's making me sin because I want him to fuck me like that redhead, and I know that makes me a whore. *Lust is a sin.* My obsession with him has overtaken my need to find my sister's killer, and for that I feel guilty. This is the way of the devil, to distract you from the path of righteousness, and I mustn't let the devil worm his way into my soul the way Ezra has.

My eyes drift to the open notebook tossed on the floor. "Ezra James."His name drops from my mouth like a delicious piece of sin, like a prayer needing to be heard. His name sounds so Biblical, almost angelic, but I guess at some point so did the name Lucifer.The more he makes me sin, the more I want to kill him.

I pull my panties up and quickly go to the sink, scrubbing the filth from my hands. I slip that too tight white dress over my head, tugging the slinky material over my curves, and then I grab my coat and hurry out of my apartment building. With each step, the guilt becomes more unbearable, and my pace quickens until I'm jogging down the narrow sidewalks, weaving my way between the people out for a leisurely evening stroll. By the time I come to the doors of the church, I am breathless and sweating, my inner demon screaming at me. The second the wooden doors open, the familiar smell of the old church surrounds me like a worn, comfortable blanket. My eyes train on the altar, but I drop to my knees halfway down the aisle. I'm that torn apart that I can't make it any further. I need forgiveness right now. "Please forgive me for my impure thoughts. For my distraction," I plead. "I shouldn't want this evil, but God, help me, because I do. Take away my desire for this man, so I may stay on the path of righteousness. Please."

Keeping my eyes closed, I wait for a peace to wash over me, but it never does. There's only silence and the sound of my own pulse drumming in my ears. After several minutes, I pull myself to my feet and leave the cathedral, finding my way to the subway, and within half an hour, I'm walking through the doors of Ezra's club. Literally walking into Sin.

It's crowded and the place reeks of sweaty bodies. I push my way toward the bar and find an empty seat at the end. The bartender approaches me and folds his arms over the counter. "What do you want, pretty little thing?" He winks, and I try to even out my breaths.

"Chardonnay."

His gaze narrows on me as he uncorks a bottle of wine. When he places the wine in front of me, I hand him my card to pay. "Is Ezra here?" I ask.

He turns from the register, his lips kicking up on one side. "You want him or something?"

"Just curious." I feel sweat dot my forehead. I have lost all control, and I am well aware of it. "If he's here, would you tell him Evie would like to see him?" I force a kittenish grin, trying to downplay the panic gripping me by the throat.

Handing my card back to me, he nods. I watch him walk over to another patron, then another. He never picks up a phone, he never leaves the bar. He hasn't told Ezra I'm here for him.

"Excuse me," I shout, and his gaze swings over to me. "Can you please tell him I'm here?"

"If Ezra wants to see you, he'll come see you. He knows you're here."

I groan and narrow my eyes at him as I down the glass of wine. I grab my purse and stand, straightening out my dress before I squeeze through the crowded bar. The stairwell is blocked off by a rope that I climb over. The door to Ezra's office is cracked, and I peer through before softly rapping my knuckles over the door.

"What is it?" Ezra slowly looks up from his paperwork. A wry smile pulls at his lips as his dark eyes focus on me. "Impatient aren't we?" He clasps his hands behind his head, and my attention immediately goes to the tight material straining over his biceps. His dirty-blond hair is messy, and I want to drag my fingers through it. Honestly, the way he looks makes me want to ride him hard while I watch the life drain from him. *You shouldn't want him, Evelyn. He's a demon.*

I did not plan this through. I'm unprepared and I don't like this feeling creeping through me like a cold fog. I take his massive frame in, swallowing as I chastise myself for the uncontrolled throbbing between my thighs.

He watches me carefully, assessing my every move. "Why are you here, Evie? Are you brave, or just stupid?"

"I can't stop thinking about you hurting me," I say quietly.

He cocks an eyebrow while his eyes flick over my body. "Stupid it is," he says with a smirk.

A primitive need oozes from him as his gaze burns through the slinky material of my too-tight white dress. The way his jaw tenses as he takes me in inch by inch makes me want to be dirty, and the fact that I find myself enjoying the way he's staring at me makes me feel guilty. I force myself to smile and I take a step toward his desk as I try to calm my thundering pulse.

This man makes me nervous. He looks brutal, he is ruthless, and I know he would kill me without a second thought if it suited him. My eyes skim over his biceps, over the dark ink winding its way around his large muscles. Ezra James drips sex with each movement, every word, and I can feel myself weakening, straying into sin with every second I am around him. I clear my throat and trace my finger over the wooden edge of the desk as I peer up at him through my lashes. I don't say a word. I don't have to. Words are merely foreplay, and at this very moment I'm already fucking him with my eyes. I need him to believe I want to fuck him like a dirty little whore. *And you do want to be a dirty little whore for him. You want to be a sinner for him.* He needs to think I would let him wind my hair around his wrist and slam me up against a window while I scream out his name like my last rite.

I slowly move around his desk, the dance of seduction playing from my hips. His eyes are honed in on me like a predator waiting to pounce on his prey. I'll play the pathetic little lamb he wants. I will walk right into his trap and bait him because I love making the hunter the prey. When I come to a halt in front of him, he wets the edge of his lips with his tongue. Bending over, I grip the arms of his leather chair, watching as his eyes challenge me, dare me.

He studies me, an amused smile pulling at his lips. "You really should run away, sweetheart."

The callous tone to his warning should make me stop, but all it does is entice me. "Why?" I whisper as I inch my face toward his. My gaze drops to his mouth then back up to his eyes. I lean in closer, and the heat from his lips radiate against my mouth. "You don't scare me," I breathe, my lips brushing against his. Every last piece of my soul shivers with want and need and fear and unholy thoughts.

Suddenly, he grabs my hair, gripping it with such force I feel my scalp lift, the burn eating away at me. "Very. Stupid," he says, breathing across my lips. "There's a fine line, sweetheart, and you just crossed it." He inches closer, grazing his lips across the corner of my mouth, my cheek, until they brush my ear." You're in the lions den, Evie."

My pulse hammers through my veins. I'm well aware I'm no longer in control here. *The devil has you in his claws now, Evelyn because he knows you are a sinner.* A fissure of fear coils around me like a snake, and he smiles. "You should have run while you had the chance little lamb." His warm breath against my ear causes chill bumps to race across my skin. His hold on my hair tightens as he rises from his chair and towers over me. There's a beat of silence as his eyes narrow, and then he jerks my head back, tilting my face toward him.

"Do you want me, little killer?" He leans in so close to me I can't breathe. "I don't fuck whores," he says with an air of disgust, then pulls away. Although I know he is wicked, I feel shame under his judgment, as though he were righteous.

"I don't want you to fuck me," I say in a breathe. "I just want you to hurt me."

Groaning, he releases me before turning away. He watches me, his feet shoulder width apart, his hands clasped at the base of his neck. "Careful, Evie."

"I want you to make me cry," I say, a slight tremble in my voice.

"Fuck." He turns and charges me, violently fisting my hair again. My head snaps back and his lips slam over mine.

The kiss is brutal and it bleeds into me. His teeth nip at my bottom lip, gently at first, but with each second, his bite grows more angry and hard. His teeth rake over my lower lip, and the metallic taste of blood coats my tongue. I can't breathe because he's consuming me. I try to pull away for fear he will completely possess me, but his hold is strong. Ezra grabs at my hips, yanking me against him. When our hips press together, I can feel the hard length of him, and all I can think about is that redhead and how much I want to be her.

He spins me around, places his hand between my shoulder blades, and shoves me face down onto his desk, my cheek meeting the cold wood of his desk with a thud. The weight of his body pushes behind me, his hard cock grinding against my ass while his free hand traces down my thighs. He's in control which means I have none. My pulse skips in panic. He's going to fuck me and kill me and toss my body into the Hudson River. I should be begging for forgiveness before I die, but the only thought in my mind is Ezra ripping my clothes from my body and fucking me before he kills me.

Evelyn, the wages of sin is death. Lust is a sin. Ezra is sin. And I don't want to be his sinner. I'm righteous and holy and I am not sin, he is! This man is making me want to bury my soul with his in hell. I push against his erection, wanting nothing more than one moment of pressure from him. And as I begin to lose myself, as I begin my descension into the pits of hell, I try to focus. All I can hear is our inter-mingled breaths, a chorus of want and need and utter sin. His hand moves to the hem of my dress, and when he yanks the material up cool air hits my exposed skin. My thighs involuntarily squeeze together, my body trying to find some form of relief from this torture he's inflicting on me. *Forgive me. Forgive me. Forgive me.* I can feel the sin bleeding through me.

Ezra reaches around, gripping my jaw in his hands, pulling my head back so far I feel my neck is about to snap. And even though I'm terrified, I can't stop pushing myself against him, I can't stop imagining my naked body pinned against his in a dance of sinful desires.

His full weight lays against my back, his lips skimming up the back of my neck until he hisses in my ear. "I can taste your fear, little killer." His teeth graze my skin and then, slowly, his teeth sink into the tender flesh of my neck, harder and harder. I groan at the pain, at the pleasure, at how wrong it is that I like the burn of his teeth tearing into my skin. His tongue swipes over the pained flesh and he releases me.

"You make me want to break my own rules, to defile you in every way. I want to break you, over and over." His teeth skim my jaw. The heat from his breath sends a sharp shiver trickling down my spine. His fingers snake around my throat, exerting a small amount of pressure and, as though sensing the impending loss of air, my throat constricts. I can no longer tell each heart beat from the next, because there is no pause. Ezra is in complete control. Life or death, that is his choice, and right now, in this world only he and I are aware of, he is my god because he alone determines my fate.

"I want to corrupt you, little killer." His grip on my throat tightens slightly and I grab at his hands, trying to pull them away. He laughs. "I'll make you hate yourself, all the while, loving it. You will beg for your own destruction." His cock presses against me again and he groans. "I want to destroy you."

I try to swallow, but I can't. I pull at his hands, but my body is becoming numb, and in this moment, when blackness is setting in at the corner of my vision, I long to be freed. Finally, he releases his hold on me, and I gasp. My chest heaves as I drag in breath after breath, drinking in the air around me. I push up from the desk, papers crinkling beneath my palms. When I spin around to face him, his eyes set on me, a smirk on his face.

I swallow. "Destroy me then." I stare at him. I can feel my nostrils flaring, and my heart is still in my throat, my skin buzzing with a mixture of adrenaline and fear and guilt and lust. The muscles in my thigh twitch because my body is telling me to flee. I should run away from him and pray for anyone who will ever encounter this man because sin oozes from his every pore.

Ezra is the kind of man I grew up fearing. He is the kind of man I have no power with, with whom I will lose all control. He is the epitome of everything that ruined me. *God never gives us more than we can handle, Evelyn.* This is my test, this man is my chance to find the absolution I need, my chance to be forgiven of my sins. I have no choice but to stay.

14

EZRA

Evie. The little killer, the monster hiding behind the face of an angel. I didn't expect to see her again. If she had any sense of self-preservation, she would have stayed away.

She pretends to be innocent, but I see straight through her bullshit. She's a killer, and that fact presents a challenge, a level to which I have never been, and that excites me. Possessing the ability to take a life takes a certain type of person: cold and calculating, unfeeling. And yet, although Evie should be unfeeling, she is scared of me, and her fear calls to me like no other. *Make me cry.* She's such a broken little doll, she's perfect. I want her. I want to ruin her, and I always get what I want. I skim my fingers over her throat and feel the fear in her thrumming pulse. *Her* fear is intoxicating.

The taste of her on my tongue, the feel of her soft throat under my hands...I only have so much restraint. I close my eyes and inhale. Images of all the things I'd like to do to her flash through my mind, and none of them are good. Some men like rough sex, hell, some like to tie women up, maybe spank them a bit. I like to hurt them, *really* hurt them. I like to bring them to the point where they believe their own death is a very real possibility, because that brand of fear is the only authentic fear there is.

She watches me, her chest heaving, her throat marked with my handprint. Her eyes are wide, her cheeks flushed. This is the perfect combination of arousal and fear. She slides back onto the desk when I step closer to her. I grab her legs, force them open, and press between them. Her head tilts back, and she stares up at me through her long, thick lashes.

"Is that you want, sweetheart?" I caress the side of her throat, brushing the marks left by my own fingers. "Destruction?"

Without warning, she grabs the back of my head, her long nails digging into my neck as she pulls me towards her and slams her lips over mine. Her tongue skims my bottom lip as her legs lock around my waist. "I want you to take everything from me," she says against my mouth.

My fingers dig into her thighs, and I yank them apart with such force she has no choice but to release me. I drag her to her feet. A look of confusion passes her face before I grab her waist and I spin her around, making her face the wall behind my desk. My fingers twitch against her skin as I skim my teeth over her shoulder.

"I take, little killer. I don't give," I say as I shove her forward. She staggers, slamming into the wall. I take her delicate wrists and yank her arms above her head, pinning her in place. She attempts to turn her head to look at me, and I tighten my hold on her wrists. "Do not look at me," I warn.

She complies and turns to face the wall again. In the following silence I can hear her rapid breaths. I can feel her heart pumping. "Good. Now, spread your legs," I say, and she hesitates for just a heartbeat. I force my thigh between her legs, pushing them apart as I lean in by her ear. "Never hesitate," I breathe against her neck.

I take both her wrists into one hand, and slowly trail my free hand over her bunched up dress before I squeeze her arse, clad in white lace. So innocent, so fucking sexy.

"Make me cry, Ezra." She rocks back, grinding against my hard cock.

My pulse grows frantic and my jaw clenches."Careful what you wish for, little killer."

Just the thought of pushing her to the edge of her capabilities makes my cock twitch. I want her to beg me to stop, but I have the feeling she never will. I may very well have to kill her in pursuit of her tears, because I will earn them.

I skim my hand over her stomach and tug her lace thong to the side, dragging a finger over her pussy. That slight touch causes her body to tremble. Moaning, she throws her head back and fights against my firm hold. I growl and thrust two fingers inside her wet pussy. She gasps as she clenches around my fingers, pulling me deeper inside her. I pump into her, each time harder than the last, and after just a few strokes, the wetness from her pussy trickles down my fingers. Her back bows and her moans grow frantic. My cock is painful now. I swear, if she rubs her arse against me one more time I'm going to fuck her into next week and teach her exactly where the pleasure pain line is.

Someone bangs on the door to my office, and I groan in frustration, shoving my fingers deeper inside of her. Evie pushes back against me and her pussy clenches around my fingers so damn hard.

The handle to the door jiggles. "Ez?" Jonty shouts before pounding over the wood again.

"Yeah," I say angrily, my fingers still buried deep inside her warmth.

"Zee's here," Jonty says.

"For fucks sake." I growl as I rip my hand away from her. I stick my fingers in my mouth, sucking the taste of her from them. "Why is he *here*?" I shout.

"Because he's a twat..."

I pull Evie's dress down and yank her away from the wall before I unlock the door. Jonty stands in the doorway, his eyes narrowing on Evie's flushed face.

"Where is he?" I ask, drawing Jonty's attention back to me.

"By the bar. Says he needs to talk to you." He glances back at Evie and smirks.

"I'm not done with you yet, little girl," I whisper in her ear before taking her by the shoulders and shoving her toward Jonty. "Take her out to the bar," I say as I step into the hallway.

On my way down the hall, I adjust the erection threatening to rip through my jeans, and as soon as I set foot into the club, I spot Zee leaned against the bar. *Fucker.* He glares at me like the prick he is. Jonty walks Evie past me to the bar, and Zee's beady little eyes follow her every move. The way he's looking at her pisses me off. He looks like he's about to come in his pants.

I grit my teeth when I stop in front of him. "What do you want, Zee?"

He grins. "You know what I want, Ezra."

"My answer hasn't changed, but the second it does, I'll let you know."

His expression remains blank and he shrugs, his gaze veering back over to Evie. His eyes drag over her body and I clench my jaw. "Oh," he laughs. "I'm sure I can change your mind."

"Lets go to my office," I say through clenched teeth. His eyes light up as though I'm about to give him what he wants. I just don't want him near Evie.

Zee follows me up the stairs and takes a seat at my desk. I shut the door and Dave hops up, circling my legs as I make my way across the room to sit down. He steeples his fingers in front of him. "I tell you what, Ezra, you can buy your-self a little more time." He grins, glancing at the TV screens on the wall. "I want *that* girl." And of course, the screen his finger is aimed at has Evie dead and center. It makes me want to rip his bloody finger from his hand and shove it down his throat.

"Tough."

Zee tilts his head to the side, his dark eyes narrowing. "I'll even pay you for her. Everything is for sale at the right price."

I clench and release my fists over and over, fighting the urge to grab his face and twist his head to the side. The pop his neck would make as it breaks would be music to my ears.

"Go and buy another girl."

"I bet she's pretty when she cries," he says, arching his eyebrow as a grin twists his lips.

"We're done here. "

"You forget that I own you, Ezra."

I snap, rising from the chair and launching across the table at him. I grab him by the throat and yank him halfway across the desk. "No one fucking owns me." I growl. "You forget who I am. I know about you and Moorcroft. I have the evidence. You implicate me and you implicate yourself. Ergo, you haven't got shit." I release him and he falls back into the chair coughing. I take out a cigarette and light it, inhaling the thick smoke, staring at Zee while he glares at me.

"You kill me, and it won't matter what you have," he says. "You'll still go down."

I shrug. "So it appears we are at an impasse. We both go down or neither of us goes down."

He smirks, tapping his index finger on his bottom lip. "Then nothing has changed. You can't turn me in, and you can't kill me, but I can take your girls Ezra. So, if you sell her to me now, I'll give you a hundred grand, and I'll leave your other girls alone...for now. But if you fight me," he sighs, "I will start picking them off. One by one, until you give her to me."

"Why her?" I glare at him. Evie is pretty, but she's not a hundred grand pretty.

"Because the second I looked at her, you looked like you were about to kill me." He laughs as he shakes his head smugly. "I told you I would take everything from you Ezra. You don't seem to care about your whores, but maybe you care about your own personal whore. Don't worry, I'm sure she'll think of you when I cut her, and then fuck her while she bleeds out."

I slam my fist over the desk. Still smirking, Zee falls silent.

"Get. Out." I snarl. "Before I snap your neck."

He slowly rises and strolls out of my office as though he has all the time in the world.

I grab the decanter from the side of the desk and take a hefty swig. I can't keep doing this. I wasn't made to bow down, and the very notion is making me irritable, likely to do something stupid. I jog back down the stairs, eager to get Evie the fuck away from here. She's perched on a bar stool with her long legs gracefully crossed, smiling at something Jonty says to her.

I point at Jonty. "You tell the fucking bouncers not to let him in here again." He nods. "Fucking shit! I would have thought that was obvious." Jonty scowls at me. I know I've pissed him off, but shit, the last thing I need is Zee in my club. And now he's seen Evie. "And put the girls on lockdown," I say. "Call them all in and tell them they work only from the club, they do not go on the streets, and have the guys walk them home. He's going to keep coming for them."

I grab the back of Evie's neck, take a fistful of hair, and I drag her off the stool. "I'm taking you home," I say.

"I don't need you to take me home."

"Do *not* argue with me." She studies my face, and she must see how deadly fucking serious I am because she slowly nods, her fingers gripping the cross hung around her neck.

I guide her toward the hall, grab Dave from my office, and we leave from the back of the club.

15

EVIE

Ezra pulls onto one of the dirty New York side streets, tires screaming as he guides the sleek Mercedes through traffic. Dave slides around in the back seat, panting. I glance over at Ezra. His posture is rigid, his knuckles have gone white from how tightly he's gripping the steering wheel. I don't like him angry because he reminds me of the devil when he's like this. I press my back to the door, trying to keep as much distance as possible between us.

An alarm dings. His eyes cut over at me and he groans. He steers with one hand, reaches across my body with the other, and forcefully pushes me back into the seat before jerking the seat belt across my hips and clicking it in place. "Shit's annoying," he says and the beeping cuts off.

Swallowing, I force my gaze away from him. He scares me, and I don't like that. Not since Zachariah have I let a man scare me. Ezra's sharp facial features, his demeanor, his course British accent; it's all so chivalrous, yet brutal at the same time. He is quite deceiving, but then again, the deadliest things usually come in the prettiest of packages. I stare at him for a moment longer. *He is beautiful in the most brutal of ways.* And now I see why they say beauty is sin, because he makes me want to sin. He makes me want to lie back on a dirty bed with filthy sheets and let him spread my legs apart. I want him to do terrible, nasty things to me. He makes me want to be that redhead, sucking back his cock in front of a window so others will want to covet what is mine.

There's a rough bump as we pull onto the Manhattan Bridge. Ezra's jaw tenses, and his arms straighten out. We drive in silence, and when we pull onto my street, I feel sick. He knows where I live.

"How do you know where I live?" I ask.

He taps one finger on the steering wheel, his eyes fixed on the road ahead. "I know everything, little killer. I had you followed that first time."

The thought of him having me followed seems romantic, and the sickness in the pit of my stomach transforms into flattery. I feel flattered. *He's more like you than you want to admit, Evelyn.*

The car stops on the side of the road and he cuts the engine. I glare at him as I climb out of the car. "Thank you," I say before shutting the door and heading toward the steps.

I hear his car door slam shut, and the click of Dave's paws trotting over the pavement. He's right behind me. I spin around and he all but walks into me. Ezra snatches the keys from my hand and storms ahead of me, opening the door to the stairwell and signaling me to walk ahead of him. Dave ducks into the doorway and disappears. Panic winds its way around me. I don't trust Ezra, he's dangerous, and I of all people know how things like this end. I'll let him follow me into my apartment and he'll kill me then dump my body into the Hudson River, because that's what I would do. I'm shaking at the idea of how he would kill me. I've never thought about what death must be like, but now I am wondering if it hurts.

"Walk, Evie," he says in a commanding tone, his accent making the order inoffensive.

He walks to my door and I stop. I'm not going to be dumped into the Hudson River tonight. "You can go now," I say as I snatch the keys from his hand. I am terrified of him, yet somehow crave him. This was not planned. This is not part of *his* plan.

"No."

I grit my teeth and anger bubbles through me. "I don't want you here, Ezra."

"I don't care what you want," he says calmly, making me aware that what I want is irrelevant.

He stares down at me, his enormous frame towering over mine, and all I can think is he's like the devil towering over an angel, that angel me, the devil him. The tension rises between us, and I become increasingly aware of his body only inches from mine. This calm heir of danger pours off him in waves, and it should scare me because I know he wants to hurt me, but I like it when he does... His eyes drop to my lips, and my lungs falter. There's a pause, and then he slams me against the wall, forcing the breath from my lungs in a rush. His mouth meets mine in an angry clash of lips and tongues. My heart hammers, I can hear it in my throat as I tear my lips from his, fighting to catch my breath.

I want to slap him for making me want his filthy lips on me. I feel my nostrils flare. I want his lips on me again, and I am going to hell for it, but I don't care. Because I kiss him again, I grab his shirt and wad it inside my fist. I press my body against his, and it's hot because the flames of hell are licking at my very soul right now. He is a sinner and I am sin and everything about this is the work of Satan. Ezra's lips move to my neck, trailing down my throat, branding my skin in the most sinful way. I moan at the way he feels all over me, moan like a wretched little slut.

"Door," he growls.

I turn and fumble with the key. His chest presses against my back, his steady breathes touching my neck. I can't breathe. I can't think. The lock clicks and I push on the door. As soon as it opens, the dog runs inside and lays down by the hearth. I walk through the doorway and Ezra grabs onto my hips, pressing me against the wall while he kicks the door closed with his foot. He's so heavy against me. I can't stop my hands from touching him, from feeling over every last inch of this man's defined muscles. *Why are my hands touching him?* His hands are in my hair and he's pulling, and it feels so good. This shouldn't feel good. It should feel dirty and wrong and vile.

His warm lips move over my neck, and then his teeth are on me, biting me, bruising me, and it's painful, but it's right because he's punishing me for wanting him like this when I shouldn't. *Make him stop, Evelyn.* But I can't because I've already fallen and there's no way to stop me until I hit the bottom. And I will hit the bottom.

Ezra tears his lips away from me, breathing heavily as he holds his face barely an inch from mine.

"The ways I will destroy you up, little killer..." he says with a growl.

Hands, and mouths, and tongues...and where did my dress go? He picks me up and lowers me to the floor. His hands grip my hips in a bruising hold as his mouth works over my stomach. I moan like a little whore, my body writhing beneath him even though I'm telling it not to. I like it. I want it. And I shouldn't...but I do. I do, I fucking do. His fingers grip the insides of my thighs, violently shoving them apart before he drags his wet tongue over me, and I whimper.

"Fuck, you taste like heaven," he growls--no he hisses. *Evelyn, you're filthy and dirty.* But Ezra says I taste like heaven. He's comparing me to heaven, and there's reverence in his tone.

His gaze locks with mine as his tongue darts out and dives inside of me. His eyes darken, turning feral, and I, in turn become unhinged. I'm hot and I don't want this to stop ever, because is this what sex should be like, like this? Like I am something he wants to worship, like I am a stream he can drink life from every day? Is this what sin really is, because it's beautiful and I want to burn in it if it is. This is sin and sin leads to hell and I'm okay with that because at this very moment I would dance in the flames of that inferno. I would pirouette with the devil himself for this. And I can't blame those bad men for wanting women like they do, really I can't...and now, Ezra's making me question myself. I don't like that, but now my hands are ripping his shirt off. His body looks like a painting in the Vatican, righteous and glorious. And how can this be sinful when it looks so holy? All I want is him naked. I want to be that redhead. I want to be a wanton slut that needs a dirty, filthy man to fuck all the wrong right out of her, so I rip his jeans off. I shove his boxers down, and I sit up, forcing him back onto the floor while I ram his cock down my throat. I trace my tongue over each vein, over every single ridge, and his hands pull at my hair again, and why does that feel so damn good?

"Fuck, Evie. Your mouth." He groans, thrusting his hips into my face. His cock slides deeper into my mouth, the tip hitting the back of my throat. "I knew those lips were made for my cock," he says through clenched teeth. And yes, they were. These lips...my lips were made for his cock and I believe that now and how I'm I supposed to kill the man whose cock my lips were made for?

And all I want right now is that cock that my mouth was made for inside me. I place my hands on his shoulders and I drag my naked, slutty body over his righteous body. It feels so right, the way his skin slides against mine, heating it. "You're making me sin, Ezra," I whisper in a voice I don't even recognize because I have been possessed by this man.

I slip my pussy over him, and just when I feel the flames of hell engulfing every last inch of my being, his lips meet mine in a violent kiss, his teeth biting down on my bottom lip, drawing blood. Blood, and then I taste myself, and he is right, I *do* taste like heaven. Maybe I have been lied to for all of these years because a devil can't taste like heaven, it's impossible. I want to say his name because I love how it feels when it rolls from my lips. "Ezra," I moan, and it sounds even better in a moan than I imagined.

He grabs my hips, flipping me over with an animalistic growl. He leans over my back and takes my wrists, holding them both in one of his large hands as he pulls them over my head, restraining me. I try to tug my hands free and he slams them down harder, threatening to cut the circulation off. He squeezes me harder and I relish in it. I moan at it, trying to contain the urge I have to scream because I want him to take me, and I shouldn't be on my floor like this, but I am. He releases my wrists only to grab my hips and yank my ass into the air.

"You don't fuck me, Evie. I fuck you." My cheek presses against the cool floor as he places a hand between my shoulder blades, pinning me, restraining me. "And I fuck hard," he whispers before he rears back and slams inside of me.

I bite my lip, a silent scream lodging in my throat. His skin is hot and smooth, his body perfect over my back and between my thighs yet so wrong and dirty and sinful that I should kill him for it. I should slit his throat, but I can't because my lips were made for his cock. *You taste like heaven, Evie.* And how can I kill someone who compares me to heaven with the reverence of a Saint? I can't even think about that now because he's thrusting inside of me so hard, but yet so gentle if that makes any sense. His hands are forcing me to fuck him, forcing me to feel him, to submit to him, like that redhead. He wants me and I want him and...I choke on my thoughts because it feels that damn good.

His fingers dig into my hips with such force it hurts. His lips move to my ear, his teeth nipping at my earlobe as he rears back and releases my shoulders. His fingers dig at my hips, pulling them back to meet his ruthless thrusts. He drags one finger down my spine and over the crack off my ass until he brushes a place that screams dirty and foul and sin. And I gasp.

"Maybe I should start with this? Have you ever been taken in the arse, Evie?" He folds his body over mine until his hot chest presses against my back and his lips are at my ear. "If your pussy feels this good I can only imagine what your sweet," his breath hitches on a deep groan, "virgin arse would feel like."

I can't say a word. I try, but I'm choking. I shake my head because now I really can feel the flames of hell consuming me, and they will burn me until I'm nothing but ash. I close my eyes, biting my lip. And then his thumb grazes over me...*there*...and I can't stop where my mind takes me. That one sensation catapults me into the dark crevices I try not to go.

"Don't you scream. Don't fucking cry either, Evelyn," Zachariah hisses as he pins me down, pressing his thick forearm over my throat. "I'll choke you with my bare hands then wrap a rope around your neck and hang you from the closet. I'll tell everyone you killed yourself just like your mother did, because you had demons inside you that wouldn't shut up."

He slams into me, the pain shooting through me like rusted nails, catching on every piece of flesh inside me. "Dirty. Filthy." He grunts as he rams himself into me again and again, jarring the tears free from my eyes.

"Please, Zachariah. Stop." I plead through tears.

"I can't stop, Evelyn. I have to punish you for making me want you so damn badly. It's a sin you know. Sex. You make me sin, and for that I have to make you hurt, make you not want to tempt me ever again. I have to purge the wicked from you with pain." I claw at

him, trying to push him away from me, but I'm so weak it does no good.

Ezra laughs and snaps me out of hell, dragging me back to the brink of his own heaven. He grabs my hair, wrapping it around his wrist and pulling me up onto my hands. "So fucking innocent."

My back bows and he forces himself deeper inside me, hitting a spot no one has ever reached before, and now I'm back in that place where everything is beautiful and blissful, because this is bliss. The tingles jolting through my body, the way I feel like an idol in his hands. My arms tremble beneath me, threatening to give way under my weight and the lack of control I'm experiencing at the hands of this man.

"Innocent, Evie," he whispers, and my face smacks the cold floor because I can't hold myself up any more, but he keeps fucking me. I'm screaming and swearing and I'm clenching around him because this feels too good, too raw, too real, and if he doesn't stop I'm going to...

"Ezra," I moan. My hands slap at the floor like I'm trying to tap out, but all he does is laugh that deep laugh that reminds me of the devil. Aftershocks of what he's done to me wrack my body, and I know now that I am his and he is mine and I can't kill him because this is salvation right here, right now.

He keeps thrusting until his body stiffens behind me with a guttural growl. Everything stops, and all I can hear is our mingled breaths, almost like the waves of the ocean crashing onto the shore after an angry storm.

His chest rises and falls in ragged swells against my back. This is how it should be.

I feel his lips touch my neck, and then he's pulling away from me. My body suddenly feels cold without him, and with that coldness comes the shame. I was that wanton slut, even though he didn't fuck me against the window, and I shouldn't have been. I let him fuck me because I wanted him to. This was no means to an end. He is still very much alive and I am very much undone. This was a sin, pure and simple.

I lay on the floor next to him, silently praying to be forgiven, but I know the prayers of someone as wretched as me won't even reach the edge of heaven. They never have.

16

EZRA

I collapse on the bed, my chest heaving and my body slick with sweat. I feel like a sixteen year-old working out months of frustration. I can't get enough of her. She takes everything I give her, and asks for more. She has no limitations, no breaking point, and it just makes me want to push her that much harder. Honestly, I'm pretty sure one of us is going to end up dead.

I turn my head to the side and glance at her. Her black hair is sprawled across the bed, her red lipstick smeared across her lips. Her eyes remain closed as she tries to catch her breath. So innocent, so breakable.

"You done yet, sweetheart?" I smirk.

She nods.

I sit up, searching the room for my clothes. I spot my boxers and stand, yanking them on. Evie watches me the entire time, her wide, blue eyes fixed on my every move.

I wonder if she even knows how far down the rabbit hole she's fallen because there is no getting out of this now. I fucking own her.

I WAKE UP CONFUSED, in strange surroundings. I reach under my pillow for my gun, only to come up empty. I frown as I study the unfamiliar room. The bare walls and sparse furniture remind me that I'm in Evie's apartment. The bed shifts beside me, and I glance over to see Evie's beautifully naked back, the fine pink scar spanning her shoulder blades and stretching down her spine.

I want to get up and leave, but I can't because Zee wants her, and he's not getting her. I slide out of bed, pull my jeans on, and stumble through her living room. There's a sliding French door that leads to the balcony. The second I open it, Dave jumps up from his spot on the floor and wriggles through it.

The frigid morning air touches my bare chest as I drag out a chair from the patio table. I take the pack of cigarettes from my jeans, and light one, inhaling a lungful of smoke. I comb a hand through my hair and brace my elbows on my knees. I can still smell Evie on me, the scent of her perfume mixed with sex makes me bite my cheek as I remember how tight her pussy felt around my cock. No woman should feel that good. It's like she was made for me, and that's just dangerous.

I should walk away, but somehow, we've ended up bound together in this shit. I don't do this shit, sleeping in a girl's house, in the same bed, but I guess I'm all heart because I'm worried Zee is either going to gut her or sell her. Ah, hell, that's bullshit. I just don't want him near her. I guess staying with her is the equivalent to pissing on her, marking my territory. And she can't stay here alone. She's like a sitting duck.

I stub my fag out on the metal balcony railing as I rise from the chair. Dave follows me back inside and to Evie's room. He sits at the foot of the bed, cocking his head to the side as he stares at her. She barely stirs when I yank her drawers open, pulling out items of clothing and tossing them on the bed.

"What are you doing?" she asks, her voice husky and sexy from sleep. The second Dave hears her voice he hops onto the bed next to her and flattens himself into the duvet as though I won't see him.

"Get up, get your stuff. You're leaving," I say without looking at her.

She rolls over, her brows pinching together. "I'm not leaving ..."

"I'd advise you do as I say. It would make my life considerably easier." I spot a suitcase on top of the wardrobe and pull it down, throwing her clothes into it.

She swings her legs over the side of the bed, staring into the suitcase. "Why?" There's a flash of fear in her eyes as I glare down at her.

I lean over her and brush a knuckle down her cheek. "What did I tell you about asking questions?" I say quietly. She drops her chin to her chest, and I notice her hands form angry little fists. "Good. There's a man who wants you, and not in a good way. So you come with me, or you die. Your choice, sweetheart."

"What are you talking about, Ezra?" She is too calm. "Who wants me?"

"Questions..." I warn as I shove a handful of clothes in the bag.

"Someone wants to kill me?"

"He doesn't want to kill you." I growl, turning to face her. "He wants to buy you." I step closer to her. "He wants to fuck you, and hurt you, and then he will sell you to the highest bidder so that they can fuck you and hurt you." I cup her jaw, stroking a thumb over her cheek. "And they will make what I do to you look like Disneyland, little killer."

Her eyes narrow. "What's his name?"

"Zee." I turn away and rip open another drawer. "He's a trafficker."

"How does he know about me?" Her jaw ticks. "What, were you trying to sell me to him before you decided you like hurting me yourself? Is that what the little tests of yours were about?"

I take a deep breath, willing myself to have patience. "He was one of my clients. And no, I whore girls out, I don't fucking sell them."

"Why isn't he your client any longer?"

"Jesus Christ, Evie. Enough!" I snap. "He was a client, he killed a girl, I cut him off. He's pissed and now he's coming after my girls, namely you. You are coming with me if I have to drag you by your fucking hair." I pick up the suit-case and walk out of the room. I don't even know what I'm doing, but all I know is I would sooner just give up and hand myself over to the UK government before I let that little ball bag win. He will not have Evie.

I drag her suitcase down the stairs, Dave, my ever present shadow, following me as I go to the car, pop the boot, and toss the luggage inside.

Evie appears a few minutes later with a frown fixed on her features.

"Get in the car," I tell her.

She opens the door, letting Dave inside before she slides into the passenger seat. She stares out the window as we pull away from her apartment complex, and I turn up the radio, blasting Gun's n' Roses around the car.

A few minutes later she turns the radio down and stares at me, fuddling nervously with her hands. "What was her name?" she whispers.

"Who?"

"The girl he killed. What was her name?" Her voice hitches and I glance at her. Her eyes are filled with tears and her teeth are buried in her bottom lip.

"Sophie."

She slams her eyes closed and nods slowly as she stares out the passenger window. I turn my attention back to the road. "Who was she to you?" I don't know Evie well, but she's a killer, a whore, not the sort of person to pity a strange girl she doesn't know. People like she and I, we are creatures of the underworld, we do not shed tears for strangers.

"My sister." Her voice is detached, devoid of emotion. Sophie was her sister? *Shit.* "Her real name was Hannah."

Sophie was a good girl and an even better whore. She was one of the broken ones, and I almost felt sorry for her. In this industry you don't often have to deal with the consequences of your actions, but now here I am, sat in a car with those consequences. Sophie was a whore, but she was also a sister. She had someone who loved her, and now she's dead. Do I blame myself? No. She knew what she was getting into when she took the job on. I gave her a means to earn money. I'm a businessman not a charity. But I know I should have been more careful with Zee, more careful with her. I didn't look out for her when I should have.

I won't let Zee get Evie. I owe Sophie that much. At least that's what I'm telling myself.

17

EVIE

I try not to think of Hannah as I look out the window. I watch the people walking on the street, staring at a family laughing, and I try to think of what that must be like. We come to a red light and my gaze locks on a man panhandling for money.

Ezra's phone rings and he snatches it from the console to answer it. "Yeah."

There's a long pause and then he slams his hand over the steering wheel, dropping his head forward. "Shit. Find her Jonty. I fucking want her back!" Another pause. "Fine. I'll go to the girl's place now."

The light turns green and Ezra floors the accelerator, the car fish-tailing as he makes a U-turn. Cars honk as he swerves in front of them. I press my back to the seat and remain silent despite the nagging urge to ask him what's going on. I know better than to ask him questions when he's angry.

Ten minutes later the car comes to an abrupt stop, the seatbelt digging into my chest.

"Get out," Ezra says as he cuts the ignition and flings the door open.

I do as told and hurry to keep up with him. We head toward the apartments on the corner of the road. They look like vintage 1930s bungalows, fresh paint on the brickwork, new windows with pretty little flower boxes beneath them. As soon as Ezra reaches the door, it opens.

A woman steps through the door and throws her arms around Ezra's neck. She's young with long blonde hair falling down her back in perfect waves. She looks like a cheerleader with her tiny shorts and tight t-shirt.

"Please find her, Ez." She's crying on him. She's giving him her tears, and then I wonder if he beat her and fucked her the same way he did me. I wonder if he told her she tasted like heaven, and the thought makes me enraged.

Ezra places his hands around her delicate waist, taking a step back as he removes her arms from his neck.

"Lola, I need you to show me the security footage from this morning." She nods, sniffing away her tears.

I follow Ezra as he walks into the building, and is greeted by a string of girls. Every one of them tries to touch him, like he is a god they worship. When they call him Ez it makes my jaw clench. His name is Ezra, not Ez. They glare at me when I pass them, judging me. I know they wonder why I'm with him, and I want to scream that it's because I'm the whore he will fuck, not them, me.

"You stay here," Ezra says to me before following Lola into her apartment.

I lean against the wall, keeping my eyes on the floor. I see their shoes walk past me, I hear them whispering to one another, and it makes me wonder if they have ever seen Ezra with a woman before. *See, Evelyn, you are special.*

I remember Hannah telling me he was putting her up in a luxury apartment. I remember her begging me to come work for him, how highly she spoke of the man she intended to kill. I couldn't bear the thought of letting a man beat me before I killed him, but now, after being with Ezra, I can see what Hannah saw in it. She realized that she could be forgiven by the very men she killed. I don't even notice that I'm walking away from the door until I come to the end of the hallway. I turn around, glancing back down the hallway. One door opens and a dark headed woman saunters out in a short purple dress. She turns to lock the door and catches sight of me. Her eyes narrow.

"Which was Sophie's room?" I ask.

She stares at me, taking several steps in my direction. I watch her eyes study my face. I see that she notices the similarities between me and my sister. "Why?" she swallows and tears well in her brown eyes.

"I'm her sister...Ezra brought me here."

Her breath hitches. "I'm so sorry." She shakes her head and leads me past two doors before stopping. "This one. We haven't touched it yet," she says and walks off.

I inhale before I place my hand on the knob and open the door. She'd lived with me before she took that job with Ezra six months ago. I missed her so much when she moved, but she told me part of her deal was she couldn't have visitors, and she couldn't go out without permission.

The inside is immaculate, furnished with the kind of furniture you see in Pottery Barn advertisements. I step inside and close the door behind me. It still smells like her, like cherry-blossom and vanilla. I fight the tears building in my eyes because I don't want to cry. I trail my fingers over the back of the sofa, trying to remember Hannah any other way than in that bag, but I can't. I round the front of the couch and sit down. I can feel her here.

"Dear God, please help me. Please guide me. Please let me kill the man who took my sister from me." I feel a tear trickle down my check, and quickly swipe it away. I skim the room, and on the edge of the coffee table is Hannah's ring. I pick it up, rolling it between my fingers. This was our bond. This was one of the ways we righted the wrong. I flip the lid and find the inside of the ring empty, only a trace of arsenic inside. Why did she not give this to the man who killed her? I close my eyes again. "Please bless me. Please forgive me, and Hannah, and Ezra..."

I feel something nudge my elbow and I open my eyes to find Dave next to me, his tail wagging as he stares at me. I hesitate before I skim my fingers over the smooth fur on his head. I know Ezra is here, I can sense his presence, feel him watching me. I stand and turn, and there he is, leaning against the door frame, his thick arms folded across his chest. My eyes trace over the ink that winds around his arms. He's like a devil, or a demon, something wicked. A beautiful demon.

His dark eyes watch me, his expression tight. "Never met a whore who prayed before," he mumbles.

"Hannah prayed."

"Huh." He cocks a brow. "She didn't strike me as the type," he says with such a coldness to his voice, I shiver. I hear what he doesn't say, he thinks we're both hypocrites. How can a whore pray?

"Sinners pray," I tell him, my chest tightening.

A condescending smile shapes his lips. "If you say so. We need to go." He turns away and Dave trots after him. And just like his dog, I follow after him.

*****BREAK*****

Ezra closes the door to the office. Jonty is sitting behind Ezra's desk, his enormous body looking cramped in the chair. He smiles at me and the scar on his face creases into a jagged dent.

I take a seat on the couch and Dave pads over to me, staring at me as he rests his head in my lap.

Ezra bristles with impatience as he waits for Jonty to finish on the phone . When he hangs up he leans back in the chair, releasing a long breath. "Nothing, Ez. I can't find shit."

"Motherfucker." Ezra inhales, scrubbing his hand over his face.

"He must be selling them within twenty-four hours, probably has some fuckers ordering them and he's just picking off the ones he needs." Jonty's eyes skirt over to me, then back to Ezra.

"Goddamn it!" Ezra groans as he slings the door to the office open.

I glance over at Jonty and immediately run after Ezra. I follow him down the hallway and then down the stairs. He storms through the club until he comes to a door marked 'Staff Only'. He punches in a code on the keypad. The lock clicks, the door releases, and there's another set of steps, descending into the cellar.

"Ezra!" I call after him. But he ignores me, pulling a cord hanging from the ceiling.

A dull yellow haze casts over kegs of beer and wooden crates. Ezra rummages through one of the crates, slinging things around. He finds a metal box and pulls it up, opening the lid and removing blocks of what look like explosives. He closes the box and shoulders past me without a word. I follow behind him, winding my way back up the stairs and to the hallway until we're back at his office.

He points inside. "Go sit."

I look at Jonty still sitting behind the desk and swallow. "I want to go with you," I say timidly.

"What the fuck do you think you are? My pet dog?" He turns away from me. "Jonty, don't let her out of your sight." And he walks off.

I grit my teeth as I watch him strut down the dim hallway and disappear around a corner. I hate the way he makes me crave him despite how brutally cruel he is.

"You going to stand there all night, or come sit down. I don't bite," Jonty says, an amused smile on his lips.

"He just left me..." I go into the office, standing close to the door.

He laughs, taking a packet of cigarettes from his pocket and holding them out to offer me one. I shake my head, and he places one between his lips, lighting it. "Word of advice, treacle, Ezra James is one mean bastard." He exhales a long stream of smoke. "Helping you may well be the first decent thing I've ever seen him do." He coughs.

"It's only because he likes to hurt me."

He chuckles again. "Yep. Sick fuck." His eyes slide over my body and bile rises in my throat. "I wouldn't hurt you, sweet thing." I take a step back and he snorts. "I'm joking. Shit. I like my balls right where they are. Ezra...he's like a pitbull with a bone. Do not touch. At least not til he's through chewing on it."

18

EZRA

J onty has had a tail on Zee for a couple of days now, but he doesn't seem to follow much of a routine. As far as we know, he hasn't been near any suspicious places. I watch from my car as Zee opens his door and climbs out of the car, clicking the locks as he walks up to a townhouse. He knocks on the door, and a woman answers, smiling wide when she see's him. He grabs her face and kisses her before pushing her back inside. Maybe this is one of his whore houses, or maybe he just has a bit on the side. Hard to imagine with his tastes.

As soon as the upstairs light comes on, I move, crossing the road and ducking down behind his car. I unzip the duffle bag and pull out two blocks of C4. Bombs aren't my forte, this is more Jonty's shit, but I can wire a simple car bomb. I wire a mobile phone to the detonator and duct tape it to the blocks of explosive.

I lie down on my back and slide underneath the car, pausing to listen for any movement from the house. Zee is probably balls deep in that woman by now, blissfully unaware, but the last thing I need is to get caught.

I tape the bomb to the chassis right in the centre of the car and turn the phone on. Zee will learn what happens when you fuck with me. I can't kill him, not yet at least, but I just need to remind him that I can. Anytime I like.

I hop up and jog across the street, getting back in my car. And then, I wait. I wait for three hours, until Zee has blown his load, put his dick away, and decides to leave the house. He steps out from the door and I press the call button on my phone. Zee pauses on the porch, and then his sixty grand BMW explodes in a ball of fire. The windows of my car rattle, and I turn my face from the blinding light. When I look back, Zee is lying on the porch, unmoving.

The only reason he's not a pile of ash on the front seat of his car right now is because of what he has on me, but he needs to remember that I'm not rational, I don't do well with black mail, and no one shafts me.

I quickly dial Jonty's number.

"Hey," he answers.

"It's done. You hit the warehouse tomorrow. I want that bastard crawling on his knees."

I hang up and pull away from the house, heading back to the club before the cops decide to rock up. If there's one thing that makes me hard it's blowing shit up. I could call Jen, but now she feels like a shitty substitute for Evie's brand of crazy.

19

EVIE

The couch cushion jolts and I hear Dave's nails tap over the floor. I'm slightly disoriented. The room is dark except for a lamp on the desk, and then I remember where I am.

"Well, what are you going to do with her, Ez?" I hear Jonty's voice coming from the other side of the closed door. "You just going to leave her here?"

"I don't know. I don't have time to babysit her but fuck, Zee will kill her."

"Give over, Ez." Jonty laughs. "You sure as shit aren't keeping her here because you've suddenly developed some sort of moral compass."

"Fuck off."

Jonty laughs again, hacking a cough. "She must really take the belt if you're prepared to go all white knight for her. Not falling for that pretty face are you?"

"Be serious. She's a fun distraction. Takes a beating better than even Jen, and sucks dick almost as well." He laughs. "I'm going home. Take her up to one of the rooms. Just watch her."

My entire body goes up in flames. Ezra told me my lips were made for his cock...My pulse thrums in my neck. He wants to play savior to me, he wants to beat me and use me and fuck me into an oblivion, well, I'll show him what a fun little distraction I can be.

The door opens, and Jonty walks in, his eyes straying over to me before he grabs my suitcase. "Come on, treacle. Got a room for you to stay in."

I sigh and stand up, following him down the hallway. He stops to unlock a door, and I can't ignore the steady string of thuds and squeaking springs coming from the room next to us. There's a fake moan, and the bangs against the wall grow faster. Jonty laughs to himself as the door swings open. He tosses my luggage inside. "Bathroom's at the end of the hall," he says before shutting the door behind him.

The room is bare except for a bed in the center of the room and a radiator beneath the window. I look over the comforter before flipping it back. The sheets smell clean, but I don't take my clothes off before climbing into the bed. I know there is no amount of bleach that could clean these sheets of the filth that's seeped into the threads. I lay my head down and Ezra's snide comment plays on loop in my head. *"Takes a beating better than even Jen, and sucks dick almost as well."*

There are seven deadly sins. I can manage several of those with a man like Ezra. Lust...pride...envy... Ezra is the kind of man that doesn't like to share. And, much to my surprise, Ezra has made me realize I am a woman who doesn't like to share. I may just be a plaything to him--a distraction. But I am *his* distraction.

An eye for an eye...

I close my eyes and drift back to sleep, dreaming of all the ways I can have him hurt me.

20

EZRA

My phone rings, and I smile when I see Zee's number on the screen.

"Zee, how are you?"

"You're a motherfucker, Ezra, a stupid motherfucker," he curses.

"No, Zee," I laugh. "You're the stupid one for thinking you can screw with me without consequences. You really think you can take on the mob?"

"Ezra, I can take on, and take down the mob *through* you."

"Not without taking down yourself. And for what? A little more money? Run while you still have the chance Zee, sell your slaves, make your money. Survive." I spit the word. "Because if you don't I'm going to keep coming for you. I might leave you alive, but I will burn your fucking world to the ground."

"I'm going to destroy you, Ezra. And when you're crawling on your knees, you will wish you had taken my offer."

My burner phone beeps and I open it, laughing as I quickly read over the text. "Speaking of burning, you might want to check on your warehouse." I laugh once more and hang up.

I smile as I press play on the five second video clip of Zee's warehouse being blown to shit. If there's one thing Jonty does well, it's a good pyrotechnic show.

21

EVIE

I've been here for three days. I know I can leave, but I don't want to. Zee, the man who killed my sister, wants to take me. I'm not ready for him. I know nothing about him, and when I asked Ezra about Zee yesterday, he grabbed me by the throat and nearly choked me. Ezra said he would handle it, and I want to believe him, but he is taking too long. And he is ignoring me which makes me angry.

I've spent every waking moment when this club is empty learning it. I know each and every place those monitors survey. I know the places they can't see. Ezra has fucked me and beat me four times in his office while clients and whores are in the hallway, and I moan and I scream because I like it, because I am a good distraction, because I am better than Jen.

With each passing hour, with every touch of his hands, I hate Ezra even more because he has infested my mind like a crippling disease. My once pure heart has been tainted and blackened because all I can think about is how he feels between my thighs, deep inside me. I find no solace in prayer now because I know what forgiveness at his hands feels like, and that is what I want. I want forgiveness. I want this sin crawling through me to be beaten out of me, purged...by the devil.

That is who Ezra is, the devil, and I want him. Part of me wants to kill him, part of me thinks I'd die without him, and oh, what a horrible place that puts me in. I feel trapped in a never ending cycle of sin and penance, and Ezra is both: my sin and my penance. And how is that even possible?

I have to cleanse myself. I must put myself back on the right path, away from the devil. And besides, Ezra must be punished for lying to me about my lips. I'll show him just how good I can be at sucking dick.

The loud music from the club rumbles up through the floorboards. I have to remember why I am even in this mess to begin with. It's not to be Ezra's sex slave, it's to do the work I was chosen to do. Ezra thinks he has the upper hand, but it is only because I am allowing him to. He thinks I am a meek little lamb ready for slaughter. But I am not. I am a hunter. I am a warrior. I use my weakness as a lure, and I will show Ezra he cannot control me. *You only have control when you make a man love you, when you kill him. Go find a sinner, Evelyn.*

Without pause, I leave the room. I peer through the cracked doorway into Ezra's office. His chair is empty, and then I hear him arguing with one of the girl's at the other end of the hallway. Quickly, I make my way down the stairs, scurrying along the hallway, my heart banging in my chest as I step foot inside the dark club. I close my eyes and stand in the doorway because the cameras can't see me here. *Please help me...* The moment my eyes pry open, they land on a man in a crisply laundered dress shirt, an air of power swirling around him like a storm. He sticks out like a beacon amongst the dingy drunks, and I know that is a sign. The moment his gaze lands on me, his eyes narrow and I motion him over with my finger and a kittenish grin. The closer he comes, the more he undresses me with his eyes. As soon as he is within reach, I grab onto his silk tie and pull him toward my face.

His brows arch, and he grins, revealing his perfect, stark-white teeth. "Are you one of Ezra's girls?" he asks.

"Yes."

The man leans in to my ear, sucking in my scent. Disgust climbs up my throat, and all I want to do is choke him.

"Are you just one of his cheap whores, or are you one of his *girls?"* he asks.

I take that comment to mean he knows about the other girls, the girls like my sister. A vision of this man taking a knife to Hannah, coming as he takes her life, flashes through my mind and my jaw clenches. Maybe this is Zee.

"Does it really matter when I'm offering services on the house?" I smirk, rubbing my hand down the front of his shirt. He groans in response and I spin around, his tie still in my hand as I lead him to the stairwell.

The stairs groan under the man's weight, causing my stomach to knot. I know this is risky because when Ezra catches me, and he will catch me, he's going to be so angry. Fear mounts in my chest, and I thrive on it. He wants to ignore me, he wants to make me feel used, he wants to make me sin over and over and not grant me forgiveness? I will make him notice me. I will make him angry. I will make him beat me. I will force him to forgive me.

The door to Ezra's office is closed, which means Ezra is back inside. I swallow the lump in my throat as I lead this man to my room. As soon as we're inside, I shut the door, lock it, and slide the deadbolt into place.

I glare up at the camera, rage building in my chest as I pull my shirt over my head. I walk toward him, swaying my hips. He undoes his tie as I trace my fingertips over his chest, slowly unfastening each button from his dress shirt. Running my hands up his sides, I slip the material from his arms and press a gentle kiss to his stomach--the stomach I will slice open in a matter of moments. He grabs my hair, jerking my head back. His free hand gropes at my breast, pinching my nipple to the point of pain. I hate him touching me, but I want him to want me. I need him to want me. I have to have him love me.

I reach for his belt and pull the leather through the buckle, and he brushes my hand away. His pants drop to his ankles. He pushes his boxers down and fists his cock as he steps toward me. My pulse hammers in my ears when his dirty little lips lay over my neck, trailing kisses across my throat. His hands slip over my body, and my stomach turns. I have to get him away from me before I vomit. I push him away, gently, even though I want to shove him so hard he falls and splits his head wide open. He stumbles before falling back onto the bed.

I take his dick in my hand, trying to control my urge to gag as I stare at it. I force my lips over it. *Your mouth was made for Ezra's cock, Evelyn.* These lips are Ezra's, but his are not mine. So this is not wrong, and although I still feel guilty, I have work to do. I have to rid the world of men like this--I peek through my lashes at the man and all I can see is Zachariah--bad men. The man groans, his hips bucking up to meet my mouth, his hands grabbing on to the back of my head. *Ezra lied, your lips are not the only ones made for him, Evelyn.* My eyes stray up to the camera. I stare at the lens, a slight smirk on my face while I swallow back this man. I will make Ezra notice me. I will make him envious.

Sliding one hand beneath the mattress, I grab the knife I took from the bar last night. My fingers slowly wrap around the handle. The thought of Ezra watching me makes me shamefully wet.

I circle my tongue around the tip of this man's dick, staring at him. "Tell me you love me."

His eyes narrow and I slip him into my mouth, then back out. "Tell me..." Back in. Back out. "Tell me you love me..." Back in, then I stop and glare up at him.

He's panting and fisting the sheets, sweat beading on his brow. "Damn it. I love you, now finish."

I smile around his cock, my fingers twitching over the knife.

"Evie!" I hear Ezra shout from down the hall. He is angry now, and anger is an emotion he can't ignore. His hard footsteps thump down the hallway, and within moments the entire door is shaking.

"Shit!" the man huffs, releasing his hold on my head.

Fear drowns his face, and I can't help but laugh.

"Evie!" Ezra yells again, and the door rattles.

The man's eyes narrow on me as he tries to stand, but before he can manage to get up, I take the knife, jabbing it through his thigh and jerking the blade through his muscle. Warm blood splatters across my bare chest. The bright red spraying from his artery looks like a volcanic eruption, spurting with each frantic beat of his heart. An agonized scream fills the air and he knocks me over as he desperately tries to get away. He takes two steps before collapsing to the floor, gasping desperately as he bleeds out.

Ezra bangs against the door again and the entire wall trembles. The hinges groan, the wood creaks.

"Evie! You open this damn door, or I swear to your fucking god that I'm going to make you beg, little girl. I will destroy you."

Butterflies flit in my stomach at his promise.

This is what I want. Ezra angry at me, threatening me before he fucks me. Making me sin only so he can forgive me. And although I know it is messed up, it is beautiful. The sinner and her sin. After all, what is more holy than being one with your very salvation? And as long as he can save me, I cannot kill him, no matter how evil he may be.

22

EZRA

Evie being here is not good. I look at her and I crave her, her fear, her pain, her desire. Every time I fuck her, I want to own her. I want to put a bullet in the skull of any guy who looks at her, and believe me, they *all* look. I've spent years fucking girls like Jen, running whores, but never touching them, and of all the women to catch my attention, it just had to be the pretty little murderer who thrives on pain as if it's her next breath.

I storm down the hall, go back into my office, and pour some whiskey in a glass. By the time I sort this shit, I'll have liver failure. Thinking about Evie has given me a hard-on, and I glance at the monitor to her room, hoping to catch sight of her in her underwear. And I do. She's in a thong, on her knees, with a guys dick in her mouth. My heart slams against my ribs and all I see is red. I yank open my desk drawer and grab my gun before striding down the hall to her room. I wrench the handle down and it doesn't budge.

"Evie! You open this damn door or I swear to your fucking god that I'm going to make you beg, little girl. I will destroy you!" I'm going to make her pay, and I'm going to kill the cunt who dared to fucking touch what is mine.

I take a few steps back and charge the door, colliding with it shoulder first. The door creaks on it's hinges, and I rear back, slamming it again. The door pops open easily, It looks like something out of Texas Chainsaw Massacre in here. At her feet lies the guy she was just blowing, still butt naked and feebly clutching his thigh. Blood is pissing out of his femoral artery, and an enormous red puddle is spreading across the floor, seeping into the carpet. And Evie, she looks like the angel of death, her white lace underwear and doll like features so innocent, yet crimson blood trickles down the top of her tits, trailing over her stomach.

A wry smile tilts her lips and she cocks an eyebrow at me as she twist the knife in her hand. "Beat me."

Narrowing my eyes, I step into the room. I stop with my face only inches from hers and she closes her eyes, her breath hitching. "Oh, I'm going to break you, Evie." She trembles and I can see her erratic pulse thumping in her neck. I grip her jaw, digging my fingers into her cheeks. "I'm going to remind you that I own you, and that mine is the only cock you wrap these fucking lips around."

"Oh, how he moaned." She smirks. "How good he said my lips felt wrapped around his cock." I grab her by her throat with enough force to take her off her feet before I slam her onto the floor. She gasps for air.

"Stupid Evie. Very fucking stupid." I say, barely containing the rage in my voice.

This is what she does. She makes me insane. I don't pretend to be a particularly morale individual, but I'm calm, I keep my shit together. If I kill someone, if I hurt someone, it's done with a rational point in mind. I don't get angry, because I don't lose control. She makes me lose control. She sends me hurtling straight into homicidal rage territory with one look, and that combined with my need for her--to hurt her...I feel like a ticking time bomb.

She claws at my hands and then bucks underneath me, rubbing her body against my crotch. Her eyes are wild, a mixture of fear and excitement swirling in those blue irises of hers. I release her and push up from the floor, pacing as I drag my hands through my hair.

"Beat me, Ezra." I hear her say.

When I spin around, Evie's leaned over the bed, hands fisting the sheets. Her arse is in the air, her white lace thong showcasing her amazing arse cheeks. Beneath her feet is the man she's just killed. My cock throbs, demanding I heed her request. Right now, she is in control, and she knows it, she's manipulated it. I fist her hair, jerk her back, and her body tumbles onto the floor. I make my way out of the room, dragging her down the hallway by her hair.

"Jonty!" I shout. "Jonty!"

"Yeah," he calls from down the hall.

"Get a cleaner into room three. Now!"

I growl as I fling open the door at the end of the corridor. It slams closed behind me, and I lock it, shoving the key in the front pocket of my jeans. Evie stands motionless in the middle of the room, head dropped. This is not how this is supposed to work. She should not want this, she should not bait me to this. And I should not rise to it. I beat women to teach them, to train them, to profit from them. This...I do this because I like it, because I crave it. No other reason.

As I approach the cross I rip my shirt over my head, flexing my neck from side to side. I grab two of the heavy chains hooked into a pulley system on the ceiling and adjust them so the cross is now upright, just like a crucifix. I turn to face Evie and her gaze is fixed on the solid wooden cross, her face blanched white.

She thinks she can provoke me, but I have been doing this for a long time. I will break her, by any means necessary. She has no physical limit, so if I have to strap her to a crucifix to mentally fuck with her, I will. "Step up to the *cross*, sweetheart," I say with a smile.

She takes a shaky breath and glances between me and her destination. I think she's going to refuse, but she slowly steps up to it and turns to face me.

"Turn around and face it. Do not look at me." She stares at me for one more fleeting second, a defiant smile gracing her lips. I'm about to wipe that off her face. "Don't hesitate," I say through gritted teeth.

I'm not even sure anymore whether I want her to like it or not, but right now, in this very second, I want her to hate it. I want her to scream and cry and beg me to stop because she sucked another guy's dick, got blood all over my club, and she needs to learn a motherfucking lesson.

She turns around, pressing her cheek to the wood. I take her slim wrists and fasten the leather cuffs around them. She's trembling, her body flushed in goosebumps. I would normally leave her legs loose, but not this time. I go to the inconspicuous set of drawers and pull out a simple pair of metal handcuffs. She flinches as I clamp the cool metal around one ankle and then the other before strapping the leather cuff on the cross to the chain. I stand and look at her, smiling at the irony of her position, strung up on a crucifix, and why? Because she likes to be beaten, to feel depraved, to submit.

I pull my belt through the loops and trail the leather across my palm before cracking it together. The muscles in her back tense and release as her head falls back a little, her hair brushing the top of her arse. She wants this. She wants this enough to kill for it. She thinks she can push me, manipulate me into giving her something she needs. She's wrong.

"Do you think you can control me, Evie?" I ask quietly, taking steady steps towards the cross.

"No." I hear her swallow amid her heavy breaths.

I stand so close to her I can smell her perfume, feel the heat from her body. She twists her head to the side, attempting to glance over her shoulder.

"Do not. Fucking. Look at me," I say calmly.

"But I want to."

"That's your problem, Evie. You seem to think I give a fuck what you want."

"And you seem to think I believe that..."

I smirk. "Do you want me to hurt you, sweetheart?"

"Yes," she breathes.

"Do you want me to fuck you?"

She hesitates. "Yes."

I move closer to her, pressing my erection into the crack of her arse cheeks, because just the sight of her naked body, the promise of no limitations, has me hard. "You want my cock buried inside you?" I say against her ear. She shivers, pushing back against me, making me grit my teeth. I'm so tempted to fuck her, to pound into her until she can't walk straight. But that's what she wants.

"Please," she begs shamelessly.

I wrap her hair around my wrist, leaving the pale skin of her neck exposed. Slowly, I trace my tongue along the side of her throat. "No," I whisper.

Releasing her, I step away, and unzip my fly. She tugs against the restraints. I smile as I yank my jeans and boxers down just enough to expose my cock.

"But--"

"Shut up." I stroke over the length of my hard cock, fisting it, imagining how beautiful Evie would look right now, bound and covered in scarlet welts. I think of everything I would do to her, everything I can't do to her because that is what she wants.

I bury my nose in her hair and pull hard on her nipple. She moans, and pushes her arse back against me. Her desperation is enough to make my balls tighten. I stroke my cock until my legs start to go numb. I grit my teeth as raw pleasure shoots through my body. I pump my dick harder, groaning as I shoot my load all over her. My eyes slam shut as I milk my cock for all it's worth. I'm breathing hard, trying to catch my breath, and I rest my forehead against her shoulder blades.

I glance down at the come all over her lower back, smiling as it drips over her arse. "You look hot, covered in my come, Evie," I say breathlessly, and she doesn't say a word.

I grab a handful of her hair and yank her head back whilst swiping a finger through the sticky mess all over her arse. I bring my finger to her lips. "Taste it, little killer," I say as I force my finger into her mouth. She licks the come off my finger, moaning as she does. She may be screwed up, but fuck, she's perfect. She sucks on my finger like a woman starved, and my cock threatens to harden again.

I grab my trousers and pull them back up, adjusting my dick before I drop to a crouch. I free her ankles from the restraints. "Spread your legs."

She slides her legs apart, and her rapid breaths accelerate. When I stand, I pull her thong to the side. I drag two fingers from my other hand through the cooling pool of come dripping down her arse before ramming both fingers into her pussy without warning. She gasps, flinching away from me.

"Take it, Evie!"

Her pussy clenches and trembles around my fingers. I pull out and then push back in again. She moves her hips, grinding them against my hand. A moan slips from her lips, and I remove my fingers, leaving her panting.

"Ezra..."

"Shut up!" I shout, anger and the raw need to possess her coursing through me.

I swipe my hand across her arse, smearing come between her cheeks. "Remember when I told you I would take your virginal arsehole, Evie?"

She doesn't reply. I laugh, grabbing her hips and pulling her back so far that her arse cheeks are spread. She's shaking, and it's no longer from excitement. I slap her arse hard before I slam my finger into her arsehole. She clenches tightly against the intrusion, trying to pull away from me.

"My come is in every hole in your body. I own you, little killer." I nip at her ear as I work my finger farther into her arse. Within seconds, her muscles have loosened and she's backing up against me, panting and moaning. I take another finger and shove it, knuckles deep, into her tight little hole. "Remember that the next time you decide to bring your shit to my front door." I grab her throat with my free hand and trace the shell of her ear with my tongue. "And the next time you put another man's cock in your mouth, I will fuck this sweet arse so hard, I'll rip you open."

I ram both fingers in all the way. She flinches and whimpers. I pull away, leaving her shaking as I turn and exit the room. She can stay there, bound, and covered inside and out with my come.

She will learn. One way or the other.

23

EVIE

My fingers are numb, my legs weak from standing here for most likely hours. This is his idea of punishment, but it does nothing for me. With each passing second my sins eat away at me. I must have the forgiveness Ezra denied me. My pulse is erratic, my breaths heavy, and I worry he may never come back for me. He may very well leave me here to die, unforgiven. And then I will go to hell.

The hinges to the door groan, and I hear his heavy footsteps cross the room. Without a single word, he releases the cuffs around my wrists. My arms drop to my sides. My fingers throb as the blood rushes back through them. I turn around and cautiously glance up at him. I don't think I want Ezra angry anymore, because, as I just learned, anger does not lead to my forgiveness, but rather my denial.

"I'm sorry," I whisper. "Forgive me?"

He releases a heavy breath and his eyes lock with mine. "I don't forgive." Cupping the back of my neck, he pulls me closer until his lips barely brush mine. "I like you, little killer. I want to hurt you and fuck you until you cry for me, because I own you, so the next time you put some guy's dick in your mouth, I will kill you, sweetheart."

I swallow and nod my head. The heat from his body feel so nice against my bare sin. He's clothed and I'm in nothing more than a thong. I like the way it feels to have him want to control me and own me. I feel innocent and dirty, wanted but not needed. I shouldn't want him because he is wicked, he is a distraction, but I am only human. His dark eyes gleam as he studies me, and I want to beg him to love me.

"Now go get your shit, you're coming with me," he orders.

I open my mouth to ask why, but he cocks a brow. *Do not ask questions.* So I nod instead.

"Good." His lips pull into a small smirk and he walks out of the room. I happily follow him because I'm obsessed with him. I'm not too proud to admit I need him, his pain, his body, his sin.

*****BREAK******

Ezra opens the door to his apartment, and Dave nudges his way in, running to the fireplace and circling his bed. The familiar scent of Ezra's apartment swirls around me as he closes the door, and I remind myself he mustn't know I've been inside his apartment--several times. He wouldn't like that.

There's a thud when he drops my suitcase in the entrance-way. "I'm going to bed." He yanks his shirt over his head and starts toward the room he fucked that redhead in. When he flips the light off, panic seeps through my veins.

"I need to go to the church," I blurt. I should just turn around and leave, but for whatever reason, now, I feel I need his approval. *Because he owns you, Evelyn.*

Ezra turns to face me. His dark eyes meet mine and I want to shrink away from him. "Church?" He laughs as he crosses his arms over his massive, bare chest. "You want to go to church?"

I can't expect him to understand this. He's not religious. So instead of explaining, I nod and head toward the door. As soon as my hand brushes the handle, his thick arm locks around my waist and jerks me back against his hard body. "You aren't going to the fucking church, Evie. It's six 'o clock in the morning, and unless you had a nice comfortable nap on that cross, you should go to sleep."

"I can't..."

His warm breath touches my neck and my thighs clench. I want him to fuck the forgiveness from me, and I realize how terrible that is. I find myself relaxing into his body when I should be running to the church instead. He's like a raging fire sucking all of the oxygen from the air, suffocating me, leaving me breathless. And I'm not sure what I need more at this moment, forgiveness, or him, and that terrifies me.

I attempt to wriggle free of his hold. "I have to go..." His grip tightens. "Please." Guilt is eating me alive.

His lips skim over my neck, heating my skin. "What do you need, sweetheart? You want to pray? You can get on your knees for me if you like." He chuckles, and his chest vibrates against my back, sending chills splintering up my spine. His comment should disgust me, and it does, but not as much as it makes me want to fall down to my knees in front of him and worship him--his cock, everything about him because he is temptation at its finest.

I break free of his hold and spin to face him. "I need to be forgiven," I say.

"For what?" He looks at me like I'm filthy, and I instantly feel ashamed.

My heart thrums in my throat, sweat pricking its way over my forehead as my eyes slowly drag over his naked chest, taking in the intricate details of the ink playing over his tight skin. *What do you need forgiveness for, Evelyn? Tell him.* I swallow. "For wanting you," I breathe the words, my voice catching in the back of my throat as I imagine fucking him.

A cocky smile tugs at his lips and he cups my face, his thumb skirting across the corner of my mouth. That simple touch causes my eyes to slam shut and my body to respond to him like a wanton whore. "You make me want to do such terrible things," I say before I swallow again. "You distract me from my work, Ezra. You make me want to sin...I should want to kill you, not fuck you," I confess before I even realize it.

He inches his way toward me until I feel his breath on my lips, until I can taste the scent of whisky on my tongue. His hands glide over my body, stealing my breath one inch at a time. He grips my thighs and lifts me off my feet, slamming me back against the door. His hot skin slides against the inside of my thighs as he pins me in place with his hips.

"Then sin, little killer," he tempts with a wicked smile. "I'll forgive you."

I want to. I want to drown in sin with him.

His fingers snake under the hem of my dress, brushing over my panties and tearing the material from my body. His firm stomach feels so right against my bare pussy, and I bite back a moan. His body is like a sculpture of Apollo or Zeus, and it's because Ezra is a false idol. A beautiful false idol I will burn in the lake of fire for worshiping. But he *wants* me to be his sinner. He wants me to go up in flames within his sin all the while granting me forgiveness. Ezra wants to be my god, and I shouldn't let him, but I can't help it. I want him to own me. I want the same terrible things as he does. I want to give him my tears. And God forgive me for that because this man's sin is so delicious.

His hands clamp down on my legs, and then he pushes me up the wall until my thighs wrap around his shoulders.

He stares up at me, one side of his lip curled in a grin. "Is this a sin?" he asks before he buries his face in my greedy little pussy.

I can't help but watch in anticipation as his hot tongue plunges inside me. It flicks over my swollen clit, and my morals come undone, bowing at his feet. How can something so vulgar look so pure? I wind my fingers into his messy blond hair, pulling at the roots as he forces me to come apart, piece by piece. Ezra strips each shred of dignity, each piece of purity away from me until I am bare and exposed. He laps me up like I am the waters of life, holy and pure. His tongue assaults my clit, determined. A chorus of moans fall from my lips, just like a hymn, and he growls, grazing his teeth across my clit. I break, screaming his name like my last rite as my thighs clamp around his face.

But he does not stop. He continues to fuck me with his tongue until I can't take it any longer. Pleasure muddles with pain and I gasp. My body involuntarily flinches away from him. Ezra laughs, slapping the outside of my thigh before he drops me to my feet. I slide down the wall, weak with every inch of his body bleeding through me, but he catches me and brings my face to his. His lips slam over mine. His tongue thrusts into my mouth, forcing me to taste myself. His erection presses against my sensitive skin, leaving me breathless, my head spinning, with the flavor of my own sin thick on my tongue.

"See," he says against my mouth. "Like heaven." He winks and steps away from me.

I drag in several breaths as guilt slams its way through me. I'm not just drowning in sin, I'm literally sleeping with the enemy. I am tainted and soiled and not worthy to carry out the Lord's work.

You are wicked and dirty and unworthy of love. I hear Zachariah's word echo inside my head and rage fills me. I've sinned, I've forsaken my plot in life for desires of the flesh. Prayer will do nothing. God will not hear my prayers until I've been punished for what I've done.

"Hurt me," I scream desperately. "I need you to hurt me." Tears blur my vision and I fall to my knees, grabbing onto Ezra's hand and pulling him toward me as I beg for my penance.

"I told you, Evie." He squats in front of me, cocking his head as he watches me crumble. "You don't control this. I hurt you when *I* want to hurt you."

I must be forgiven. Pulling my hand back, I slap him across the cheek so hard his head turns to the side. He grates his jaw from side to side, his nostrils flaring, his chest rising in ragged swells. He *will* hurt me.

Growling, he backhands me across the face. I tumble to the floor, the coppery taste of blood welling in my mouth. I swipe at my split bottom lip. I need more than this to be forgiven. Then his hand slams around my throat, his body on top of mine, and in that small amount of pain I feel an ounce of relief.

"You hit me again Evie, and I will leave you in a pool of your own blood."

"I need you to make me bleed. Make me bleed." I scream so loud Dave goes scurrying from his bed, darting into the open bedroom.

"What the fuck?" He brings his face inches from mine. "Why are you so determined to make me hurt you, huh?" Ezra's eyes lock with mine, his uneven breaths cooling my bloodied lips.

"I need forgiveness..." I choke, my pulse frantically drumming in my ears.

"Why?" His eyes flicker, and I think that is rage firing behind his black eyes. His fingers tighten around my throat, and I claw at his hands, panicking as my air starts to dwindle. I want pain, not death. My work is not done. He squeezes harder, his nails breaking my skin before he suddenly lets go of me. I gasp and cough, staring up at him from the floor.

"Why?" He repeats, more calmly.

"Because..." I drag in a hard breath, trying to still my pounding heart. "It makes me feel clean."

He leans over me again, his hands on either side of my head. His stare is accusing, and I close my eyes to avoid his judgment.

"You realise that makes no sense, right?"

"You don't understand my religion." My eyes flash open. He studies me, his eyes flicking over my face. And I watch him silently assess me. The more of his beauty I take in, the more like the devil he seems. His eyes are empty, dark and bottomless, his lips wicked in every way. His body is a temple of temptation. *He's the devil, Evelyn. He'll take you to hell.* "To be forgiven, there must be pain," I say. "Pain cleanses me of wicked things like you, Ezra. It bleeds it out of me."

"Oh, I can bleed you, sweetheart, but you're a whore and a murderer. I'm pretty sure your God will want a damn site more than a little pain before he lets you through the pearly white gates." My teeth grate against each other. "You're just a filthy little whore..." he whispers into my ear.

"You wanted this. You asked for it, Evelyn." Zachariah releases his hold on my thighs. "You pretend like you don't love this, but just like any other wretched little slut, you only want things that are sinful. There's not one righteous thing about you." His hot breaths blow across my bare flesh, causing bile to rise in my throat. "You tell anyone about this and I'll slit your throat in your sleep, I promise you," he whispers as he lifts his heavy frame off mine. I can't stop the dirty feeling crawling all over me. I can't make the throbbing pain between my legs stop.

Zachariah throws his undershirt at me as he walks to the door. "Clean that shit up, you dirty whore." He grabs the doorknob and turns to look at me, at the broken mess he's leaving behind. "You better pray to be forgiven for tempting me like that, Eve. *Just like the woman you were named after, tempting a righteous man to sin. Shame on you." He opens the door and disappears, and I sink. I sink into this feeling of self-hatred, of loathing, of worthlessness and shame. I am a sinner, and the only thing that can save me is if I repent.*

That little demon inside of me screeches at the top of its lungs and all I want to do is take a knife to Ezra's throat and watch the very last drop of his ruby red blood spill out onto the floor. He is no different than Zachariah. He is no different than any other man. I am not a whore. I am not his whore. I am good.

24

EZRA

Evie freezes, her expression blank. "I am not a whore," she screams. "I kill bad men. I kill horrible men. I do good. You are sin, Ezra!" Her chest heaves as she drags in deep breaths.

I move away from her, propping my back against the nearest wall and running a hand through my hair. She's still lying on her back, staring up at the ceiling, talking to God I guess. I knew Evie was a little off. No girl should be able to take a beating like this one, but she's *fucking* crazy. People don't just get like this, they're conditioned, brain-washed. Just as I've been programmed to feel no remorse for the things I do, Evie has been programmed to feel ashamed, to feel as though she is breaking some sacred bullshit.

She believes that her faith will save her, that her God will grant her forgiveness.

My mother used to tell me that God loved her, that one day he would hear her prayers and we would be saved. My mother died a drug addicted whore at the age of twenty-six. She was a filthy slut who fucked dirty, nasty men for money to feed her habit. Religion never did shit for her, and it sure as hell hasn't done anything for me. Religion is a cop out. It's an excuse for people to wallow in their messed up lives because 'God will save them.' Guess what? The only person who can save you is yourself. If there is one thing I have no time for it's religion.

Evie continues to mumble beneath her breath, begging for forgiveness, repeating she's not sin. I won't lie, a chick like this...I'd usually kick her to the curb and high tail it out of there. But in my world of easy sex, killing, and money, it takes a lot to truly intrigue me, and Evie amuses me to no end. There's something about her that draws me in, and it's more than just her tight pussy and love of the belt. She's so insane, she makes me look boring. She's just asking to be possessed and owned, truly owned, not because she wants to please me, or fuck me, but because she needs it.

"You want to go to the church, I'll take you to the damn church." I sigh.

She turns her head to the side, glaring at me. "You don't understand." She shakes her head. "What you just made me do, that kind of disgusting sin has to be beaten out of me." She pulls herself up to her knees.

I skim my knuckles down her cheek. "I will fuck you when I want to fuck you, sweetheart, and I will hurt you when I want to hurt you."

"Please, Ezra." Her eyes drift shut. "I've never felt as clean as I do when you beat me."

Those words force my dick against my fly. "Strip, Evie." I can't help myself. She makes me do this shit with her words.

Am I enabling her crazy shit? Of course I am, but sometimes creatures as depraved as we are must find each other in the darkness.

Without a word, she pulls her dress over her head, and tugs her lace underwear down her long legs. My eyes follow the scar down her spine to her arse.

She glances over her shoulder at me. "Please," she begs.

I grit my teeth as I yank my belt open and pull it through the loops. I grab her hair and yank her head back. "Bend over the sofa," I order.

She bends over, giving me the perfect view of her arse and pussy. I'm going to beat her and fuck her until she can take no more.

A COUPLE OF DAYS PASS, and I'm starting to think that Zee took my advice and ran. Letting him walk away after taking my girls makes me want to break shit. It's not in my nature to lay down, but sometimes you have to be smart.

Of course, nothing is ever that simple.

There's a knock on the office door and Jack walks in, carrying a box. "Delivery for you boss."

I briefly glance up from my laptop. "It's probably for the bar." I dismiss him.

He shrugs and dumps it on my desk before walking out, and I go back to placing the liquor order.

"Are you not going to open that?" Evie asks from her spot on the sofa.

I glance at her and cock an eyebrow. "Impatient?" I take a pair of scissors from the drawer and hold them out. She stands up and wraps her fingers around them. "I want these back." I say before releasing them. Before I know it I'll find some poor bastard with a pair of scissors buried in his nut sack.

She rolls her eyes before cutting the tape across the top of the box. I go back to the spreadsheet. Evie fiddles with the plastic packing, and then she screams. I jump and Evie swats the box across the desk. She's leaned over, her face white, and her hand plastered over her mouth like she's trying to hold back vomit.

"What the hell, Evie?" I push up from the chair and pick the box up off the floor. Inside is black plastic, like a bin liner. I move it aside, and inside at the bottom of the bag, is a pair of tits. Crystal's tits to be exact. I recognise the small rose abover her left nipple. I take a deep breath and shove the plastic back over them.

Evie is still holding her stomach, her face white. "Don't tell me you're freaked out by some severed tits. Go and get Jonty."

Evie glares at me, her chest still heaving as she walks from the room. Looks like my message wasn't clear enough. Crystal was dead the second he took her. I know that. Blowing his car and warehouse up, that were scare tactics, what he's doing is tearing down my business, so I'm going to take down his.

Between Alexei and Seamus I can work the Mexican Cartel, I can disrupt not only his supply of girls, but his import channels, as well as his end buyers. I have more reach than he can possibly imagine, and he really underestimates me.

25

EVIE

The sound of tires bumping over the alleyway pulls me from my sleep. I roll over in the bed, and watch Ezra, sleeping soundly on his side.

I enjoy him touching me. I let him fuck me, every day, every night, for no other reason than pleasure. I swallow at the thought of how he feels pinned over me. My skin tingles at the memory of him beating me, cleansing me. The street light streams in through the window and causes shadows to nestle within the deep ridges of his Ezra's muscles. A man whose body is as honed and perfected as his is looks nothing short of holy. Everyone needs a god. Everyone need something that makes them feel safe. And I worry that Ezra is becoming a god to me.

I trace a fingertip over his bicep with feather light strokes. He has no idea that had he let me in his bedroom a few weeks ago, I would have killed him. Instead of lying here, sleeping peacefully, he'd be in a coroner's bag, cold and rigid. I don't like to think about my Ezra in a coroner's bag. It makes me sad.

Dave trots up on my side of the bed and sits, his head thumping over the floor, and his head cocking to the side as he studies me. When Ezra shifts in the bed and groans, Dave's ears perk up. I swing my legs over the side of the bed. Pain throbs through my ass and legs, and I flinch, even though that pain reminds me I have been forgiven. I glance at the clock and realize it's past noon. Ezra is still asleep. *Sloth is a sin, Evelyn.* His arm is thrown out to the side, the sheets barely covering his hips. He looks dangerous even in sleep, but maybe that's because of the skulls and daggers he has tattooed over his chest, the depiction of hell that trails down his arm.

I sit on the edge of the bed, unsure of what to do. Dave shuffles forward and rests his head in my lap, whimpering as he looks up at me. Brushing him off my lap, I reach for the thick curtain and pull it back. Sun pours into the room, and I stare out at the skyscrapers. Guilt slices through me because I'm alive and I'm sleeping with a man my sister wanted to kill.

Temptation is clouding my judgment, derailing me from my goal. I came after Ezra because I needed someone to connect me with the murderous pervert who killed Hannah. And even though Ezra's given me the name 'Zee', I've done nothing because he's told me not to. And I could, if I wanted. I could find him. Actually, Zee wants me, so all I'd have to do is make myself available...but I want to be good.

What am I doing?

I try to convince myself I am only with Ezra, in his bed, letting him defile me because he will protect me, because he will eventually lead me to Zee. *Evelyn, no one will protect you. They never have they never will. Ezra is only a man who wants to get his dick wet. Kill him.* I don't want him. I don't love him. I do love him... *You want him so he can beat you and treat you like the filthy little whore that you are.*

Dave wines, tucking his tail, and I wonder if he heard that little voice too.

IT'S BEEN NEARLY a week since I've allowed Ezra to take me, since I've pretended he will protect me. He's sitting behind his desk, smoking a cigarette, making call after call and cursing whoever's on the other line. He makes me go everywhere with him, and he tells me it's because I can't be trusted, and I can't, but I think more than that, it's because he wants me with him. At least that's what I want to believe.

"How do you know it was one of my girls?" he asks. "Maybe your wife's been doing the dirty on you." He laughs. There's a long pause before he rolls his eyes and slams the receiver down, immediately standing up and heading toward the door. Ezra yanks the door open, and Dave eyes him from his spot on the sofa next to me.

"Jonty!" Ezra shouts. "Tell SJ to get her arse in here." He paces, combing his fingers through his hair.

The door opens and a busty girl with burgundy hair struts inside, her tits pouring out of the tight shirt she's wearing. She doesn't even glance at me as she steps close to Ezra. Dragging her eyes over every last inch of his body, she smiles and bats her fake lashes.

"What do you need, Ez?"

Ez? A sudden impulse to grab that woman by her throat and choke her shoots through me. He is not hers, he is mine.

His eyes narrow at her before turning away to sit at his desk once again. "Have you got the clap?" He blurts.

"I'm careful." She sighs and crosses her arms over her enormous chest. "You know that."

"No," he huffs, dragging a hand over his chin. "I don't know that, because short of standing in the room whilst you fuck the guy, I can't guarantee that you'll do what you're told." He slams his fist down on the desk. "Rob is pissing blood, and now he has to somehow try and drug his wife with the damn antibiotics. He's not happy, SJ!"

She shrugs. "You think I'm the only woman besides his wife he sticks he wrinkled little dick in?"

"I think you're cheap enough to offer bareback extras." he shouts.

Her eyes cut over at me and Dave growls. "The only person I give bareback extras to is you, Ez," she says with a smirk before turning back to face him. And now I want to stab her in the back of the head.

Ezra scowls at her and slowly rises from the desk, moving toward her. She pushes her breasts out, setting her eyes on his like she wants nothing more than to know what it feels like to fuck him. I watch him lean closer to her, and my heart pounds. He's too close to her. He's close enough he may kiss her. I panic when he grabs her hair the way he grabs my hair. Ezra jerks her head back so hard her legs buckle, and he forces her to her knees in front of him. She whimpers from the pain, but instead of letting up, he only tightens his hold.

"Do not fuck with me. You won't like the consequences." Tears fill her eyes as he yanks her hair harder. "Now go and take your diseased pussy to the doctor, and don't come back here until you've sorted that shit out." He lets go of her hair and turns his back on her as though he's too good to waste his time on her any longer. I almost feel sorry for her. Almost, but not quite because she is a filthy whore.

Just like your sister, Evelyn. No, my sister was doing good work, just like me.

 The door clicks shut as SJ leaves, and Ezra drops back into his chair with a heavy sigh.

Hannah slept with Ezra, Evelyn. Her lips were made for his cock too. You are not special. I close my eyes, confused and lost, willing that voice to be quiet. I wonder if my sister slept with Ezra. If that girl that just left did. I wonder how many women beside that redhead have been slammed up against his window in a too-tight white dress.

"Did you fuck her?" I ask, my heart racing at the thought. I'll have to kill him if he did.

"I don't fuck whores."

"You fuck me..."

 His gaze crashes into mine, sucking all the air from my lungs. "I need to go and handle some shit." He turns away from me. "Stay here. Don't get into trouble, and do not kill anyone."

He just dismissed me the way he dismissed that dirty, diseased whore. I narrow my gaze at him as he walks out the door. He fucks me, then he ignores me. Anger swells in my chest. I stand, snatching his keys from the desk before following him down the hallway.

"You can't keep me here," I shout.

Ezra slams to a halt and I almost plow into him. He turns, crowding me with his large frame. "When are you going to learn, sweetheart? I do what I like, and you will listen, or you will suffer the consequences."

My blood turns to lava burning through my veins. I feel like I'm going to burst into flames. My nails slice into my palm, and I grit my teeth as I watch him disappear into the club. I should just leave. I should go home. I don't need him because he is a distraction. He will not save me, he is lying just like my father did, just like Zachariah did, just like everyone in the town I grew up in did. He is a liar and I don't need him to keep me safe.

I shove my way through the grimey, sweaty men crowded in the bar, my gaze locked on the back of Ezra's head as I reach for the door. The cold air stings my cheeks when I step onto the sidewalk. I'm breathless and angry. If he wants to protect me, he will come bursting through those doors, pissed and yelling the second he realizes I am gone. When I make it to the end of the block, I turn around to watch the door. Ten minutes pass, fifteen, and Ezra hasn't come after me. Rejection eats away at me, and I want to cry. He has warped my mind. *Show him, Evelyn. Make him notice you.*

Exhaling, I hike my skirt up as I lean against the side of Sin. Ezra wants to ignore me, so be it. I have a job to do, and if he's not going to help me, I can't waste any more time. I rake my hands through my hair and pull the neckline of my dress down, exposing half of my breasts. Within moments, there's a whistle and I glance up to find a man standing in front of me, puffing a cigarette.

"How much?"

"One-hundred." I notice a wedding band glint beneath the streetlight. *Adultery is a sin.* "Two-hundred bareback."

"Two-hundred it is," he laughs.

I turn and walk down the alleyway. The red lights to Ezra's car flash when I press the unlock button.

"Wow, you must be a damn good fuck," the man mumbles beneath his breath, eyeing the shiny Mercedes.

"I aim to please," I say, grinning as I open the backdoor.

26

EZRA

E vie is driving me insane. I like the girl, and I love sinking my dick in her, but damn, she bitches more than anyone I know. I talk to the whores, and I can see her plotting all the ways she could end them. She's hot, but you know what they say, the hot girls are always crazy. Well, she redefines that shit.

I stay on the club floor and help Jack behind the bar, mainly to stay away from Evie because if I don't, I'll either kill her or fuck her--perhaps both. I work the bar until we close.

Once the bar is quiet and the doors are locked, Tony, the bouncer leans on the bar. "Hey, I'm out, but your girl wanted me to give you these." *She's not my girl.* He holds his hand out and drops a set of keys into them. I glance down at the black fob with the Mercedes logo on it. This can't be good.

"Thanks," I grumble, before stalking straight past him. I open the door that leads to the stairs and whistle. Dave comes running down the stairs a few seconds later and follows me out of the club.

The second I open my car door I'm ready to kill her. "Shit." I slam my hand on the roof. There, on the back seat, is a guy, eyes wide open and staring lifelessly at the ceiling. His head is at an odd angle and his jaw is hanging open. *She snapped his neck.* What is she? Jackie-fucking-Chan?

I slide into the driving seat and turn the ignition. I am not dealing with that shit. She can dump the body, and I swear, if she put his dick in her mouth, I'll make her dig her own grave next to his.

The tires screech as I floor it into downtown, heading for her apartment. Dave whines the entire way to her place, glancing in the back like the zombie apocalypse is about to rise.

I park the car in the shadow of the building. The last thing I need is someone looking in the window and spotting the dead guy chilling out on the back seat. I can't fucking believe her. She's lost her shit. Dave throws himself out of the car so fast I'm sure he's shit himself. I slam the car door and climb the stairs to her apartment. My temper is bubbling and I try my best to rein it in because this is what she wants. She wants me to be angry so that I beat the living shit out of her, and believe me, I fucking want to.

I bang on the door, bracing my forearms against the door frame. I count to ten in my head over and over again, trying to get a hold on my temper. "Evelyn!" I shout.

27

EVIE

I pace in front of my bed, clutching the poison inside my palm. I kneel down to pray. I clasp my hands. I can't find the words because all I see when I close my eyes is Ezra. *Hannah.* Closing my eyes, I try once again. "Dear Father..." *You are a sinner, Evelyn. Can you not see? You are a lie. A blasphemer.* The memory of Ezra fucking me, his face buried in my soaked pussy loops in my head. I'm trying to pray and all I can think about is fucking him. I scream and push myself off the floor. And pace again.

I'm not even sure what I'm doing anymore. I'm obsessed, possessed by him. He is the devil and he has drug me down to hell. My gaze lands on the Bible I took from Matthew's apartment. I killed him. Murder is a sin. *But he was a bad man.* Everytime I've killed a man, I picture Zachariah. I see his face, I hear his voice. I kill these men in an attempt to kill his memory, and it doesn't work. I kill bad people...

"Dear God, forgive me," I breath the prayer, but my stomach knots because there is no answer. I can't feel God anymore.

There's a loud bang at my front door. The moment I hear Ezra shout my name, my heart leaps and those butterflies flap in my stomach. I hurry to stand, checking my makeup in the mirror before I drop the vial into my purse. He pounds over the door. "Evelyn!" he growls, and I rush to the door. *I will be forgiven. Ezra will see to that.*

Smiling, I open the door. Ezra's large arms are braced in the doorway, his head tilted down, his eyes glaring up at me. "Really? In my fucking car."

"I couldn't kill him in the street." I cock a brow and stare at him, daring him. "I kept it clean."

He steps closer to me, slowly inching his face toward mine until I feel his warm breath on my lips. "Did you fuck him?"

"No." My heartbeat quickens, drumming into the back of my throat. He told me I'd be in a pool of my own blood next time I put another man's dick in my mouth. Even though I didn't touch the man--because my lips were made for Ezra's cock, because I love Ezra--I don't think he'll believe me. He's going to kill me and toss me in the Husdon River, laughing as I float downstream.

"Did you put his cock in your mouth?" he asks, his brow twitching, his voice dangerously low.

"No, Ezra." I swallow, fighting not to blink, because if I blink he'll think I'm lying.

His hand shoots out like a snake striking its prey, and his fingers clamp around my throat, cutting off the air. "You're walking a fine line, little killer." The muscles in his jaw tick as he stares me down. "Your temper tantrums are getting old. When I tell you to stay, you fucking well stay." I should want to fight him. I should be scared and be desperate to get his hand away from my throat, but I'm not. I like that I can make him this angry. He releases me, shoving me away from him.

"You don't own me, Ezra," I say quietly.

Laughing, he steps behind me, slowly circling me like a vulture. "That's where you're wrong, sweetheart." He fists my hair from behind, yanking my head back so hard my scalp burns. He pulls in a deep breath, inhaling along my neck line as he nips at my throat. that sensation forces chill bumps over every last inch of my skin. "I do own you. You disobeyed me, and for that there are *always* consequences. Especially when your actions involve a dead body and my leather seats."

And I want those consequences...

I swallow, my heart pounding because I need him angrier. "I didn't make him bleed. It's just a body, Ezra."

He growls in my ear. "You ever seen a dead body shit itself? Because I have. You're lucky the guy didn't prolapse all over my fucking back seat." My eyes drop to the ground. "Now," he says, "are you gonna walk to the car, or am I going to have to drag you?"

I know I don't have to go with him. I know I shouldn't, but part of me wants nothing more than this--this possessiveness of his. I have never craved the attention, the affection of a man, but the way I crave Ezra is enough to kill me.

"Just let me get my purse," I say as I turn away. I just need to have my poison with me in case I have to kill him.

I can let him think he owns me. I'll even let him believe he can control me, because as long as I am only allowing him to think this, I am the one in control. I tell myself these things even though I know they're nothing but lies because Ezra does own me.

I grab my things from my dresser, flip off my lights, and lock my door. When I come back out of my apartment, Ezra glares at me and I swallow. "Are you mad?" I ask.

He turns, walking down the stairs in front of me. "Oh, I'm mad, little killer. I'm just biding my time, because what I have in mind for you, you won't be able to sit down in the car when I'm done."

I smile, my heart swelling at his promise.

****BREAK*****

Ezra's weight crushes over me. My shoulder blades make a loud crunch as he forces me against the hardwood floors. The cold edge of the knife grazes my stomach as he cuts my shirt down the middle and tears it from my body. The cool air causes me to tense. He gently trails the tip of the blade between my breasts and down my stomach, my skin prickling from the touch. With the slightest amount of pressure he could slit me open and gut me, but he won't do that because he wants me. He needs me just as much as I need him, and I see it in the feral look in his black eyes. This is what I need, just as much as he does.. This is why he can't ignore me. I need to be wanted.

His lips brush over the path he just traced with the blade. As he kisses me skin, he drops the knife, and it clatters to the floor.

I shouldn't enjoy this, and I am well aware of that, but there are a lot of things that shouldn't be pleasurable that are. I want to be his idol. I want to be a sin he feels guilty for, but how wicked must something be to make a man as depraved as Ezra feel guilty?

"I'm going to make you regret pissing me off, Evie," he promises, and butterflies flit in my stomach from the thought of it. "And no, I'm not going to hurt you, not physically anyway. You'd like it too much, my depraved little killer." He tenderly kisses my stomach before his teeth sink into the skin, and I smile because he lied. He will hurt me.

He reaches for the knife and, cocking a brow, he traces the inside of my thigh. His eyes glint as he sweeps the blade over my panties. And my heart stalls, my breath hitching. This is dangerous, he holds the power and I am powerless. But I need someone to control me and Ezra can.

He lips the edge of the knife beneath the lace at my hip, and the material slowly shreds. He smiles before he drags the blade across my stomach and cuts the other side, his hands angrily tearing the tattered lace away from my body. He shoves my legs apart and stares at me--at the dirtiest parts of me. There's something empowering in being completely naked in front of a man who looks at you like you are something holy and divine.

A deep grin sets on his face as he takes the knife and carefully traces over my bare pussy, sliding the flat edge over my clit. The cold metal feels good rolling over my warm skin. The possibility that he may hurt me causes my adrenaline to spike.

"This time, you will beg me to stop." He breathes those words against my skin before he stabs the knife into the wooden floor. His thick fingers dig into my thighs as he forces them apart with such violent strength my muscles burn. My pulse hammers with anticipation. I want his sin. The moment his warm mouth lays over me, he consumes everything, and he becomes my god. There is nothing but Ezra and me and our sin. This beautiful, tragically filthy sin.

Groaning, he spreads me open and thrusts his tongue inside me. My back bows away from the floor as a blissful heat consumes me. His forearm lays over my hips and pins me to the floor to keep me from moving. His tongue circles my clit, sucking. I need something to hold on to, to ground me because it feels as though he is ripping my very soul from me. It's as though the rapture has come and sucked me away from this earth and into another realm. I grab onto his head, scratching my fingers through his unruly hair. Never have I felt so wanted, so desired, so innocent as I do when I am in the hands of my absolution. I moan. I recite his name over and over, attempting to push against him and force his tongue deeper inside me, and then... he stops, and I feel like I've been tossed into the pit of hell. He rears up onto his knees, his wide smile sadistic like the devil's.

I'm so undone I can't form words, and before I can even let out a single breath, he grabs onto me. With one swift movement, he flips me over. My chest slams against the floor with a thud. His firm hands hold my ankles and yank my legs apart for him to use me how he pleases, and I feel his body nestle between my thighs. I want to look at him, but when I attempt to glance over my shoulder, he pushes my face into the floor.

"Don't fight it, little killer. You'll only make it worse."

I don't want to fight this. I want whatever he can provide me; pain, denial, forgiveness. I would take anything from him. Because he makes me sin, and then he forgives me.

He rubs his hand over my ass, groaning, and then that gentle movement is replaced with blinding pain. A loud clap echoes from the walls as the breath is knocked from me, my ass throbbing from where he spanked me. Ezra lightly brushes his hand over my pussy, and I lift my hips, begging him to touch me, to grant me release from the throbbing pressure building inside me. I want him inside me, I want him fucking me. I want to be his whore, his naughty vice, his little killer. The need I have is so great that I scream from pleasure when he plunges two fingers inside me, finger fucking me so deep his knuckles dig into me.

"So wet for me, sweetheart," he groans, pulling his fingers out.

He chuckles as his slick fingers slide over my asshole. The good girl inside me whimpers and my demon laughs. This is dirty. This is sinful. That innocent part of me wants to pull away from him, but the disgusting whore inside of me won't allow it. The last time he put his fingers in my ass, I liked it. I wanted more. I wanted his cock in there because that would make me his dirty little slut.

He grabs the back of my neck, squeezing. "I'm going to fuck your arse, Evie." He shoves his thumb in, hissing in a breath as he twist it in my asshole. An uninhibited moan escapes my lips and I press myself back against him, forcing his thumb deeper before he yanks it free.

He slips his two fingers back inside my pussy and I clench around them. I choke on a groan, clawing at the hard floor in an attempt to stay grounded.

Slowly, he spreads his hand out and buries his fingers harder into me as his thumb brushes over my ass again. There's slight pressure as he threatens to push his thumb back inside that filthy part of me. And oh, how I revel in that threat. I delight in how dirty that simple action makes me feel.

I've spent my entire life trying to cleanse myself, trying to be pure, but with Ezra all I want to do is wallow in filth and squalor. His thumb presses against me, and he slips the very tip inside my ass only to pull it away. And I moan. His fingers dig into me. I slap at the floor, pushing my ass against him, demanding he take me. His heavy breaths blow over my low back, and he groans just before he slips his thumb in my ass up to the knuckle. Two fingers fuck me in the pussy, one finger in my ass, hard and fast. I feel like I'm shattering, being pulled apart at the seams. I'm sullied and tainted, all the while being worshiped by this man defiling my body.

Ezra brutally fucks my body with his hand. The hold his other hand has on my neck tightens as he leans forward, pressing his bare chest against my back. "Who does this pussy belong to, Evie?" he asks, growling in my ear.

"You," I say, moaning as I writhe under his hold.

"And this." He pulls his thumb from my ass before pushing it deeper inside me. "Who does this belong to?"

"You." I gasp, desperately. "My body is your temple."

Ezra touches me in the darkest, most sinful of ways, dragging me willingly into the abyss of hell with every thrust of his hand. He's taking me to burn with him. The moment I feel the flames threatening to engulf me, just when my body trembles and my core clenches, he pulls away. I want to curse him, but I refuse. His teeth rip into my shoulder, sinking deep into my skin. The pain should tear me from the swath of pleasure instantly, but it doesn't, it drowns me in a form of wicked pleasure. Ezra's pleasure.

"Ezra, please," I beg, not even sure what I'm pleading for. I want to come. I want him to hurt me. But all he's doing is teasing me with empty promises.

He releases my neck, and grabs both my hips, yanking them against him. He grinds his cock against me, forcing me to feel the erection straining through his pants. "Is this what you want, Evie?"

That is what I want. Every inch of it, buried deep inside of me.

"Fuck me," I say, an edge of hysteria to my plea. I'm near tears and desperate. If he doesn't grant me some form of release I will kill him.

"Oh, don't worry, little killer." His cock presses against me again causing my pussy to throb painfully. "I'll fuck you." He laughs.

The metal of his belt buckle clinks, and that beautiful noise causes my heart to bang against my ribs. I'm salivating like a beast conditioned to that sound because it only ever brings to me the things I need.

"Don't look at me, Evie," he warns, and even though I want nothing more than to disobey, I won't because he is right, he does own me. He can give to me, or he can take away. When I'm bad he takes, and when I'm good he gives. I want to be good.

I feel heat between my legs and I hold my breath. Every last inch of my body is over sensitized and needy. I wait patiently. Quietly. Obediently. And then I feel his cock press against my pussy. I push against him, and he fills me. My muscles tense and I exhale from the instant relief. It's as though a prayer has just been answered. He is my heaven and he is my hell, and my body is his temple. A long moan slips past my lips followed by a string of pleas. I fight back the tears threatening to spill from my eyes because he is giving to me when I need it most.

"You want my cock, Evie?" he asks, his accent making him sound more refined than someone like him should.

"God, yes." He's making me take the Lord's name in vain.

"This isn't about what you want," he says angrily then he slaps my ass with such force it feels more like a blow. The smack echoes from the walls. "*This* is your punishment."

He pulls out of me, and I realize what he is doing. I fist my hair, tugging at it with anger. I feel lost and used. I want to hurt him because he is depriving me, not only of my pain and forgiveness, but from him. I collapse to the floor panting. The tears brimming at the edge of my eyes.

Ezra rubs the head of his cock against my ass and I tense. "I'm going to come inside your tight little as, Evie. I will claim you, and I will own you because this..." he laughs, the pressure tremendous as he threatens to push into me, "...this is mine." He growls as he forces his way inside me. There's tearing and stinging and burning and fullness. I gasp and hiss at the pain, unable to catch a breath. Everything inside of me tenses, my nails scratch over the floor-boards. I want to endure this pain because it is the only pain I will get from him right now. And I need it.

"Take it," he says on a groan.

I inhale several times and force myself to relax and accept his intrusion into my body. I feel him slip deeper, and I tense around him, coaxing a feral groan from his lips.

"Good." He breathes heavily, his voice almost sounds drunk. "Good girl."

He removes one of his hands from my hip, rubbing it over the small of my back. He pushes inside me deeper. I feel myself tear more, but I want to be good for him. I want this pain, so I push back against him, my stomach knotting from the way it feels to have him buried so deep inside me. *Let him own you, Evelyn. Let him possess you.*

"Fuck." He freezes and his cock twitches inside me. Slowly, he pulls all the way out, then forces his way back in.

I slam my ass back against him, groaning at the uncomfortable feeling. I don't give him a chance to move, I tuck my hips away and then push back down around him again and again, fighting the tears away. Both his hands grab desperately at my hips. His fingers dig into my skin with each movement. I want to make him come. This pain is forgiveness, and it is pleasure, and if Ezra forgives me, then he will pleasure me more.

He groans, squeezing my hips hard enough to bruise me as he stiffens behind me. There's a moment where all I can hear is my hammering pulse and his staggered breaths. "And now," he pants, kissing the back of my head as he pulls out, "you really are a dirty whore, sweetheart. *My* dirty little whore." Without another word, without another touch, he stands and walks away.

I flip over on my back, my pussy throbbing and desperate for release. I hate him. I want to scream, but I bite that urge back. Anger and embarrassment and guilt slam through me.

"You dirty little whore. You like it when I fuck you, because the only time you have the slightest bit of righteousness in you is when my dick is deep inside that worthless pussy of yours." Zachariah shoves my face into the pillow, holding me down as I fight against him. "Fight me, and I'll fuck you so hard you won't be able to walk to the church to ask for forgiveness."

I wanted to be something to Ezra, but I am nothing. I am a pathetic whore. Worthless. I am not worthy of God, I'm not worthy of love, I'm not worthy of anything besides being a vessel a man can use and toss to the side. It was foolish of me to believe that Ezra thought I was innocent, that he wanted me. All men are liars. My throat tightens and burns as I fight the emotions, the identity I don't want to own.

You really are a dirty whore, sweet'art. I close my eyes and those tears I've been fighting for what feels like my entire life trickle down my cheeks.

When I hear his footsteps over the floor, shame drowns me. I attempt to cover my face with my hands because he wants my tears, and I don't want him to know he has them. I try desperately to wipe them away from my cheeks before he sees them.

"Don't hide from me, Evie," he says, grabbing my wrists and ripping my hands from my face. "Your tears are beautiful."

Never have I felt so stripped, so bare in front of a man before. Ever since I took my father's life, I've used men. And I've killed them for using me, but Ezra, he'll kill me long before I'll ever kill him. I have no control with him. He is a man I should hate, but I'm terrified I may love him. This need eating away at me for acceptance, the way I obsess over him, they way I want him regardless of the consequences...I am willing to go against my own instinct, to betray everything I've ever held sacred, and all for him.

"Do you know why I do this to you?" he asks.

I shake my head, because I'm afraid of what he'll say.

Leaning toward my face, he wipes a tear from my chin, and presses a soft kiss to my lips. "Because I want to see you break, little killer. And now, I own you body *and* soul." His eyes focus on the tear rolling down my cheek. He smiles and trails his tongue over my tear. "Your tears are mine, and now, y*ou* are mine."

A sinner and his sin.

My breath hitches in my throat, my pulse threatening to burst through my chest. You covet what is yours. You protect what you own. He owns not only my body, but my soul, which means I am forgiven.

28

EZRA

I was broken when I was just eight years old. It made me stronger, it made me invincible. And finally...Evie has *finally* broken. Her small body trembles as those illusive tears track down her face. I have watched countless whores break under the belt, screaming and begging me to stop before snapping. In some way, I own a piece of each one. But Evie's submission, her tears, they are the sweetest of them all because she cannot be broken through pain or force. She had to be mentally broken--she had to be destroyed. We must be broken before we can be fixed, and now, I will fix Evie because she is mine.

I scoop her up off the floor and pull her against my chest. She presses her face into my neck, her tears wetting my skin. I let her fall apart. I *want* her to fall apart, and until now I had no idea how much I needed her to fall apart.

I need her. I need to possess her because for whatever reason, she is my weakness. And weaknesses must be controlled before they consume us.

THE ICY AIR stings my face as I walk down the street. Jonty's at one side, Evie's at the other, and Dave's ahead, pissing on every lamp post, pile of trash, and sleeping homeless person he finds.

Ideally, I don't want to be bringing Evie with me for this shit, but I can't leave her unsupervised, and the only person I trust with her is Jonty. But for this particular job, I need him.

As soon as I round the corner, I see the kid huddled under a doorway. He's standing close to one of the whores as they make an exchange.

These dealers are like cockroaches, and the distributors who supply them are looking for any way in. My club runs whores. Whores do drugs, and the kind of guys who fuck whores do drugs, ergo the place is like a gold mine for that shit. And where there is demand, I will always supply. Drugs aren't my thing, too risky, but the family moves in those circles, so we have guys to run it. Guys from who we take a cut. These guys are pushing all sorts of dodgy crap and they sure as shit aren't cutting us in.

I pull my gun from the waist of my jeans and click the safety. The guy's head jerks up like a spooked animal. His gaze swings to me and then he runs.

"Stupid motherfuckers."

"Well..." Jonty huffs.

I glare at Jonty, and whistle one shrill blow through my teeth. Dave takes off down the street. Only time he ever moves that fast.

"Please don't let him get hurt," Evie whispers.

I roll my eyes. "He's not a poodle, sweetheart."

Evie chews on her bottom lip as she watches Dave charge the guy, jumping and hitting him in the back. The guy goes down, and Dave's teeth lock around the man's wrist, his head shaking from side to side as he unleashes a series of growls.

The guy screams and tries to yank his arm away. I smile as I approach him. "The harder you fight him the deeper his teeth go," I say as I crouch down and pat his shoulder. "Best to relax."

"Please," he whimpers. I say nothing for a long moment before clicking my fingers. Dave releases him, but proceeds to stare and growl. "What do you want?" he asks, scrambling away from me.

Jonty grabs the guy by the throat, pulls him to his feet, and drags him into the shadows of a nearby alleyway where he pins him to the wall. His feet flail above the ground, his legs thrashing wildly as Jonty's forearm presses against his windpipe, quickly cutting off his air supply. Dave stands behind us, pacing and snarling frantically. The taste of blood sends Dave into a frenzy, he'll be a nightmare for days now.

I point to Dave and look at Evie. "Keep a hold of him." She grabs him by the collar and yanks him away. I step up beside Jonty, narrowing my eyes on the shitbag pinned against the wall. "I thought my message to DeCosta was clear the last time," I say calmly. It couldn't have been any more clear. I sent him his dealers body back in a bag. A bin liner to be exact. "Do you know the effort I had to go to, cutting that bastard up? I ruined my favourite suit all to drive the point home, and now…now I find you here, which means I wasted my time, and I really hate wasting my time." I sigh. The guy continues to gasp and choke as his oxygen dwindles.

"Enough," I say.

Jonty steps back and the guy's body falls to the floor, slumping against the wall. I bend down in front of him, my hands resting on my thighs. "I figure that sending him back a dead guy didn't work." I press my hand over my mouth and shrug. "So, I guess I'll send him back a live messenger this time."

"Thank you," he gasps. "Thank you."

I smile at his words. "Don't thank me yet. I said alive, not unharmed." I lean in closer to him. "There are some fates worse than death my friend," I whisper.

His eyes go wide, all bravado slipping. I take out my pack of cigarettes and place one between my lips. "Left or right?" I ask.

29

EVIE

Ezra flips the top to his silver lighter open and the click echoes from the brick walls. There's a slight smirk on his face as he flicks the flint. The amber light from the flame lights his face up, making his dark eyes glint.

And I want him so badly.

He inhales a long drag, his eyes narrowing on the guy slumped against the wall as he blows a cloud of smoke in his direction.

"What?" The guy coughs. "Left or right what?"

"Left or right, pick. You're boring me." Ezra sighs. "And when I'm bored I tend to get a twitchy trigger finger. So pick boy."

"Left! Left!"

Ezra remains crouched in front of the guy, taking another puff from his cigarette as he holds out his hand. Jonty places a switch blade in his palm, and the guy immediately attempts to scramble away from Ezra, but Jonty's boot lands over his hand. His screams bounce around the alleyway.

Dave growls, threatening to break free of my hold, and I tighten my grip on his collar. Ezra holds the knife up, smiling as he slowly hovers it over the guy's right hand.

"Left. I said left," he shouts frantically.

Ezra shrugs. "You took your sweet time." He hacks off the guy's pinky finger, and hysterical wails flood the street. Jonty clamps a hand over the screaming guy's mouth as Ezra moves to the next finger, sawing through flesh and bone.

He is torturing this guy. It's not only my pain he likes, he likes anyone's pain, and I don't like that. I want to be the only person he enjoys hurting. "Ezra!" I shout, and he glances over his shoulder at me, the cigarette gripped between his lips.

"What?"

"That's not nice." My eyes lock on the guy fighting behind Jonty's grasp. "You shouldn't torture him like that. It's wrong."

Ezra throws his head back and laughs, taking the cigarette from his mouth and holding it between his blood covered fingers. "Not nice? He can live without his fingers. The poor fucker whose neck you snapped?" He waves the knife in the air. "Not so much." He turns back to his work, severing through another finger. The man's screams weaken into moans.

I narrow my eyes. Ezra doesn't realize it's his fault I snapped that man's neck. When he wouldn't hurt me, when he ignored me, he forced me to do something in order to obtain my forgiveness. "No, Ezra. That was quick, you are dragging this out which is just sadistic. Just kill him."

The guy's eyes pulse open and he tries to shake his head, mumbling under Jonty's hand. Ezra rolls his eyes, takes another drag of smoke, then slams the blade down over another finger. The man's feet kick at the ground, his back arching from the pain as Jonty holds him in place.

"Live, Evie. *Live* messenger." Ezra stands, stepping away from the guy writhing in pain. "Some of us aren't fucking psycho's."

I glance down at the guy's mutilated hand, watching the blood pool in the veins of the cobblestone street. He cut off every finger except his thumb. "You left his thumb?"

"I'm not a complete bastard. It's opposable thumbs that separate us from animals after all."

He is evil. Only an evil person would make someone suffer like this. I kill people, but I do not drag it out. I let them be forgiven. I pray for them before they die. I send them to heaven...or hell. But I grant them deliverance, Ezra just destroys them. Like the devil. He is destruction.

Jonty pulls a cloth from his pocket and wraps the man's maimed hand in it.

Ezra flicks his cigarette into the alley and takes a step back toward the man clutching the blood soaked cloth to his hand. "You go back to your boss and you tell him that the next time I find one of his dealers on my turf, I'm coming for him personally," Ezra says. "And what I'm going to do to him will make this look like foreplay. Understood?" The guy nods frantically. "Good." Ezra grabs the collar of his jacket and hauls him to his feet. He staggers a few steps before Ezra slaps him over the shoulder. "Off you go." The man walks away, swaying and leaning on the walls for support.

He's just letting him leave? "Ezra!" I grab onto his arm. "Why did you let him go? Won't his people come after you?"

Closing his eyes, he tilts his head back, and groans. "Questions, Evie!"

I direct my gaze to the ground. Ezra snaps and Dave jumps up, following behind him as he walks away.

"Ah, he's a charmer. Don't take it personally, sweet thing." Jonty winks, flashing me a smile. I nod, and walk alongside him, and then he whistles "Knocking on Heaven's Door". It's now I realize that it was Jonty Ezra had follow me that night and again, the idea that Ezra had me followed feels so romantic.

30

EZRA

I wake up and the smell of Evie's perfume assaults my senses. She's here, in my bed. I drag my hand down my face. This is ridiculous and stupid. Now is not the time to be obsessed with a girl, and as much as I would rather stab myself than admit it out loud, I am obsessed with her.

I've had Alexei and Seamus working on tearing down Zee's empire, and so far we've cut almost all of his supply from Mexico, as well as his most import routes to Europe and America. We have him under siege, suffocating him. Sooner or later he will have to fold, or he will have nothing left, making this entire ploy to bring me on side with him pointless. Although, I think this has gone far beyond business, it's personal now. I've heard nothing from him since the tits, and honestly, it's making me twitchy. Maybe I should be pleased. No news is good news, right?

Either way, Evie should not be my priority, and yet the girl is like some sick sort of sick crack. She's all consuming and I can't get enough of her. I glance across the bed to where she's laying on her side, spooning Dave. Her fingers brush over his side and he groans.

"I thought you didn't like dogs." I smirk.

She glances over her shoulder with a smile. "He's grown on me."

She didn't have much choice. He's like her damn shadow.

I get up and take a quick shower. I'm toweling off when I hear voices in the other room. Who is that? I wrap a towel around my waist and storm through the apartment to the entrance. Evie stands with the door ajar, talking to someone. I come up behind her and open the door wider, staring over her head at Jen. Her red hair is pulled into a loose braid over one shoulder. Her toned body covered in a skin-tight red dress. Now, when a woman turns up on your door dressed like that, it's for one reason. I glance down at Evie who is wearing one of my shirts with nothing underneath. Her hair is a wild mess that looks like she just got royally fucked. She leans back into me, pressing her arse against my crotch. She's a possessive little thing, and it makes me smile.

"Jen. How are you?" She flashes me a seductive grin.

Oh, this is going to be fun. I like Evie submissive, but I like her even more when she gets her claws out.

"I'm good, Ezra," she says, acting as if Evie isn't even here. "I haven't heard from you in a while. I was worried."

No, she was burned because she's surplus to requirement.

"Well, come in." I almost laugh when I feel Evie go rigid and then turn, ducking under my arm.

Jen steps into the apartment, a smug smile on her face. Evie plops down on the sofa with her arms folded across her chest and a face like thunder.

"Take a seat," I say, waving toward the couch. I watch Jen glance at Evie with disdain. "Evelyn, this is Jen. Jen, Evelyn." Evie's eyes narrow on me before darting over in a glare at Jen. Jen's eyes are set shamelessly on my bare torso, and Evie notices, her nostrils flaring. Oh, this is too good. Any minute now and I might get to see a catfight. A *hot* catfight. Although that would probably end with Evie slitting Jen's throat.

The longer Jen stares, the harder Evie glares at her. "I'll go make us some coffee," Evie says, far too sweetly as she hops up from the couch.

"Uh..." I jog after her. "It's fine. I'll do it." She scowls at me, and this time, I do laugh. "Wouldn't want anything unsavoury slipping into our guests drink, now, would we?"

"Then I suggest you get that whore out of your house." Evie's eyes narrow on me

"That's no way to talk about my friends," I cock an eyebrow at her, "sweetheart." And I wait for the explosion.

I can literally see her blood boil to the surface. Her face reddens and she stomps her foot over the floor like a child. "She is not a friend. She wants to fuck you, and I swear to God, Ezra. I will kill her."

"Can you blame her?" I laugh, loosening my towel and pushing it down my hips slightly.

"Drop that towel one more inch..."

I grab her hand, pressing it to my now semi-hard cock. "And what, little killer?"

"Do you want her?"

I grab her around the back of the neck and yank her close to me, grinding my boner on her thigh. "Not the way I want you."

Evie scowls at me, and I lean in, teasing her mouth with my tongue. Her lips part and I sink my teeth into her bottom lip, making her hiss.

"Fucking redhead." She pulls out of my grip and grabs the towel, undoing it and allowing it to fall to the floor. "Fucking slut," she mumbles. I pull back and cock an eyebrow at her. "You're not hers," she says. "You're mine." She falls to her knees, and in one gulp, shoves my cock into her warm mouth.

I throw my hands out against the breakfast bar for support and she grabs the backs of my thighs for leverage. "Fuck, Evie!" She takes my cock until she gags, and damn, that's hot.

"Ezra?" *Ah, fuck. Why did I let Jen in here?* Oh, yeah, so it would piss Evie off. I cross my arms on the counter in front of me and bend over.

"Hey."

Evie sucks me harder, pumping her hand up and down my base. Shit. I fight to keep my eyes from rolling back in my head.

"How have you been?"

Really. Now? She wants to make small talk, now? "Fine. I'm, yep. Good." My voice hitches when Evie lightly drags her nails over my balls. I drop my head forward, squeezing my eyes shut.

"Are you okay?" Jen asks.

"Mmm-hmm."

"Is that girl your girlfriend?" Her voice wavers, and Evie stops moving for a second. Of all the times for me to have to answer that question, it's when the crazy bitch I like to fuck has her teeth millimeters from my cock.

"Uh, it's..." Evie's tongue presses against my Jap's eye and I jerk. "Complicated," I choke. The next thing I know, her finger's pressing against my arsehole. I clench my cheeks together, but she shoves her finger up there anyway. I would be mad about it, but holy shit, my balls explode, and I do mean explode, down her throat.

I slam my palm down on the counter and clear my throat in an attempt to cover the groan. Wave after wave ripples over my body and I clench my fists because Evie won't let up.

"Are you sure you're okay, Ezra?" Jen asks.

When I finally stop coming, I manage to focus on her. "You should go. I'll call you." Evie rams me in the hole again and I wince. "Or not," I cough.

"Oh, um...okay." Jen takes her bag and is about to leave when her gaze moves to my left. I glance at a very smug looking Evie who is wiping the corner of her mouth whilst glaring at Jen like she's about to stab her. Without another word, Jen leaves.

I turn to face Evie who looks like butter wouldn't melt. My legs are numb, and I have to grab the counter for support. "My arsehole! Really?"

She shrugs, then turns and trots out of the kitchen.

"Some things are fucking sacred, Evie!" I shout after her. "A man's hole is one of them."

31

EVIE

I'm trying to be a good girl and not kill anyone. Ezra has me work at the bar on the nights he has to handle business. He said keeping me busy would keep me out of trouble, but he underestimates me, really he does because my little demon still beckons me. The thing that's the most concerning is that sometimes, when I'm laid next to Ezra watching his chest rise and fall in deep swells as he sleeps, it tells me to kill him. But I can't do that because I love him. I don't want to kill the one thing I love.

I managed to work behind the bar for three weeks without killing anyone. And then two weeks ago, Ezra made me mad, and I had to kill someone so I wouldn't kill him. I thought I could stop with that one, but there are so many bad men in the world, and Ezra won't let me have any control.

I can't get the way Jen looked at Ezra this morning out of my head. I can't get the memory of him fucking her up against his goddamn window out of my head. *He still hasn't fucked you up against that window, Evelyn.*

"Sugar," the man says, ripping me away from my thoughts. "My beer."

"Miller Light?" I ask, reaching for a glass.

"That's what I said the first time, dumb bitch."

Heat covers my face and I clench my jaw.

Forcing a smile, I nod my head and turn away from him, gripping the glass as I walk to the tap. It only takes a swift movement of my hand to pop the top to my ring and dump the poison into his glass. When I spin around to hand his beer to him, he has no idea I've done anything to it. To be honest, Ezra having me work behind this bar has been the best idea he could have ever had. It makes it all too easy to kill these disgusting men. They drink their drink. They start to feel sick and leave. They'll either collapse blocks away, or on the subway train. And in this part of town, scummy men found unconscious on a subway train are usually chalked up to an overdose.

He brushes his fingers over mine when he grabs the glass from my hand. "You're a pretty thing. Too bad you aren't one of the whore's here. I'd pay good money to sink my dick in your tight little pussy." He winks and takes a sip before he turns away from the bar.

I wish I could watch him gasping for his last breath. But I'm being a good girl, so I can't.

Several minutes later, the crowd around the bar thins out, and I take the opportunity to go to the bathroom. As I am washing my hands, the door flies open.

The man from the bar laughs as he drags his eyes over my body. I don't bother to turn the water off, and I quickly move toward the door, but he slams it closed and deadbolts it. I back away from him, my heart pounding violently as he staggers towards me. There's a sick smile on his lips as he grabs my hair and slings me against the wall. He groans when he presses me against the grimy bathroom tile. "All women are whores," he says. "Which means your pussy is mine."

I yell, but he covers my mouth with his dirty hand. I sink my teeth into his skin, the taste of sweat and grease filling my mouth, but he doesn't budge. He grabs my skirt and shoves it up around my thighs. I struggle against him, trying to kick my legs, but he has me positioned in such a way I can't move. His rough hand works beneath the edge of my panties, and I try to squeeze my thighs closed.

"Mmm," he groans next to my ear. "I like a little fight, sugar. I like dirty little whores that are fighters."

I choke on a sob and my mind comes to a screeching halt. I know all too well that I can do nothing to stop this. I am too small, too weak, and this man will take what he wants from me. I focus on the water still running in the sink and try to take my mind elsewhere. I try to ignore his fingers prodding and poking me while he groans. I go back to the place I used to go when Zachariah would take me. Numb. Empty. Useless.

The man presses his forearm over my throat, choking me as he keeps me pinned in place. I know why this is happening. It's because I've found pleasure within my penance. When Ezra beats me, I like it and in order to be forgiven you must endure pain. This is my punishment. This is my pain.

The man takes a wad of cash from his pocket, holding it up in front of my face. "Whores get paid to fuck."

He shakes the cash at me and uses his fingers to pry my lips open. I try to fight him. I keep my lips tense, but he leans over my throat with more force. I can't breathe. My lungs burn, and I gasp for air. When I do, he crams the money inside my mouth, shoving it down my throat with his thick fingers. I cough and gag, spitting the filthy paper out.

"Too good to take my money?" he laughs.

I hear someone try the door, and there's a loud bang, but the deadbolt won't give. No one has ever saved me. Not my father. Not the police. Not God. And I accepted years ago no one ever would. The man jerks his fly down, the sound of the zipper seems so loud. The groan he makes as he pulls his cock from his pants causes my stomach to knot and my heart to race. I want to die. I'd rather die than let this man take me, but I'm helpless, and a coward.

There's a loud crash. The metal hinges groan as the door crashes to the floor. Everything happens so fast, and suddenly, the man is torn away from me. I collapse, my legs weak. Ezra's enormous frame towers over the man, his elbow kicking back as he punches him in the face again and again. He drags him to the sink and pushes him face down in it. All I can think is that it looks like Ezra has just placed the man's head on a chopping block.

"You picked the wrong girl to screw with," Ezra says calmly before he pulls his gun from his pants, places the barrel against the back of the man's head, and pulls the trigger.

My ears ring from the loud bang of the gun. I can't catch my breath. Ezra glances over at me, his chest heaving. One of his hands still holds the man in place over the sink, the other is braced against the mirror, gun still in hand. "You okay?"

I should say something. I know I should, but what do you say to the first person who's ever saved you. The person who saved you when even God wouldn't. *Maybe God sent Ezra to save you, Evelyn.*

"Evie!" He shouts and I jump.

Tears sting my eyes, my heart pounds frantically in my chest. I should tell him thank you, I should fall at his feet and worship him, but all I can focus on is that he's still holding onto that filthy man. "Why are you holding him like that?" I ask.

"I don't want blood all over the bathroom."

I nod, but don't move from my spot on the floor. I stare at the man Ezra has bent over the sink. I listen to the blood drip, drip, drip down the drain, and my vision blurs. I finally mean enough to someone that they think I'm worth saving. The rage, the anger, the possession. In his own way this is how Ezra loves. I know that now. This is the most meaningful moment of my life, and I want to wallow in it. I let the tears pour down my face, and I don't try to hide them. This time, I give my tears to Ezra. I hear a thud as he drops the body and without a word, he bends over and lifts me into his arms, carrying me out of the restroom.

Jonty is standing outside the demolished bathroom door, his face expressionless.

"Get a door back up and block the bathroom off," Ezra orders. "And call in the cleaners." I twist Ezra's shirt in my hand, and lay my cheek against his chest. He is my safety, my harbor, my savior. He will protect me.

He's different.

He's special.

He's mine.

And no one else will ever have what we do. Bound in sin and blood.

I'll always be a good girl for him.

32

EZRA

I pace in front of Evie's hunched over form. Dave is next to her on the sofa, protecting her.

"Damn it, Evie. Did you take him into that bathroom to try and kill him? And tell me the fucking truth or there will be consequences, and not the kind that you like."

She stares into her lap, one hand stroking over Dave's back. "No..." she breaths and her eyes flick up at me, tears building behind them. " He just followed me into the bathroom. I would never touch another man Ezra. Never. I would never forsake you like that again. I love you."

Love. As much as I hate the concept of it, I can't help but like it because no amount of pain in the world holds as much power or control as love.

I smile. "Do you, little killer?"

"Yes." Her eyes dart up to mine and she holds my gaze.

"Good."

IT'S BEEN TWO DAYS, and Evie has been following me around like a kicked dog. I hate the fact that he touched her, and it makes me want to kill him all over again.

I go to the bedroom to check on her, and find her on the bed, curled on her side and spooning Dave. He barely even acknowledges me anymore. He's got shit all loyalty. I've left her here for the last two nights while I go to the club. One of my guys keeps an eye on the flat just in case. Whether to keep others out or her in, I'm not sure, but I can't run shit and keep an eye on her too.

I sit on the edge of the bed and glance down at Evie. I'm shit in these kinds of situations. When you grow up surrounded by whores like I did this shit seems standard. Guys will often try and take it too far with a whore, thinking that because she sells herself she's fair game. The fact is, nothing is free, and the guy that touched Evie is not the first guy I've had to remind of that. But, in the end, it's part of the business, you deal with it and you move on. Evie is not dealing with it. I need to bring back my little killer.

"Okay. Enough. You *were* a whore. You got felt up. You should be used to it, sweetheart. Now get your arse up and get in the shower." I yank the duvet away from her and Dave grumbles. "You're coming to the club tonight. I need someone to work the bar." She rolls onto her back, her gaze blankly fixed on the ceiling. Dave takes that as his cue to leave.

"I am a whore. I am dirty. I am sinful and wicked and the reason the righteous men fall. Zachariah was right. I deserve the bad things that happen to me because I'm not a good girl, Ezra. I want to be your good girl, but I am bad." She glances up at me. "It will happen again because I am sin."

I drag a hand over my face. "You are not a whore," I groan. "And who the *fuck* is Zachariah?" She releases a staggered breath and covers her mouth with her hand as tears spill down her temples.

Jealousy is not something I'm accustomed to. I take women, break them, possess them, and pass them on. Evie is different though, Evie is mine, and the thought of some-one-- *anyone* touching her makes me want to end them. I don't know what it is about her that makes me this irra-tional person, but I can't control my shit around her. She is not just business, she's personal.

"Who. Is. Zachariah?" I want to know who told her that she deserved this life, that she was no better than a whore.

All the colour has drained from her face and her eyes are distant. "A boy that I grew up with," she whispers. I move, straddling her tiny waist and leaning over her. I grip her chin and force her to look at me. "And where is this boy now, Evie?" My voice remains level despite the anger brewing in my chest.

"I don't know."

"Well," I inhale, "your *boy* was wrong. Shit doesn't happen for any other reason than shit luck."

"It was my fault because I was pretty. Had I not been pretty, he wouldn't have wanted me."

What do I even say to that?

"Ezra," she sits up, her gaze dropping to her lap. She takes a deep breath, and her eyes flick up, brimming with her tears. "Do you love me?"

She can't be serious. I rub my hand over my stubble and stare at her. In a way, I care about Evie. I want her, I own her, but I will never love her. I'm just not capable.

I look in her hopeful eyes. "No," I say.

Her lip trembles and she nods. "Because I am a bad person..."

"Don't do this shit. I just don't, there is no reason."

"Because I'm a whore--" Tears track down her face. I hate tears, unless I'm the one causing them. No one else should have the power over her to make her cry. Only me. Her tears are mine.

"No!" I growl. "I want to fuck you, and I *don't* fuck whores." I cock an eyebrow at her. "What more do you want?"

"You don't understand. I am a whore. I always have been. I have always been a temptation without even trying. Zachariah was chosen by God. It was my fault he strayed. He was righteous, and everyone knew I forced him to sin. He was punishing me so that I could be forgiven, but I hate him for it." She shakes her head before she continues her rambling. "God loves sinners, but he hates the sin, and I am sin, Ezra. I am sin, so even God can't love me."

I can't deal with her crazy shit. "Have you listened to yourself?"

"You don't understand how my religion works." She shoots a confused look up at me. "Everything happens for a reason."

I frown at her and clench my fist, struggling to maintain my calm. "Evie, I told you once and I don't like fucking repeating myself. Religion is bullshit. Your god is bullshit." I uncross my arms and close the space between us, wrapping my hand around the back of her neck. Her eyes flutter shut and her breath hitches. "I'm the only god you need, little killer. I'm the one who will protect you, and I'm the one who will rain down hell on anyone who hurts you."

She closes her eyes and bows her head. "Please forgive Ezra for the things he doesn't understand..."

I roll my eyes and drag my hand down my face.

She opens her eyes and her gaze locks with mine. "I love you, Ezra."

33

EVIE

He will love me. One day.

I lay in the bed, staring at the ceiling. I feel dirty for telling Ezra about Zachariah. I know he thinks I'm dirty now. *Evelyn, there's no way he'll love you now.*

Closing my eyes, I try to pray, but I can't find the words. My mind is too possessed by Ezra to pray. The bedroom door creaks, and a sliver of light spills in from the hall. I hear Dave's collar jingle as he rounds the corner of the bed. He rests his head on the edge of the mattress. "I'm not bad," I whisper, and he licks my face before jumping on the bed. He steps over me and curls up by my legs. I lay my hand on top of his head, stroking over his ears as I fall asleep.

Blood trickles over my lip from where he just hit me, and my eyes won't move from the knife in his hand. I want to scream, but I know if I do, he'll slit my throat like he's promised me time and time again. His fist meets the side of my face with a smack, and I fall to the floor.

"I'll purge the sin from you one way or another," he growls. "Fuck it out of you or beat it out of you. Doesn't matter to me."

I attempt to roll over on my stomach, hoping he will allow me to shamefully crawl away, but he straddles me and fist my hair with the hand the knife is in. "Stay still," he says, pressing my face against the floor. "You are sin, Evelyn. You look like sin."

I feel the sharp tip of the knife pressing against the top of my spine. And I swallow the screams threatening to break from my lips. "Please, please don't do it," I beg, but all that does is make his hold on me tighten and he bares down on the knife, slowly dragging it down the length of my back. It burns and I scream, my muscles tensing.

"I'm doing this to save you. I'll mark you so everyone will know you are tainted, but saved through forgiveness." He hisses in a breath as he makes a horizontal mark across my back. The blade stings, setting fire to my skin as he slashes his way across my body. "You're blood is so red." He groans, and I feel his breath blow over my skin. His wet tongue traces over the fresh wound, and a sated moan rumbles from his lips. "I can taste your wickedness. It seeps through your veins, Evelyn. And through blood absolution shall be found."

I wake, sitting up in bed breathless and dripping with sweat. I glance over to Ezra's side and he's gone. I feel lost without him, and I hate that. At one time I felt I was strong. But he makes me weak. The things Ezra says to me--they are wrong. They are blasphemous, so why do I love him? He is not God, but for some reason, I want to believe he is. My mind is so consumed with Ezra, and if I'm honest, when I close my eyes to pray, I'm tempted to pray to him. And I am going to hell for it. *You've forgotten about Hannah...*

My mind jumbles and gridlocks as I try to reason with myself. Father lead our community, teaching us that a man is to be a woman's master, that men are righteous and the only way a woman can find religion. A master is a god. Ezra is my master, so can't he be my god? Maybe I'm not wrong for the way I feel.

Evelyn, Ezra is not righteous. It is wrong to love him. He is taking you away from God.

But if I pray to Ezra, my prayers will be answered. He will save me.

My faith is wavering, and all over a man who is the epitome of everything I once hated. I'm sure the devil is laughing over the irony. I'm questioning everything in my life, and to be honest, I'd rather give up on God and love Ezra without conviction .

What are you saying, Evelyn? Are you a blasphemer?

What am I saying? My heart beats violently, my palms grow slick with sweat. I throw the comforter off of me, grabbing my clothes from last night off the floor as I head toward the living room.

I have to ask forgiveness. I need to be in the presence of God. Maybe Ezra's presence blocks out the presence of God. I must go to the church and pray--then I'll have Ezra beat me to pay my penance. I no longer feel driven for anything other than Ezra. It's Ezra that drives me to kill those men when he makes me angry. It's his acceptance and forgiveness and approval I am so desperately seeking, no longer God's, and I have to change that. I need to be surrounded by holiness. And nothing in this place is holy.

34

EZRA

My phone vibrates against the desk as the screen flashes.

"Yeah," I answer.

"Ez, we got a problem," Jonty grumbles. "Cops are here to see you."

"What now?" I hate cops. They're a ball ache I really don't need right now.

"Not sure. Want me to bring them up?" he asks.

"Yeah, fine." I hang up. As if I don't have enough shit going on today.

A few minutes later there's a knock on the door and Jonty leads them in. Two guys in suits. Detectives.

"Mr James. We are Officer Wilson and Officer Rowe. We need a few minutes of your time."

"Well then take a seat." I gesture across the room to the sofas facing each other.

They both give me serious looks before sitting. The older guy has a scowl on his face that looks like he's just sniffed dog shit. I'm sure they know what this place is, what I am. The problem is they can't prove shit. Every now and then one of the girls gets careless and gets picked up, but they never talk, never claim any association with the club or me. It's an unspoken rule. I don't even have to enforce it. In this line of work, you keep your mouth shut and your legs spread.

I cross my leg, resting my ankle on my knee. "What is this about?" I ask, my voice laced with boredom.

The older guy leans forward and places his elbows on his knees. "Four men have turned up dead in the last two weeks. Poisoned. Arsenic."

I cock an eyebrow. "And?"

"The victims are random, nothing in common except one thing...." He pauses, apparently for dramatic effect. "They were all regular visitors to your..." his lips snarl, "*club,*" he says the word with distaste.

I frown. I want to play it off, but even I'll admit that's suspicious.

"Have you noticed anything out of the ordinary?" the other officer asks.

I shake my head and frown. "No."

They ask me questions about shit that really doesn't seem relevant. Have you seen this guy here before, do you remember this night, where were you on this date at this time.They lay out pictures of bodies, crime scenes. Some of the guys I vaguely recognise, but of course I don't tell them that.

Eventually, with very little information, they leave, handing me a business card as they go. As if I'm going to call them. In my world, you fix shit yourself, and I'm pretty sure I know exactly who the killer is.

As soon as they're gone, I grab my laptop and start trawling through the CCTV footage. These guys could have been in here any time over the last few months, but I think I remember one of those guys being in here last weekend, just four days ago.

I search through the stored surveillance on my laptop and pull up the footage from that night. I fast forward until I see the guy leaning on the bar with his drink. He talks to various girls. I fast forward again, but hit pause when I see Evie pouring his drink behind the bar. I hit play again, watching the scene unfold. Her bright red lips pull up in a smile. He pauses with his near empty drink half way to his lips as though he's physically stunned by her. I don't blame him. Evie has that effect. I watch her closely. She glances straight up at the camera. Her dark hair and pale skin contrast dramatically under the lights in the club, and I can't help but think she looks like an angel--an angel of death. He places his empty glass on the bar and Evie takes it, tossing it to the side as she mixes him another cocktail. Her eyes are locked on him with that sly grin over her face the entire time. Something is going on here. This isn't right. A fissure of unease works it's way through my chest. She touches her finger and then gently swirls the glass in her hand. It's so quick I almost miss it. I rewind the footage and watch again and again.

Her ring. She's touching her ring. She spiked his drink. Shit. I can't work out who's more stupid, her for thinking she'd get away with it, or me for thinking she could control herself enough to do something as simple as serve some drinks.

I'm striding out of the club when my phone rings.

"What?"

"She left boss. I followed her to the church," one of my boys, Jonny, says, and I hang up.

35

EVIE

The incense is too strong in here this morning. It burns my throat, but I don't cough. I close my eyes and bow my head and kneel down like a good girl. It's been so long since I've been in here, I feel a slight unease.

"Forgive me for my sins..." I swallow because the only sin I can think about is Ezra and his cock, and that is wrong because I'm in a church. I clear my throat and try again. "Forgive me for my sins, and please help me find the evil doers in this world, the sinners, so that I can end their suffering."

The door groans, but I keep my head bowed because it's probably just that homeless man coming in to find heat again. I wait to hear him singing the chorus to "Billy Jean", but I don't hear it, and suddenly, I get chill bumps.

"Evelyn!" Ezra's voice booms through the sanctuary and I swear I can feel the floor threatening to burst into flames.

I keep my head down because he's in my safe place. I don't like him in my safe place. It makes me nervous. *He shouldn't be here, Evelyn. Something is wrong.* I grab my temples willing that nagging voice to shut up, and then I pray silently to be forgiven for swearing at the alter. I hear his heavy steps echoing down the aisle. I can feel the vibrations through the floor.

He fists my hair, jerking my head back, and now I have no choice but to look up at his towering frame. His lips twist into a menacing smile, and I close my eyes to finish my prayer.

"You've been a bad girl, Evie," he says.

"And grant me strength. Amen."

He yanks me to my feet and grabs my chin so hard my lips purse. He slowly inches his face toward mine, his black eyes flashing with anger. "Pray, little killer," he whispers, his breath touching my lips. "You're going to need all the help you can get." His grip tightens to the point I'm certain I'll be bruised, and I close my eyes, flinching away from his harsh gaze. "Four in the past two weeks...you've been a busy girl. Tell me, did you fuck them, or just kill them?" Anger ripples off him in waves.

My heart leaps into my throat, and I swallow it down in to the pit of my stomach.

"Shhhh. Not in the church!" I whisper frantically.

What are you afraid of, little killer. My demon mocks Ezra.

He growls low in his throat, and all I can think is that it sounds like a hellhound. When he releases my face, he grabs me by the back of the neck, his fingers digging into my flesh, catching several strands of hair and pulling. *He knows Evelyn.* Each breath that comes from him is deep and hard and sounds like a rumbling fire. He marches me down the aisle, and all I can think is this is my death march because Ezra is crazy and I know that.

The large wooden doors creak when he shoves them open. A gust of cold air whips around me as he guides me to the sleek Mercedes still running and parked at the curb. He opens the passenger door and pushes me down into the seat before buckling my seat belt.

I don't look at him. I can't look at him. I promised I'd be a good girl, and he thinks I've been bad. He slams the door with such force the entire car rocks. I swallow because this is not good, Evelyn. Not good at all.

As soon as he slides into the driver's seat I can feel his eyes boring into me.

"Ezra..." I breathe, my heart pounding in my chest.

"Did you fuck any of them, Evie?" His voice is calm, and I know that is not good. My gaze lands on his ticking jaw, then strays to his hands tensing on the steering wheel. Every muscle in his arm is popping out, the motion causing his tattoo of the Grim Reaper to come to life. "Did you?" he asks again.

"What?" I gasp. "Fuck who?" My heart skips several beats when my eyes meet his. I've never seen them so dark and black. They are bottomless, like the pit of hell I'm about to be thrown into...or the Hudson River.

He grips the steering wheel harder, diverting his gaze out the front windshield. "Did you think I wouldn't find out? You were picking them off in the club?" He scrubs a hand over his jaw. "And now I have the police all over my arse because a modern day Jack-the-fucking-Ripper is killing off my customers." He finally looks over at me, and I can see him accusing me, I can see him judging me, and now I know I should have killed him. I should have killed him because then this wouldn't be a problem, but then...I love him.

His eyes narrow and my heart stops, no, it plummets. A cold sweat breaks out all over me and I'm dizzy. The fight or flight response kicks in and I reach for the handle of the door, but Ezra's forearm is there slamming me back against the seat and pinning me.

"Answer me." And that's a hiss, not a growl. A hiss. He's going to slit my throat and leave me in the gutter right in front of this church.

"I didn't..." I swallow, trying to catch my breath. "I didn't fuck them." My voice shakes, my body trembles, and Ezra's eyes are still on me. "I didn't fuck them!"

His arm moves away from my chest, but then, one by one, his fingers wrap around my throat, squeezing. I gasp for breath, clawing at his hands as he yanks me forward, placing my face inches from his.

"Who owns you, Evie?" His voice is a low rumble.

"God," I manage to whisper, and I can tell he doesn't like that answer because his fingers dig harder into my skin. My vision dips in and out, and he's going to choke me to death. *Ezra would never hurt me. I'm his little killer. I'm his little Evie. I'm not the red-headed slut in the too-tight white dress. He wants to love me.*

"No," he breathes, his lips brushing across mine. "Try again, little killer." The pressure on my throat loosens slightly as he waits for me to answer him.

And as bad as it is to say, I say it. "You."

"Say it again, Evie.'" His voice booms around the car, and those butterflies flit around in my stomach.

Why do I like him angry like this. I'm throbbing between my legs and he's choking me and yelling at me and he's angry. And I like it because no one's ever owned me, and people protect the things they own, the things the covet. I want to be his precious little killer because then I will be safe. Forever and ever, Amen.

"Who. Owns. You?" His eyes flicker in anticipation, a small smile creeping over his full lips.

"You do, Ezra."

His fingers unwind from my throat as his mouth slams over my trembling lips. He kisses my hard, dragging my bottom lip between his teeth. I bathe in the pain. When we sin we need to be punished, and punishment is pain. I moan against his lips, reveling in his possession because I am his.

Tearing his lips away, he looks at me like the bad girl I am. "What am I going to do with you, sweetheart?" His lips twist into a smile, his face softens. "Seems you have a little habit."

Sweet'art. I narrow my gaze on him.

"Habit?" I ask.

His hand trails across my neck before falling back to his lap. "How many have you killed, Evie?"

"It doesn't matter since they were sinners." In that instant his eyes flicker and I realize he thinks I'm crazy, even though I'm not. "They were bad men, Ezra. They're filthy and nasty and perverts and they sin, Ezra. *They sin!* Their hands never leave you, you can't wash that filth away. You can't pray away that grime, and it seeps into you so far...I need to kill them." I gasp for a breath and know I only sound more deranged, but it's all true. "I have to kill them. I have to kill them."

36

EZRA

"I have to kill them," she says it with such steadfast belief.

I release a heavy breath and pinch the bridge of my nose. "Shit, Evie." She's going to get caught if she keeps going. She's messy, uncontrolled. She might as well just leave a trail of bodies all the way to her front door the way she's going. In fact, no, make that my fucking door. I glance at her, and she's looking at me with wide eyes, her teeth gnawing nervously on her bottom lip .

"You can't just kill people," I say.

"I don't just kill *people*. I kill the people that need to face judgment." She's holding that damn crucifix, twisting it between her fingers.

I lean my head back against the headrest. "I don't give a shit if they're Mother-fucking-Theresa, but you're leaving bodies everywhere. You might as well write my damn name on their foreheads and leave them outside the club door. The police are all over me." I shake my head, because this is so fucked up. "You need to stop...whatever *this* is."

Her eyes pulse open and she shakes her head furiously. "I can't stop. I can't stop." She inhales, her nostrils flaring and her jaw clenching. "Please don't make me."

I drag a hand through my hair in frustration. "Jesus, Evie."

She buries her face in her palms. This is warped, even for me. Without saying anything, I pull away from the curb. She stays silent as we wind through the heavy New York traffic. Her gaze remains fixed out the window, her knees pulled up to her chest. She looks fragile, and for the first time I feel like I really see the damaged depths of her.

I turn the radio up and don't look at her until I pull up outside my flat. I climb out of the car, but she doesn't budge. I sigh as I walk around and open her door.

And, of course, now she won't look at me. "Evie?" Nothing.

For fucks sake. I lean over and release her seat belt. She's still balled up on herself, and I take her wrists, yanking her arms away from her legs.

"No!" she shouts.

I don't have the time or patience for her shit right now. A better man might have, but I'm not a better man. I'm a bastard. I forcibly drag her from the car, throwing her up against the side of it. "This can be easy, sweetheart, or--" She starts thrashing wildly. "Hard way it is." I slam the car door and click the lock.

Tears streak her face as she tries to pull away from me. "Please," she begs.

I bend down and grab the backs of her thighs, throwing her over my shoulder. She screams like a fucking banshee, squirming around and hitting my back.

"Don't kill me. I don't want to go in the Hudson River. Please!" Her fists pound over my back, and I keep walking towards the lift. Once I'm inside I press the button for my floor. The doors slide shut and all I can hear are her heavy sobs. "Please don't kill me," she whispers again.

I roll my eyes. "I'm not going to kill you, Evie. Shit, you're the one running around like a mass murderer."

The lift stops and the doors open. As soon as we're inside my apartment I relax. She can lose her shit all she likes in here. I drop her on the couch and she lands in a sprawled heap. I turn away from her and grab the bottle of whiskey from the kitchen, taking a heavy swig straight from the bottle.

"Do you hate me?" She swipes at the tears on her cheeks.

I take another gulp of whiskey. "No," I sigh. "You kill people. I kill people. Shit happens. The world keeps turning."

"You kill people, Ezra." She glares at me, still clutching her crucifix. "I kill *bad* people."

I narrow my eyes and point at her. "I don't get caught. I don't leave them on the back seat of a fucking car, and I sure as shit don't kill four guys all from the same place in a two week motherfucking period!" I approach her, towering over where she sits on the sofa. "You'll go to jail Evie, and then you'll go to a psych ward because, according to the law, killing for God is not a legitimate reason to go on a killing spree."

Her face washes white, and she swallows. "Do you still think I taste like heaven?"

I drag my hand through my hair, ready to damn well rip it out. I don't even know what to do with her anymore. "Evie, what the..." The buzzer for the front door rings and I take the opportunity to walk away before I lose my shit.

Evie is addictive and something about her has me by the balls, but she's crazy, hell maybe it's *because* she's crazy that I want her so much. In my world, I live on the edge. Being with Evie is like constantly walking a tight-rope--breaking her, owning her, whilst constantly wondering when she'll snap, when I'll push her too far. I'm waiting for the day when she tries to kill me, and when that day comes I'll beat her until she bleeds, I'll fuck her until she cries me a crimson river.

I yank the door open and the young guy on the other side of the door jumps back, wide eyed. He shoves a bunch of white roses in my face and practically runs away. There's a small card addressed to Evie shoved in the middle of the leaves. I slam the door and storm back into the apartment.

"Who is sending you flowers?" I dump them on the table, offended by whatever pussy bought her fucking flowers. "And why are they sending them to *my* house?" I yank the envelope open and read over the short two lines.

Evie,

Ezra can't protect you forever. I so look forward to our time together.

ee.

I'm going to kill him. I don't care what he thinks he does or doesn't have. I'm going to tear him apart one fucking limb at a time. And then I'm going to shove my gun up his arse-hole and rape him with it before I pull the trigger.

I grab the vase of flowers and launch it at the wall. Dave leaps up from his bed and jumps onto the sofa next to Evie, cowering against her.

Evie clutches Dave, pulling him into her lap. "Who..."

"From now on, you do not leave my sight unless I tell you to. No more of this sneaking out bullshit, Evie." I point at her. "And I swear to your fucking God that if you disobey me, I will leave you in that club, chained to that cross, and let you really get in touch with your religion." I throw the card on the sofa next to her and she picks it up, her small hands shaking as she reads over the words.

"I don't want to stay with you. I don't like you like this," she whispers.

I lean over her, cupping her face firmly and dragging my thumb across the corner of her lip, smearing her lip-stick. "Who owns you, Evie?" I ask, my voice husky.

"You do..."

"And who protects you, Evie?"

Her eyes lock on mine, tears welling within them. "You do."

I fist my hand in her hair, wrenching her head back and bringing her face to mine. I slam my lips against hers, stroking the side of her throat with my free hand. "I do," I mumble against her lips.

37

EVIE

E zra isn't mad at me any longer. I promised I'd be a good girl, and I think he believes me. I follow him as he heads toward the door, shoving his gun in his waist. I don't want him to leave me.

"Just stay here." Ezra glares at me. "I'll be back in an hour. I've got my phone, you've got Dave, Jonny is outside. Lock the door."

"Please, don't leave me."

He sighs and drags his hand down his face. "Evie, I can't take you with me to this, and you sure as hell aren't going to the club. I'll be right back." He opens the door and shoots me one last glare. "Don't you fucking leave." The door slams shut. "Lock it. Now," he shouts from the other side.

I quickly push the deadbolt in place and glance back at Dave who's laid on his bed and staring at me. I fall back on the couch, and Dave jumps up beside me, resting his head in my lap.

"What do we do now?" I ask and his tail slowly wags.

I turn the television on, and wait. An hour and a half later, Ezra's still gone. I can't help but feel there was a reason he didn't want me to go with him. One I wouldn't like. What if he's lying to me? An overwhelming urge to know what he's doing consumes me. It's Tuesday. I glance at my watch. It's five o'clock. Every Tuesday at five o' clock he goes to the local Starbucks and orders a latte' while he waits to meet someone. I glance at the door, and I know I shouldn't leave. *He wants you to believe his lies, little killer.* I have to know what he is doing, and why I couldn't come.

"Want to go for a walk?" I ask, pushing Dave off of me. He circles around me, jumping and barking, his tail going crazy. I quickly fasten his leash and we leave the apartment.

The city workers are shoveling the fresh layer of snow off the sidewalk. Dave whines when his paw sinks into the wet snow. I yank on his leash, forcing him to walk. I'm not stupid, I see the guy get out of the black Audi parked across the street. I feel him following me. I know he'll tell Ezra, but I'm just walking the dog.

The closer we get to Starbucks, the harder my heart pounds. There's something romantic about watching him when he doesn't know that I am. I slow my pace and stop at the corner of the window. From here I can see the table Ezra always sits at. He's staring down at his phone, one hand on his cup. My lips curl into a smile, but then fire engulfs me. That redhead, Jen, has just sat down at his table. She crosses her legs, her grey dress riding high on her thighs. Ezra glances up at her and arches a brow befre looking back down at his phone.

Dave pulls on the leash, whining. "Stop it!" I hiss.

I watch Jen swipe her filthy little whore hands over his arm. I want to cut her fingers off.

She tosses her loose, red curls behind her head and laughs. And I want to shove a dirty rag down her throat until she gags.

Dave growls, pulling harder on the leash and I'm tempted to let the damn dog go. Ezra smiles at something she says. He never smiles at me like that. He loves her. And I love him. And all he does is own me. I want him to love me, not her. Jen stands up and walks over to Ezra, leaning down and pressing a kiss to his cheek. I will kill her. He fucked her against that window-- the window he's never fucked me against. He buried his cock deep inside her. He made her his. And he still wants her even though he saved me. I am his sinner, but she is his sin. *You must kill him, Evelyn. He is a liar. A user. He has come between you and your work. Grant Hannah peace. Kill him.* I don't want to kill him. I love him. *Who do you love more, God or Ezra? Kill him.*

I feel tears prick at my eyes as I spin around and snake my way through the crowded sidewalk. Dave trots ahead of me, wagging his tail. I feel guilty because poor Dave is going to be without a master. I'll have to keep him, it would only be right, and then I can still have some piece of Ezra with me.

"Please don't make me kill him. I love him," I plead under my breath when I reach his apartment building.

Love is a sin. Ezra was mine. The way she pressed her slutty-lips against his cheek--he didn't push her away. He smiled because he wants her naked and pressed against his window, not me. My heart is angry and it drums against my ribs the more I think about it. My mind is a jumbled wreck of lies and betrayal and rage and confusion. I thought he was the devil, I thought he was a god, and now I think he's nothing more than a filthy, worthless man. A pervert, a whore. The kind of man I kill because it is my job. I must remember my job...He made me believe my religion was pointless. He made me question my motives. I may love him, but I must kill him.

As I climb the stairs to his apartment, tears stream down my face. I don't want to kill him, but I have no choice. I'm going to do what I should have done long ago. I let the devil in and I sinned. I sinned. I sinned...but now I will make it right.

As soon as I walk into the apartment, Dave shakes the snow from his coat and hops onto the couch.

"I'm so sorry Dave," I whisper as I walk to the dresser and open my make-up box. I pull out my foundation, carefully painting it onto my face, covering each blemish, every imperfection with each stroke. I dip my brush into the charcoal eyeshadow, sweeping it over my eyelids. I take my time drawing a perfect line around my eyes with the black liner, making certain to coat my lashes in a thick layer of mascara, and finally, before I leave the room, I cover my lips in blood-red lipstick. I look like a porcelain doll, like something breakable and valuable. And that's what Ezra wants. Looks mean nothing. The devil was an angel, a beautiful angel, and he damned all of mankind to hell.

******Break*****

Dave has been pacing and whimpering ever since we got back. I'm certain he can hear my little demon, and it's angry.

"Forgive me for straying," I whisper as I twist the cap to the whiskey and pull the vial from my purse. "Forgive me for letting that man defile my body. Forgive me for believing his lies."

I dump a cup of ice into a glass and then pour the whiskey over it, watching the golden liquid weave its way between the cubes, listening to the ice crack beneath its heat. Taking the vial, I pop the cap and dump the powder into the drink, my stomach knotting as I watch the poison dissipate. I don't want to do this. I tuck the empty vial safely away in my purse. "And forgive Ezra for the sins he's committed. Amen."

That last one hurt...

I glance out the window, and see him coming toward the entrance of the building. I begin to count in my head. *One. Two. Three...* I perch myself on the kitchen counter, crossing my legs. *Eleven. Twelve. Thirteen.* My heart thumps against my chest, my insides jittery with anticipation. I shake my hair out and adjust my cleavage, before I lean back. I place one hand on the cold granite while holding Ezra's drink in the other hand, and I wait. *Forty-five, forty-six, forty-seven.* The seconds seem like torture, and part of me wonders if I am strong enough to do this. I glance down at the drink, tempted to throw it down the sink. *Don't do it, Evelyn.*

I count out the one hundred and twenty seconds of extreme agony as I wait for him to come to me, to his little killer. I hear his keys jingle, the lock clicks, and the hinges to the door creaks as he opens it.

He walks into the kitchen, stopping when he sees me sat on his kitchen counter on full display. *Beauty makes all men weak, even gods.* His eyes narrow on me, and he tosses his keys on the counter.

"What are you doing, Evie?"

"Waiting on you." I grin. "What took you so long?" I ask, smiling deeper. The image of him grinning at Jen replays in my head, and all I want to do is pour this drink down his throat and watch him gasp for his last breath. *Patience, Evelyn.*

He grips my chin, dragging his thumb over my bottom lip like he always does. "What have I told you about asking questions, little killer?"

I hold the drink out, the ice clinking against the side of the glass. "I poured you a drink." My pulse hammers through my veins because I know if he figures out what I'm doing he will beat me and fuck me and kill me. If he finds out, I will be floating in the Hudson River by dawn.

His gaze locks on mine and pins me in place. He cocks his head to the side while a small smile plays over his lips. "How nice of you."

Ezra steps toward me, taking the glass from my hand. His stare is unwavering, and it narrows accusingly on me, his eyes flickering.

I can't breathe.

He moves closer, grabbing my thigh. He uncrosses my leg and shoves the other to the side as he steps between my thighs. The heat from his body spreads over my bare skin, and I almost regret what I'm about to do because I will miss this. His fingers dig into my skin as he brings the glass to his lips. My heart pounds in my chest and my hands shake. One large gulp, that's all it will take, and this dance with the devil will be over. I will be free of my sin, cleansed in the eyes of God.

The glass touches his lips and then he stops and laughs. He holds the glass out to me, pressing the cool edge of the tumbler against my bottom lip. I swallow hard, keeping my lips pursed as he pushes the glass harder against my mouth. My eyes lock with his, my pulse now threatening to rupture my arteries. His hand darts out, and he grips my jaw.

"Drink it," his brow lifts, "little killer."

I turn my face from him. I want to cry because he knows, and I'm going into the Hudson River tonight. Sweat pricks its way over my skin. I panic as I glance at the door, trying to devise a plan to get to it. I know Ezra will never let me out of this house alive.

"Drink. It." His grip on my jaw tightens and he shakes my face. "Drink it!" he growls, his eyes rolling with storm clouds, the cold unpassing threat of death glinting within them.

The glass drops from his hand and crashes to the floor, glass shattering in every direction. I attempt to jump from the counter, but he catches me with his arm, and jerks me up against his hard chest. All I can imagine is him taking a shard of that glass and slicing through my neck, or maybe he'll pull the gun from the waist of his jeans and put a bullet through my head. He's going to roll my body up in his bed sheets-- the sheets he fucked that redheaded slut on, he'll wrap my dead body up in those and put me in his trunk. He'll drive over the bridge and then toss me into the river, watching with a sick grin on his face as the murky depths swallow me whole. And I'll go to hell because I've yet to be absolved for my sins. The fear pulsing through me is making me dizzy and nauseous.

A grimace forms on his face as he wads my hair up in one hand, and places his other hand on my shoulder. His angry eyes lock on mine, and he squeezes me so hard that I buckle under the pressure. He swipes my legs out from underneath me with his foot, and I go down hard. Out of instinct, I attempt to catch myself with my palms, and they smack over the kitchen tile. I keep my chin from smashing into the floor, but shards of glass slice into my palms. The floor is slick with the poisoned whiskey, and when I try to crawl away from him, my hands slip out from under me. Ezra straddles my back, his full weight pressing over me. I feel my hair twist as he wraps it around his wrist, and of course he pulls on it before shoving my face down against the wet floor. He's rubbing my face over the floor just like you would a dog that has messed on the carpet, and I feel each tiny piece of glass as it tears into my skin. *He's going to make you ugly, Evelyn. He's going to scar you so you will never be a temptation again.* And I hope he does scar me. I hope he makes me ugly. Ezra smashes my face harder against the wet floor, and glass crunches beneath my cheek.

Each heavy breath he releases blows over the back of my neck. His warm, soft lips brush my neck, and he kisses it, sending chilbumps racing over my skin.

"Lick it, sweetheart," he says sweetly in my ear, twisting my face to force my lips against the wet floor.

I attempt to kick him off of me. I scream, I cry, I flail underneath him. I taste the whiskey on my lips, the poisoned whiskey meant to take his life that will now take mine.

"Lick. It." he orders, and shoves my mouth against the floor again.

The alcohol stings the jagged cuts on my cheek. I know the poison is seeping its way into my bloodstream, and I feel my stomach churn. My pulse bangs in my ears and my body trembles. I will die, in the matter of fifteen minutes, I will be dead. And although some people may find peace in the moments before they die, I cannot because there is no peace in death when you know you are going to hell.

I feel Ezra lean down next to me face. "Defiant to the end, Evie." He gently strokes my cheek. "I can practically *taste* your fear," he whispers against the side of my throat. His weight lifts away and I hear his buckle clink, followed by the rustle of his clothes coming off. When the heat from his naked body presses against me, I smile. In a sick way it comforts me to know I won't die alone. But even more than that, I welcome it because even in death, I am his.

38

EZRA

I brush my free hand over her cut cheek then swipe my bloodied fingers across her lips. "Look what you made me do," I whisper. Her perfect face will be scarred, her milky skin forever blemished by her own mistakes, her own stupidity.

I grip the back of her neck, pressing her face against the floor and she whimpers. Poison is seeping into her blood stream, crippling her body slowly. It's so beautifully ironic that the very poison she tried to kill me with is now burning through her veins. I can feel the fear in her trembling heart beats. I can hear it in her erratic breaths. And there is no fear more pure than the fear of death. Her defiance turns me on almost as much as her fear.

"You've been a bad girl, Evie." I fist my cock with my free hand, stroking the length of it. "And what happens to bad girls?" I ask in a hiss, yanking her dress up so hard I hear the stitching shred.

She attempts to lift her head, but I force her back down.

"They're punished," she chokes through tears.

I gently kiss her cheek. "I'm going to hurt you, Evie." I breathe against her skin. "I'm going to fuck you while I hurt you, and you will cry for me, little killer." I watch the pulse at her neck slow from the poison tearing through her veins. "Did you forget who owns you, sweetheart?" I cup her arse and grab her lace underwear, ripping it from her body.

She barely gasps. "No."

I smile, dragging my hand between her legs and pressing a finger into her wet pussy. She's wet because she likes it, she likes this, to be owned and punished for her *sins*.

"Then tell me, why would you try to kill me?" I press another finger inside her, and watch her jaw tense as her pussy grips me. She's no longer fighting me.

"I saw you with her," she says, her voice slurring. I pump my fingers in her harder and she moans. "I know you want to fuck her."

I smile, because I know she saw me. Jonny called me, told me she was standing right outside the coffee shop. I do so love winding her up about Jen, her jealousy turns me on. Her trying to kill me turns me on even more.

Laughing, I lean down and trace the shell of her ear with my tongue. "You're right. I do want to fuck her." She bucks underneath me and I press my fingers deeper inside her. "But I don't want to own her." I pull my hand away, grabbing her hip and yanking her arse up. Her jealousy, that sense of possession... I bite my lip as my cock demands that I beat her, choke her, fuck her to the pounding rhythm of her own terrified heartbeats.

Splinters of glass bite into my knees as I rear up over her, but the pain only drives me. I release her neck and grip my cock, guiding myself to the entrance of her tight, hot pussy and slamming balls deep inside of her. I throw my head back on a groan. Nothing feels as good as her. I can feel the panic clawing it's way through her as her life threatens to leave her. Even as her heart slows and her strength wanes, she's still wet for me because she knows I own her, body and soul.

I stare down at the back of her head, at her pale skin, her dark hair tangled in my fingers and, if I could, I think I would love her, because in all her fucked up glory she's perfect. I thrust into her harder, forcing small, breathy gasps from her throat. She makes no attempt to lift her face from the floor, but her fingers try desperately for purchase on the slick tile. Her strength starts to fail her and her body sags within my hold. I bury my fingers into her hips and pull her arse back up.

"Say it. Who owns you, Evie?" My pulse is hammering through my veins like a freight train. This isn't want or lust, it's need. I *need* to hear her say it. Right now.

"You..." she gasps. "Do..."

I slam into her harder, more brutally, and she whimpers. That one sound sends me over the edge and I come, still fucking her relentlessly. Until her limbs finally give out completely, and she blacks out.

I always knew she would try to kill me at some point. She can't help herself. Death is like an addiction for her, and now she knows what it tastes like.

39

EVIE

Y ou can't blame him. You tried to kill him, Evelyn.

Some things we deserve, and I deserve this. Death is the final punishment, and it seems fitting that Ezra be the one to end me. I can feel my heart struggle. Beat, beat, pause...beat, beat--beat--pause...My fingers tingle. The colors around me smear together, and a loud noise like a waterfall floods my ears as my blood pressure plummets. I feel death gripping me, it's cold claws digging into my heels preparing to drag me down to the pit of hell.

The heat of Ezra's body vanishes, and coldness wraps around me like a prickly blanket. All I want is for him to come back to me, swathing me with his warmth. I don't want to die alone on this floor. My sluggish heartbeat echoes in my ears. My lungs tighten, burning as they falter. I close my eyes and embrace the darkness that beckons me. *Evelyn, my child. Do not fear the darkness.* And I was wrong, there is peace in death. There is a cold, dark, lonely peace found only within your last breath.

The nothingness is ripped away by a blinding fire eating its way through my veins. I fear it's the flames of hell devouring my very soul. Then, the blackness is chased away by a white light tearing at the edge of my vision. My ears ring. My eyes are heavy. There's light and pain and...warmth. And in this moment of life, this chance at re-birth, I realize that death is peace and comfort, and life is hell. Death is not a punishment, life is.

Hot water laps around my waist and trickles down my neck. I hear the soft hum of "Knocking on Heaven's Door" by my ear. Gasping, I sit bolt upright, and send water sloshing over the edge of the tub. A hand brushes the damp hair away from my face. I glance over my shoulder and there he is, my Ezra.

He smiles, leans up in the tub, and swipes a finger across my lips. "You brushed death, little killer." Leaning in closer to my neck, he whispers against my ear. "But you are mine, and not even the devil can have you."

My eyes flutter shut and I swallow hard. I am his. Forever his. He saved me when he could have killed me because I am his. He is my god, for the devil would never save one of God's own children. I was wrong. Ezra was made for me. He is the strength I lack, the safety I've always craved. He is sin, I am his sinner.

"I am yours," I whisper, laying my head back against his chest to stare up at him.

"And yet, you try to kill me." He cocks a brow.

"You were with her. You smiled at her."

He grips my chin, rubbing his thumb over my skin. "Were you jealous, little killer?" he asks, and I can hear the smile in his voice.

"Yes."

"Did you imagine me fucking her?"

"Yes." I narrow my eyes at him and grit my teeth. "Over and over and over..." I can't get the image of Ezra pressing the redhead up against that window out of my head. I hate her. I don't want to kill Ezra, but I want to kill her.

"Good." He smirks, brushing his lips over mine. "Because when I saw her today, I imagined fucking her, over," he leans in, nipping my earlobe, "and over."

I hate his cruelty almost as much as I need it. I shove him away and stand up. The sudden movement sends water splashing everywhere. My head is still groggy and I lose my balance, catching myself on the wall. Slowly, he stands and reaches for me, but I jerk away. Despite my whirling head, I manage to climb out of the tub, nearly stepping on the syringe and vials lying on the floor. I stare at the empty glass containers, now fully aware that he knew I would try to kill him. He was planning for it, he had the damn antidote. And when I tried to kill him, he decided to show me what death was like. He wanted to show me just how much he owns me. I growl, grabbing a towel and wrapping myself up as I stagger out of the bathroom.

"Evie..." Ezra laughs.

"I hate you, Ezra!" I scream.

And I do. I hate him, and I love him. I despise him. I need him. I know he'll ruin me, but I know he'll save me because he's my absolution. I lean against the wall for support, my legs buckling beneath me. His heavy footsteps stomp down the hall, and I try to force my feet to move, but stumble. He catches up to me, grabbing me by the hips and dragging my body back against his.

His hot breath touches my neck. I relax into his body, and tears stream down my cheeks. I've become so tangled in this web of sin and wrong and hell that I'll never get out. I love him even though I shouldn't.

"I could have let you die." He kisses the side of my throat. "But I didn't," he says just before his teeth sink into my skin.

Those words sink in and I choke on the sob working its way up my throat. I fold over and Ezra forces me to stand back up. I was broken before, and yet he broke me. I thought surely there were no pieces inside my tattered soul left to shatter, but he shattered me. He promised me I would cry for him, and he was right. The emotional pain he is twisting inside my chest like a jagged knife is far worse than any physical pain he could inflict. It strips me bare. Love is weakness. And Ezra knows it.

His teeth leave my neck and he spins me around to face him. "I own every depraved inch of you." He grips my jaw, his eyes narrowing on me. "Do you understand?"

Nodding, I swallow. "Yes."

"I want to fuck Jen. I do not want to own her. I do not need her." His hand drops from my jaw and his fingers slowly pry my towel open.

I watch as he drinks in my naked body, and in this moment I think he is worshiping me. He's staring at me like I'm something rare and precious and holy. And suddenly, I wonder if he *wants* to love me. His fingers skim along the curve of my waist as his eyes slowly drag over my body.

I can't help myself. "Do you love me, Ezra?" I ask.

His eyes flicker and he takes a step, then another, backing me against the wall. "No," he whispers as his hand trails between my breasts and up to my throat. His fingers squeeze as he bites down on my shoulder.

He takes me again, claiming me, showing me how he owns me, and how I will never own him.

He doesn't want to love that redhead, but he wants to fuck her. And I want to kill her for that.

Ezra's in the shower and I'm sitting on his bed, staring at his phone. I hear the water shut off and quickly snatch it from the dresser and throw it under the bed. Dave goes running underneath the footboard, his tail wagging.

"No, bad dog!" I hiss under my breath when he nudges the phone out from under the frame. He scampers away, tucking his tail between his legs as I pace.

I turn the ringer off as I glance around Ezra's apartment, trying to find somewhere to hide his phone he will never think to look in. As soon as I walk out into the living room, my gaze strays over to the kitchen and lands on the top of the cabinets. I hurry to climb on top of the counters and place the phone as far back as I can reach. I hop down when I hear the bedroom door open, quickly opening the refrigerator and pretending to rummage for something to eat.

"I've got to go out," he says. "Stay here."

I'll stay here. I'm not leaving. I watch him go back to his room and dress. He'a cursing when he can't find his phone. I watch as he tears his room apart looking for it. When he comes back out, he glares at me as he takes his keys from the counter. He opens a couple of drawers and then goes back into the bedroom. "Evie, have you seen my phone?" he shouts.

I swallow. "No." My heart pounds in my ears. I don't want to lie to him, but it's for the best. I can't have things coming between us now can I?

"Fuck. I swear Dave, if you've eaten another phone..." He points at Dave and then heads for the door, slamming it shut behind him.

As soon as he leaves, I clamor up onto the counter and feel around on the top of the cabinets for the phone. I feel it under my palm and snatch it up, jumping from the counter. I lean against the wall as I scroll through his list of contacts until I see her name. I hate that he still has her number in here. He only has it because he wants to fuck her. My fingers ball into a fist and my gaze narrows on her name. I scroll through all their messages. *I want to fuck you.* Another message: *I want to fuck you.* Then another: *I want to fuck you. Around 4am?* And another: *I need to fuck you.* My stomach knots because he told me he didn't need her, but the text he sent her two months ago, probably the night I watched him slam her against the glass said he did need her. Anger bleeds through me as I angrily tap out a text.

I want to fuck you. Now. Be here at seven.

I haven't even put the phone down before it dings. *Gladly.*

Heat spreads over my face. That filthy, desperate whore. She saw me wipe his sin from my mouth, and she's still eager to fuck him. She doesn't care that I am his.

I have a surprise for you when you get to my apartment. I text.

DING. *Can't wait, Ez.* <3

I throw the phone across the room and I hear Dave's feet scamper over the hardwoods. A few seconds later, I feel him nudge my leg. I look down and he's staring up at me, his tail wagging.

"He's ours, Dave. We have to kill her to make sure he stays ours."

He barks. He knows I am not a bad person.

*****Break****

When I open the door, Jen's eyes widen just before the scan over my body.

"Jen, right?" I say, smiling. It's six forty-five, ambitious little bitch. I already want to choke the life out of her. One of her perfectly sculpted brows twitch up. "Where's Ezra?"

"Oh," I swallow hard because I want to break her neck right now. "Ezra wanted me to tell you he's running a little behind." I open the door wider and Jen steps in, her eyes never leaving mine. The door slams closed. I know I shouldn't kill her because she's not a bad person, but she wants what is mine. My heart beats hard in my chest at the thought of watching her eyes roll back in her head. I make my way to the kitchen and grab the two drinks from the counter. Handing one to her, I ask, "Did Ezra not tell you about the arrangement?"

"No." She eyes me cautiously as she takes the drink.

I step toward her, brushing my finger over her cheek. "Ezra wants me," I whisper and she jerks away from me. I lean in closer to her, the floral scent of Coco Mademoiselle floating up to my nose. "And he wants you." I watch her swallow. "And he wants to watch us together. Then fuck us together." I see her pulse accelerate. "And I want to fuck you, then watch him fuck you." I press a gentle kiss to her neck. When I pull away to look at her, she nervously downs her drink. "He told me how good your pussy feels, Jen. He likes it."

"I'm well aware," she says.

I run my fingers over her arm, pressing another kiss to her throat. "Will you play with us? Will you fuck me for Ezra?"

Using her thumb and index finger, she wipes her mouth. "I'd do anything for him." She glares at me, daring me as she smirks. She may think she would do anything, but I will kill for him.

She tips her drink back and polishes it off. I take the empty glass and set it on the counter before I grab hold of her hand, pulling it to my lips and sucking on her finger. "I think it would be a nice surprise for him if we go ahead and get started before he gets here. Don't you?"

I lead her back to the bedroom, my skin buzzing with excitement. I turn to face her, immediately dropping my robe and exposing my naked body. Jen smiles and steps toward me, her gaze raking over my body. There's a spark of excitement in her eyes, probably at the idea of pleasing Ezra. She would happily share him to please him, but I would never share him. I am his. He is mine. I love him. She simply covets him.

I brush a teasing finger over her arm before I grab the straps of her dress and tear them down her body. She gasps as the material falls from her chest, exposing the lace bra that's forcing her fake tits up underneath her chin. "Have you ever been with another woman," I ask.

"Only for Ezra." She smiles, biting down on her lip. Rage ignites inside me. There are so many things she has done for him that I haven't done, and I hate her.

"Strip for me," I say, smiling seductively. I don't want to simply kill her, I want to own her, the same way I own all of the wicked people I kill. She needs to worship me, she must see the light before she plummets into the depths of hell.

She slowly slips her dress off, then her black underwear. I step closer to her, brushing my mouth across hers as I caress her breast. Jen swipes her tongue over my bottom lip, and I place my hands on her shoulders, pushing her back onto Ezra's bed, forcing her down onto the same sheets he fucked me on this morning. I grab her ankles and yank her to the edge of the bed. Her red hair splays across the sheets and I want to cut it from her head. I shove her thighs apart and I stare at her. Anger and jealousy well inside of me as I look at the filthy part of her that's been wrapped around Ezra's cock, at the part of her that his milked pleasure from him. I want to slit her fucking throat, but instead, I run a finger over her wet pussy before I step between her spread legs. I lean over her, licking across her hard nipple as I shove a finger inside her worthless pussy. She moans when I bite down on her breast. She wriggles on the bed when I insert another finger. I want to know what Ezra has had. *Because when I saw her today...I imagined fucking her, over and over.* I want to know what it is about this slut that has him wanting to fuck her because I can be better than her. I drop to my knees beside the bed, slowly raking my tongue over her slit before circling her swollen clit.

She groans and I stare up at her. "Do you like that?" I whisper over her sensitive skin. She nods and I lick her. I taste her. She doesn't taste like heaven. And when she's fisting the sheets and moaning, I suck on her clit and finger fuck her until her pussy clamps down around my fingers. There is nothing to her. She is a cheap whore with cheap moans and a cheap pussy. He shouldn't be tempted by her. He shouldn't want to fuck her when he has me.

I climb onto the bed and I kiss her, letting her lick her own sin and filth from my lips. Within moments she groping me. Her nails dig into my ass, and if I'm honest, I don't think she really cares if Ezra shows up or not. That's how cheap she is.

Her mouth is on me, gently licking over me. I imagine it's Ezra's mouth on me, his hands roaming over my body. And I arch my back and I moan. I can feel everything build in my stomach, my body wanting to go weightless from the flick of her tongue. *She wants to take him from you, Evelyn. She wants him to own her and love her and she wants to make you cry.* I let my hand drop to the side of the bed and feel beneath the mattress for the knife I stashed earlier.

"Do you love him?" I ask.

Jen glances up at me, her tongue flicking over my clit. "Yes."

I moan, riding her face as my fingers find the metal handle and I pull it out. I fist her hair with my other hand, my breathing falling ragged. My body tenses and my muscles clench from the pending orgasm. I take the blade and jab her in the back of the neck just as I find my release. Jen screams as I moan, as I come hard for her and Ezra.

She's rolls onto her back, dazed. Blood spills out over the white sheets and I straddle her.

"He's mine. Not yours. Mine," I say as I slowly drag the knife across her throat. Without him, I am lost and I don't want to be lost. This is self-preservation. This is self-defence. This is love.

40

EZRA

I drop my keys on the coffee table as soon as I walk through the door. Dave runs up to greet me, but Evie is nowhere to be seen and neither is Jen. Jonny called me, so I know she came here twenty minutes ago, and I know she hasn't left. Why would she be here?

The silence in the flat is broken by a low moan, and Dave's head cocks to the side, his ears perking up. I frown and listen as another long, breathy moan echoes down the hallway from the bedroom. Dave takes off down the hall. I clench my fist and grab the glock from the kitchen drawer. If Evie is fucking another guy I'm going to kill him, then I'm going to kill her.

All I see is red as I turn the corner into the hallway. Dave paces outside the bedroom door and I signal him to go away, which he does begrudgingly. I count to three in my head before shoving the door open, gun raised, ready to make it rain blood. But I'm too late, because all I can see is blood, fucking everywhere.

My feet remained glued to the spot as I take in the scene. Evie is naked on the bed, her dark hair falling down her back. She's straddling Jen, a knife in her hand. The white sheets are stained red, as well as parts of the carpet, walls and even the ceiling. Evie leans down over Jen and their tits brush together.

"He's mine, not yours. Mine," Evie whispers and then she slashes her throat. Jen takes several staggered and gurgled breathes. Evie sits up, flicking her black hair behind her shoulder.

I clench my fists. I don't even know what to do here. Evie's naked and killing another naked chick. And it shouldn't be hot, but my dick is pressed against my fly because of her words: 'he's mine'. I shouldn't be such a fucking neanderthal, but I am. And then there's the fact that, yet again, she has killed someone, and if the club wasn't bad enough, now she killed a girl I used to fuck in my own bed.

I storm towards her, and she jumps away from Jen's now completely lifeless body.

Evie disobeyed me, and by doing this she is laying a claim, making a point, staking ownership. End point, she disrespected me.

As I close the distance between us, her eyes drop to the floor like a child who knows they've done wrong. I bring my hand back and backhand her hard enough that my hand stings. She gasps, clutching her face. When her eyes meet mine, they're filled with tears, her expression that of a wounded animal. But she is not the innocent prey, she's the predator.

Her lip is bleeding, her face still covered in a smattering of cuts and scratches, some deep enough that I had to stitch them.

"Ezra," she pleads.

I grab a handful of her hair and yank her head back, dragging her up against my body. Even through my shirt I can feel her hard nipples pressing against my stomach. The truth is, she's insane, and yes, I'm spitting mad that she just killed my ex-fuck doll...but I'm not. I'm so turned on I can't see straight, and this is why she's perfect for me, every messed up, beautifully insane, damaged inch of her.

There's a moment, a heartbeat of hesitation. "I distinctly remember telling you, no more killing," I say calmly, trembling.

Blood trickles from the corner of her split lip. Evie's throat and chest are coated in Jen's blood, and she's staring up at me with those big fucking blue eyes of hers. She looks just like the beautiful monster she is, and I fucking want her more than I have ever wanted anyone or anything in my life.

"You said you wanted to fuck her," she whispers. "So I took away the temptation." My blood is hammering through my veins, my dick throbbing in my jeans.

I pull Evie against me, forcing her to stand before I grab Jen's ankle and drag her lifeless body across the bed. It hits the floor with a thud.

"Stand at the end of the bed. Spread your legs and grip the footboard," I instruct, brushing my lips over her bloodied lip. She nods and stumbles to the end of the bed. "Do not look at me," I growl, unfastening my belt and pulling it through the loops.

Her breathing is erratic, her small body trembles. Fear? Excitement? Who knows with her.

I haven't taken a belt to anyone since the last time I hit her, and that was weeks ago. The belt should be a punishment, but she likes it far too much for that. I'm about to change that.

I drag the leather across my palm, smiling. This right here is power, and it's like a drug. I swing the belt back and bring it down across her back in a way that I haven't since I was fifteen years old. She screams as it lashes her skin, and I laugh.

"Is this forgiveness enough, little killer?"

I bring it down again, exerting every ounce of force into the swing, and this time the skin breaks, a thin line of blood blossoming through the split skin. She cries out and her legs buckle, her grip loosening on the footboard.

"Stand up!"

Her knuckles turn white as she clings to the wood. I swing the belt again, using all my force, and another line of blood blossoms, crossing over the first. I hit her again and again, until the blood coats her skin and my arm is weak.

"Please. Ezra!" she begs.

"Please what?" I say, out of breath.

"Please," she whispers pitifully, her body shaking.

"Look at me, Evie." She turns to face me, her gaze locked on the ground, her dark hair hanging over her face. "Look. At. Me."

She slowly lifts her eyes, and there they are, her tears glistening over her cheeks so beautifully. Zee was right about one thing. She is beautiful when she cries.

"Are you sorry?" I ask.

"No." Her eyes drop back to the floor. "I didn't like that you wanted to fuck her."

There it is again, that possessive streak in her that makes me want to sink balls deep inside her.

I pull my shirt over my head unzip my jeans, pushing them down with my boxers. She watches my every move as I come around the bed and take a seat on the edge of it.

"Come here, Evie."

She slowly moves around the end of the bed until she's standing in front of me. Pink lashes from where the belt wrapped around her sides are visible across her torso.

I grab her hips and yank her toward me, my fingers digging into her sides as I slide my knee between her legs and part them. When I pull her again, she falls forward, her knees landing on the mattress, her legs spread either side of my thighs.

"I want to fuck you." I pull her into my lap, pressing my dick against her pussy. She bites her lip as her fingers cling to my shoulders. "You look so beautiful when you cry, Evie." She closes her eyes and another stray tear slowly rolls down her cheek. I lean forward and lick it from her face. "I love it when you cry for me."

Gripping the back of her neck, I drag her to me and slam my lips over hers. I taste her blood on my tongue when I dive inside her mouth. Her body presses against mine and her nails sink into my skin until I hiss.

She slowly lowers her warm pussy onto my cock, and I groan, wrapping my arms around her, holding her. She whimpers, and her back bows away from my hold. Blood slicks my arms as I trail my hands down to her arse, gripping it as I force her to ride me. She moves, sliding over me, throwing her head back.

"Look at me, Evie." I want to see her pain, her fear, her pleasure, and her devotion.

Her gaze lifts to mine, focusing on me as she continues to move over my cock. "Do you love me?" I ask.

"Yes." Tears build in her eyes again, and I want to own them. "I love you so much, Ezra," she says between deep breaths.

"Enough to kill for me?" I whisper as I cup her cheek, dragging my thumb over her bloodied lip and smearing it across her jaw.

"Yes." Her eyes are still locked intimately on mine.

She rides me harder, grinding over my dick, her arse pressing down on my balls. I roll my hips and meet her every thrust.

"I should punish you again just for putting blood all over my bed--*our* bed." Her breath catches, and I skim my lips over her neck, inhaling the scent of her perfume mixed with the metallic twang of blood. My hands slip over her sides, blood still oozing from her back. I hope it scars her. I want to permanently mark her. I want her to remember this, to be reminded.

She drags her nails over my shoulder blades and tosses her head back. I duck my head and bite down on her nipple. A deep, satisfied moan slips from her lips because she gets off on pain. Her nails slice through my skin. And then she's coming, her pussy clenching around my cock like a vice. I grab her hips, pushing her to move faster, until I come inside her tight little pussy, moaning her name like the fucking prayers she's so fond of.

She presses her face into my shoulder, breathing heavily. I grab her waist, pick her up, and throw her down on the bed. She hisses when her back touches the sheets. I lean over her, my hand next to her head as I cup her pussy. She bucks away from my touch and I smile before pushing two fingers inside her, feeling her own wetness mixed with my come. She moans for me and I pull my finger away before pressing it into her mouth. She sucks me, swirling her tongue around my finger like it's my cock, and I push my finger deeper until she gags. When I pull away from her lips, Evie reaches up and cups my jaw.

"Do you love me, now, Ezra?" she asks.

"No," I tell her. She flinches as though I physically slapped her, and I don't care, because no matter how beautiful her blood soaked body and her tear stained face are, she disobeyed me. "You're a monster, little killer," I whisper against her skin. *A perfect monster.*

If I were capable, I might love her. I crave her on a level that is nothing short of obsession, but love is not for people like us. She should know that.

41

EVIE

I've laid awake most of the night, tossing and turning. How pitiful is it to be so deeply in love with a man that you forsake your religion, only to have him tell you he will never love you. Love is the one emotion I will never earn from him. He wants to own me, not love me. I have tarnished my soul. I have failed my sister. I have strayed. And all over a man who should be everything I hate, but has become everything I love.

The warm morning sun peeks through the window.

I must leave. I must be forgiven. I must right my sister. This life does not matter, but where I will go when I die does. Carefully, I slip out from beneath the comforter. Dave lifts his head and looks at me. His paws tap over the floor as he follows me to the bathroom. He stays with me, whimpering while I get dressed. When I make my way to the door he follows me, sits down at the door, and whines. If I leave him here, he will sit at the door and whine, and that will wake up Ezra.

"Come on then," I whisper as I open the door. And we leave. No one will follow me, because Ezra is here to watch me.

There's only a block left before we reach the cathedral. I glance down at Dave trotting alongside me.

"He doesn't love me, Dave," I say. His ears perk up and he stops, sitting down on the sidewalk. I kneel beside him and pet over his soft head. "I tried to make him. But he doesn't." His head cocks to the side and he pants. The bells to the tower ring out, and we resume walking to the church.

I watch the people pass by me. I see people who are happy, who have love, who have their faith. I see all the people whose lives are not the crumbling, decaying mess that mine is, and I hate them for it.

When I stop in front of the steep stairs, Dave halts, whining. "Come on," I say, and he reluctantly follows me up the steps. The familiar smell of wood polish nearly knocks me over when I step inside. I make my way to the altar, stopping to glance over at the confessional on the side wall. I've tried prayer, I've tried the penance of pain I was taught cleanses you, and I can't help but wonder if maybe confessing my sins may help me find the peace I've been seeking.

You don't need penance, little killer.

Ezra has wriggled his way into my soul so deep, that even the voice of my little demon sounds like his. I'm unraveling fast, and I need something to stop me. This spiral leads to death and pain and punishment, and at one time that scared me, but now I crave it. I feel lost and saved at the same time. I no longer really *feel* the need for penance because with Ezra there is *always* forgiveness. And that is blasphemy.

Blasphemy is unforgivable.

I open the small wooden door, and Dave walks inside, sitting in the corner and glancing back at me. I hesitate before stepping inside and taking a seat. When I sit straight up, the motion pulls at my tight, beaten skin and I have to lean forward to lessen the pain. The screen slides back, but the priest remains silent. In all my years with religion, I have never set foot inside a confessional. The way I was raised to believe, forgiveness never came by confessions, only blood.

I look at Dave and he places his head on my lap, his big brown eyes staring up at me. His tail taps against the wood as he wags it. Dave is all I have. Dave and God. I close my eyes. I want to feel remorse, but I don't. I'm not sure what to do or say, so I think about all the movies I've watched where someone goes to confession. And I say what they say. "Father, forgive me for I have sinned.

"Go ahead my child. God's listening."

I hear footsteps outside the booth, and I fall silent. I don't want anyone else to hear these sins. I swallow. "I'm afraid I no longer believe...I..." I choke on a sob.

"It's okay. We all fall short."

The door to the confessional groans, and I fear the priest is coming to console me. Dave's ears perk up, and he growls.

"Please," I hear the priest whisper followed by gurgled breaths. I glance up to the metal screen, and there's a thud on the confessional wall. Dave's growl grows more threatening, and he places himself between me and the door.

"Evie." My name pours through the screen in a hiss. My heart stops, adrenaline jolting through me like an electrical current. Dave barks. I reach for the door to the booth, but it's jerked open and off its hinges.

"Did you like the flowers I sent you? I do hope they didn't get you into too much trouble with old Ez."

I can't breathe. I can't move. I stand, backed into a confessional, Zachariah blocking my exit, a blood stained knife clutched in his hand. Dave's ears lay flat against his head and he jumps at Zachariah, latching onto his forearm.

"Stupid fucking mut!" He takes the knife and jabs it into the side of Dave's thick neck. Dave yelps and falls to the floor. I scream, my heart threatening to burst through my chest. Zachariah's laughter rumbles into the steeple as he kicks Dave across the floor, a trail of blood smearing over the tile. "A fucking animal is the only thing that would ever try to protect you."

He grabs onto my shoulders and yanks me into the open sanctuary. I scream again, and he punches me in the stomach. The wind is knocked out of me and I fall to the floor. Zachariah takes a fistful of hair, slinging me around like a ragdoll as he drags me toward the altar. My scalp burns, and I grab onto his hands to try and lessen the pain. I glance frantically at the door, willing someone to walk through it. My gaze locks on the open confessional booth. Father Pritchard lies sprawled out on the stone floor, blood pouring from his throat, and next to him is Dave.

I kick and scream, clawing at Zachariah's hands, but all he does is laugh. "You've been a busy little whore, haven't you, Evelyn?" He yanks me up the steps before he bends over and jerks me to my feet. He holds me up so I'm level with his face. I dangle from his grip, my toes barely touching the floor. "How I've missed you little Evelyn," he hisses in my ear before I feel his tongue trail up my neck. "Dear, sweet, innocent, *Evie.*"

My stomach knots just before he throws me down. I immediately roll over on my hands and knees and try to force myself up, but I feel his boot press down on my lower back, slamming me face first into the worn carpet of the altar. More of his weight presses over me. My vertebrae pop, my chest pressed so flat I can hardly drag in a breath. The next thing I know, Zachariah flips me over and straddles me. His lips curl into a sadistically satisfied smirk, his blue eyes burning into me.

"I've waited so long to have you again, Evelyn. I missed you." He squeezes my breast and I want to cry, but I refuse to shed a tear for him. My tears are Ezra's. He laughs. "Always so resolute, Evelyn. Hannah was always a screamer, but not you. Do you remember the time I made you scream?"

I remember the blade slicing my back open. I remember him calling me a sinner, and a whore while he carved the cross on my back. *Let a righteous man mark you so you can be saved, Evelyn.*

"Those were the days," he laughs. "I killed Hannah, just like I'm going to kill you. How far you both fell, bathed in the fires of hell, selling yourselves to the highest bidder. Your father would be so disappointed," he says. "Hannah sold herself to *me*, without even knowing who I was. I blindfolded her while I fucked her, and she moaned like the wanton whore she was, and then, I killed her."

I close my eyes. I will not cry. But the thought of Hannah, trapped, beaten, raped, and alone with him breaks a little piece of me. We ran, we saved each other, but in the end he found us, just like I knew he always would. My pulse races, my mind reeling.

He leans in, pressing his lips to mine as he holds the blade of the knife under my chin. "You are mine, and yet you let that filthy pimp touch you!" he screams.

"It wasn't filthy because I loved him."

He growls and grabs my throat, lifting me up and smashing my head against the floor. Black spots dot my vision. My head spins. Pain ricochets through my skull. I attempt to buck him off of me, and a deep frown sets on his face, his eyes going void as the tip of the sharp blade bites into my flesh.

"You never fought me before, Evelyn, you liked it." *I did not. I hated you for it.* "You liked it because you are a filthy whore. Why start fighting now?" Keeping the knife to my throat, he grabs the collar of my dress and rips it down. The sound of the material shredding echoes in my ears.

Zachariah's free hand glides over my exposed flesh and bile hits the back of my throat. I hum "Knocking on Heaven's Door" in an attempt to disassociate myself. The farther up my thigh his hand goes, the louder I hum. Ezra was right. I am a monster. The things I've done have not been justified, ever. I am sick. Tortured. Fucked up. We're all fucked up, and the only penance for a person like me is death. I didn't do this for God, I did it for myself because I am sick. Because I get off on having power over the people I blame for making my life hell.

I take peace in the thought that there is no hell. I've already lived through that. I've already served my sentence in the abyss, and in death I will find peace. I will find nothingness. The demons will stop screaming, the nightmare will end, and I can stop loving a man who will never love me back.

42

EZRA

I wake with a start. The bed is cold and there's no trace of Evie. I glance at the clock and it's only seven thirty in the morning.

"Evie,"I call, but there's no answer. When I climb out of bed I realize Dave is gone as well. After last night, I cannot believe she's defied me *again*. Anger consumes me as I quickly get dressed and make my way downstairs. I slam the car door and crank the engine, my breaths uneven and ragged. I clench and release my fingers on the steering wheel as I floor it through the awakening streets of New York towards the church. Evie is a creature of habit. If she's not with me she's either killing someone or praying over the fact that she killed someone. She killed last night, and I can almost see her on her knees pleading to her god for forgiveness. I'm not sure she has this sin and forgiveness shit quite worked out.

As soon as I spot the enormous stone building, I pull the car over to the side of the road, the tires screeching to a halt at the curb. I will drag her out of there by her hair if I have to. It's bad enough that she killed my ex-fuck in my own damn bed last night, but now she defies me again by sneaking out of the house. She likes to push me, I swear.

The heavy wooden door doesn't budge when I push against it. I try it again, the wood creaking as I ram it with my shoulder. *Maybe the church is a nine to five thing.* I'm about to walk away when I hear a noise, barely a squeak, but it sounds like a faint scream coming from inside the church. I could be wrong, but I've learned over the years to trust my instincts, and right now my gut is screaming at me to get inside that church.

I jog around the back, my heart pounding in my chest. At the very back of the building, beside a bush, is another door. I try it, fully expecting it to be locked, but it gives way. The moment I step inside, my senses are assaulted by incense.

I pull my gun from the back of my jeans, and press my thumb against the trigger as I make my way through the back of the church. There's muffled voices, and when I step into the main part of the church, the first thing I see is my dog. Dead. I clench my jaw and my chest tightens. Next to him, half sprawled from the confessional box is a priest. That never bodes well.

"Please forgive me. Please bless my soul..." I hear Evie mumble through sobs and screams.

Panic rips through me. I raise my gun and hold it out in front of me. I round the corner, coming to a halt when I reach the bottom of the altar. It takes me a second to really process what's going on in front of me. Everything around me seems to slow. My blood pressure rockets. The only thing I can hear is the blood ringing through my ears. All I can see, all I can think about is Evie. She's stripped, bleeding, and Zee is fucking touching her. The bastard is standing on the pulpit with Evie naked and bent over in front of him. He has her pinned down by the back of her neck, her cheek pressed against the marble. His hands roam over her body. She's crying, praying, pleading with her god to save her.

An ice-cold rage creeps over my body, and my mind sharpens, focusing solely on the task at hand. Possession demands that I rip his head from his body for touching what is mine.

I close one eye, steadying my hand as I aim at his head. Zee catches the movement and yanks Evie's body in front of his, pressing the blade of a knife against her throat. She whimpers when he pulls her against him, and then, her eyes find me. Her expression looks so broken, so defeated that I can't help but wonder what he's already done to her.

"Ah, Ezra." A sick smile twists his lips. "You made it. I had a feeling you might show up, you seem rather attached to my little sister here."

My eyes shift back to Evie, and she slams her eyes closed, twisting her face away from Zee as much as possible. Brother? Zee is her brother.

"I thought it was only fair that I take something of yours. Seeing as you fucked my business up for me. Oh, but then...I had Evelyn long before you ever did." He laughs, groping at her tits. Rage descends, consuming me completely. "Oh, she didn't tell you about me? That's not nice, Evelyn. After all, we were so close when we were younger." He drags his lips over the side of her face before licking her cheek. She trembles, leaning into the blade at her neck in an attempt to get away from him. "Introduce us properly, Evelyn."

"This is Zachariah," she chokes, and I watch the tip of the blade dig into her skin.

"Ah, ah, ah. I said *properly*. Like you were taught."

"Ezra," she sobs my name like it's a prayer, "this is my brother, Zachariah."

And as his name rolls from her lips, I suddenly remember everything she's ever said, every crazy rambling that I dismissed, all her religious bullshit, her self-hatred. Zachariah is the one she grew up with, Zachariah is her brother. Zee is the one who broke Evie.

You don't understand. I am a whore. I always have been. I have always been a temptation without even trying.

Zachariah was chosen by God. It was my fault he strayed. He was righteous, and everyone knew I forced him to sin. He was punishing me so that I could be forgiven, but I hate him for it.

God loves sinners, but he hates the sin, and I am sin, Ezra. I am sin, so even God can't love me.

"I'm going to kill you." My voice is calm, free of emotion even though my body is on fire with rage.

"You can't kill me, Ezra," he laughs. "Remember? Surely you aren't going to go to prison, all for a filthy," he hisses in her ear. "Dirty." His hand gropes at her tit and I have to bite the inside of my cheek to stop myself from losing it. "Whore."

Evie sobs, her chest heaving as shame morphs her features. "I am a whore. I am a filthy whore," she cries. Her tear filled eyes land on me, pinning me in place. "And that's why you can't love me. I cannot be saved. I am sin. And he is sin. Kill us both." She drags in a breath. "Absolve me, Ezra. Let me know forgiveness."

Zee snarls as he yanks her hair, jerking her head back and pressing the tip of the blade against her perfect skin.

"Please, God, forgive me," she pleads.

I watch a single drop of blood trickle down her neck. When my gaze lifts back to hers, something inside of me breaks, cracking wide open. I imagine him slicing her throat open, spilling her blood all over the cold stone floor of the church she loves so much, and a sharp pain rips through my chest. He might have made her a monster, but it is I who broke her, it is I who own her, and it is I alone who will make her bleed.

"I told you, Evie," I aim the gun and pull the trigger, "I'm the only god you need." The bang echoes off the walls of the church, and then all I see is blood.

43

EVIE

The gunshot echoes from the cathedral, and there's a thud behind me. Pain tears through my shoulder, burning and ripping. I can't breathe. I collapse to the floor on my hand and knees, my heart pounding in my chest. Warm blood spills from the bullet wound and stains the floor beneath me. *He shot me!*

Zachariah groans. I glance behind me and see him lying on the floor, writhing in pain as he clutches his chest, blood bubbling between his fingers. Ezra squats in front of me and grabs my chin. "Evie." He forces chin up. "Focus, look at me."

"You shot me..." I gasp for breath, staring at him behind my tears.

Cocking an eyebrow, he smirks. "I always said I would make you bleed, little killer." He reaches to the altar and takes the altar cloth, pressing it over the bullet hole. "Hold that tight," he says before yanking his shirt over his head and pulling it down over mine, covering my naked body.

The shirt has his warmth. He gently slips my arms through the sleeves, and I wonder why he's doing this. He was supposed to kill me, absolve me, but he saved me. I drag in a breath at the thought of that, and all I can smell is him-- Chanel Blue. And I smile because I really am his.

I glance back over my shoulder at Zachariah. A noise reminiscent of a bubbling spring echoes from the walls as the blood pools in the back of his throat. I should feel something. Relief, satisfaction--something. But as I stare at him, watching him struggle to draw his last breaths, all I feel is disgust and anger.

"I hate you!" I attempt to stand, but my legs fail me. "I hate you!" I crawl on my knees toward him, pain shooting through my shoulder. I groan as I struggle to straddle his large frame. I drop the cloth, grabbing the knife he's dropped beside his head. My chest heaves, my heart hammers violently in my throat. This is my moment when all those sins will vanish. This is how my absolution comes. Through blood. Through the blood of the man who broke me when I didn't want to be broken, and while the man who possessed me when I needed to be possessed stands over me like a shepherd.

I lean down next to Zachariah's ear, my gaze focused on the weakening pulse thumping in his neck. "You are sin," I whisper, and with one swift movement, I slash the blade across his throat. I watch blood spill from the fresh cut and I drop the knife because this is not enough. I wrap my hands around his throat, my fingers slipping in blood as I squeeze. Staring into his bloodshot eyes, I see fear, and that makes me smile.

"You are wrong," I say. "I am not a whore. And may you never be forgiven."

His eyes flutter before they roll into the back of his head. And in this moment I know I am absolved. The little demon inside of me withers away and vanishes.

I climb off Zachariah and sit beside his body, staring at my blood soaked hands.

When I look up, I find Ezra leaning against the side of the pulpit, his ankles crossed as he inhales on his cigarette. "Feel better?"

"You can't smoke in here, Ezra."

He exhales a cloud of smoke, that arrogant smile creeping onto his lips. "There's a dead guy on the altar, a dead priest in the confessional, not to mention my dead dog." He groans, and his emotionless face slips into grief for just a fraction of a second.

My gaze veers down to the front of the sanctuary, and my heart falls to the pit of my stomach. I manage to stand, using the edge of the pews to guide me as I stagger toward the entrance. I fall to my knees beside my friend, stroking a hand over his bloodied fur.

"I'm sorry," I whisper. I drag him into my lap, clutching him as I rest my chin on the top of his cold head. Ezra's hand rests over my shoulder, but I don't move. "He tried to save me, Ezra." Tears sting my eyes and my chest tightens.

"He did his job then," he says dismissively, frowning at Dave's body. I know he's upset, but would never show it. I can feel his grief. Even though he thinks he can't love, he loved Dave.

He hands me his phone before leaning down and scooping Dave's body from my arms. "Call number one and tell them to come do a pick up for two. Give them the address then hang the phone up." He turns and walks toward the doors.

I find the number, call it, leave the message, and hang up. I follow Ezra outside, the cold air nipping at my bare legs when I step out of the doors. People on the sidewalk stop and stare at us. There's snow on the ground and Ezra's outside of a church with no shirt on, carefully placing a dead dog into his trunk, while I stand on the steps of a church wearing nothing but a man's t-shirt and covered in blood. I hurry down the stairs and climb inside the car afraid that someone will stop us.

Ezra gets into the car, slams the door, and pulls off as soon as he starts the engine. "You need to get that stitched up. And then we need to run," he says without taking his eyes off the road.

All I can think is he said *we*. He saved me, and he said we.

"Why?" I ask, hoping he'll give me some deeper reason than the two dead bodies in the church.

"What did I tell you about asking questions, Evie?"

44

EZRA

I have no idea what's going to happen now, but I know I can't risk hanging around to find out. I glance at Evie. Her legs are pulled up on the seat, her chin resting on her knees. Blood has soaked through my shirt, but she seems unphased.

I've pointed a gun at hundreds of people, pulled the trigger countless times and never felt anything except the need to do what must be done. This was different. This was personal. There was no way Zee was walking out of there alive, regardless of the consequences. I made a choice-- shoot her to kill him, and for the first time in my life, pulling that trigger was hard because I didn't want to lose her.

I dial Jonty's number and his groggy voice comes over the car speakers. "What the fuck, Ez? It's not even nine o' clock."

"I need you to get me two passports, cash, plane tickets out of Newark to Russia, some clothes for Evie, and a new car. Meet me at University Hospital, by the airport."

"What happened?" He's suddenly alert.

"Zee. He's dead. We're leaving."

"Shit. I'll call Seamus, and I'll meet you there as soon as I can," he promises before hanging up.

I've never run from anything in my life. I always face shit head on, and I annihilate anyone who gets in my way. This situation is different. I can't stand against the entire British government. I need to lay low at least until I know what the consequences of Zee's death will be. For all I know he was bluffing, but he was a wiley fucker.

I STAND IN THE DOORWAY, watching as the doctor stitches Evie's shoulder. Her gaze is fixed on the ceiling, her eyes unfocused.

I should walk out. I should leave her here. Both our lives have gone to shit since the very first time I took that belt to her. She's become my addiction, and I've become her coping mechanism for all the shit she's been through.

She asks me to hurt her, she wants me to break her, and for what? Because she thinks she deserves it. She thinks she will be forgiven by her god, and welcomed into heaven with open arms. I've always said that Evie is insane, but I guess it's no wonder. She is conditioned into believing that she is something wrong, unworthy, that she is nothing and no one, when the truth is, to me she is everything. I've never wanted to possess a woman before, but I want to own every-fucking-thing about Evie. I want every tear, every breath, her hopes and dreams, her fears and desires. Everything she is, is mine. My world is potentially about to fall apart, and I should let her go, but I won't. I'm obsessed with her to the point I don't care what is best for her, only that she is with me. She should have walked away back when she had the chance, before I fucked her, before I killed for her. Twice.

So, I will run, and I will take my little killer with me.

The nurse finishes dressing Evie's shoulder and straps her arm into a sling before leaving, offering me a small smile.

"What happens now?" Evie asks, her eyes fixed on the ceiling. She seems lost, and I don't know whether her question is for me or more for herself.

"Now, we go to Russia."

She turns her face towards me, a small frown marring her forehead.

"Because of what Zachariah said about prison?"

I nod. "I have powerful friends there. Untouchable friends."

45

EVIE

We landed in Moscow an hour ago, and a Bentley brought us to this house. Ezra promises this man can help us. *Us. Because I'm his now.* The dim room is filled with thick cigar smoke, and there are several men gathered around a kitchen table, rifles slung over their shoulders, playing poker. Every few seconds one of them shouts something out in Russian, and the others laugh and yell back. Although I feel uncomfortable, I know Ezra will keep me safe because my tears belong only to him.

The large man sitting in front of me makes my stomach kink and twist. If I thought Ezra was the devil, I was wrong. This man looks elegant, almost like a king sat on his throne. His posture is perfect, his suit fitted just right, but calculated evil plays out behind his bright blue eyes. Everything about him is cold. And I know, this man must be the devil. His eyes hone in on me. He smirks as he gently takes my hand and drags it towards his lips. My hand trembles when he kisses over my knuckles. His eyes stay trained on me, his lips still touching my skin. "I'm Alexei, my sweet little lamb." His accent is so harsh, so thick.

I nervously glance at Ezra, his fingers tapping over his thigh. "Don't make me hurt you, Rone," he growls.

Alexei chuckles. Smiling at me, he drops my hand. "Such temper." His gaze cuts over to Ezra. "So, how you kill Zee?" he asks, his broken English causing the hairs on my arm to stand on end. The devil would have a Russian accent. "Did you gut him? Spill his blood all over floor? Tell me you cut his sagging balls from his body and ram them down his throat, eh?" He laughs, and that laugh rumbles the floor.

Ezra chuckles, smiling as he takes a drag of his cigar. "No time, my friend. No balls in throats this time." Ezra glances at me, his eyes tracing over my shoulder as though looking for signs of weakness. It aches, but I don't care because that pain means I am his, and because of that, I will willingly take any pain Ezra inflicts on me.

Alexei's nostrils flare, the anticipatory grin fading from his face. "Pity," he mumbles as he grabs the bottle of vodka from the side table. He turns it up, and I watch bubbles form in the neck as he sucks in gulp after gulp. When he pulls the bottle away from his lips, he wipes his mouth with the back of his hand, then shoves the vodka in my direction. "Want a drink?" he asks, laughing.

I shake my head and scoot closer to Ezra. One of the men playing poker pushes back from the table, the legs of the wooden chair scratching over the floor. My pulse quickens as he moves toward us. He stops beside Alexei and leans over his shoulder, whispering something in Alexei's ear.

Alexei's eyes flicker and he nods. "MI5 know. They look for you as we speak." He shakes his head. "But they are no concern to me. I handle them. I kill them. Like dirty gnat on my food." He slams his thumb down on the table and wiggles it. "Smash them into the table."

Ezra laughs, picking up the vodka bottle. "Even you can't take out MI5, you crazy bastard."

"Ah, ah, ah." Alexei motions with his fingers. "Bring me Olga."

The man standing next to him rolls his eyes before he turns to walk away.

"For you, my friend," Alexei pats Ezra on the knee, "I can do anything."

Ezra takes another swig of vodka, grinning around the lip of the bottle. The man returns and drops a large missile with a naked woman pained on the side onto Alexei's lap.

"This is Olga," he says as he pats it. "She take care of the MI5."

I grab onto Ezra's arm, clutching to him for dear life because this man will kill us all. Each time his hand taps over the shell of that missile, my heart threatens to stop. "Ezra, can we leave?" I whisper.

He pats my thigh, a smile pulling at his lips. "Fucking hell, put that shit down. It's probably from the cold war." He shakes his head. "Look, I just need to stay out of the states and the UK for a while."

To Ezra, this is familiar, safe. This is his church. This is his religion.

Alexei places the missile on the table in front of him, stroking over it one last time. "You stay here. My house always open for you, my friend." His brows lift and his eyes drift over to me. "Olga keep you safe."

I swallow as I stare at this man. I have never seen such insanity. I would like to kill him, but I know I can't. I have to be a good girl for Ezra.

Ezra downs a swig of vodka, raising the bottle to Alexei before he stands. They lean in toward each other, patting each others backs without letting their chests touch. And Alexei turns to leave the room. He glances over his shoulder, a small smirk playing on his lips as his gaze drifts from me to Ezra. "Don't get blood on carpets. Expensive to clean. Put down towel." He walks through the doorway, laughing. "And don't break bed, eh."

I LAY ON THE BED, reading a book. I glance out of the window at the bleak sky heavy with snow, and I wonder whether heaven and hell exist. I wonder where Hannah is. The door creaks open, disturbing my thoughts, and I glance over.

"Evie, there's a guy downstairs with a knife through his dick and a slit throat." Ezra eyes narrow accusingly on me as he locks the door. "Did you kill him?"

I swallow hard and my eyes go back to the print on the pages. Ezra takes the few steps from the door to the bed, grabbing my chin and forcing me to look up at him. My heart slams against my ribs as his fingers dig into my face, and I drop the book. "Answer me," he says in a growl, lowering his face to my neck.

"He touched me."

His gaze locks with mine for a second and then his hold loosens. "Then good," he says against my throat. His teeth skim over my skin and I sigh. I want him angry at me. I want him to punish me because that is the closest thing to love with Ezra, possession.

My lungs falter at the thought of what he'll do to me, of the beautiful ways he will beat me. "Hurt me, Ezra."

His hands roam over my body, peeling open my robe before sweeping his touch between my breast and up to my neck. I relish in the way his fingers feel as they wrap around my throat, one by one.

"No," he says, and my heart plummets.

His thigh spreads my legs apart, and I quickly unfasten his jeans and push them down over his ass. His hard cock presses against me, slipping over my wetness before he thrusts deep inside of me. The initial shock of him filling me causes my back to arch from the bed, and he groans, clenching his jaw.

"You don't need me to hurt you, little killer." His lips brush my cheek, his teeth nipping at my jaw.

But I do. I want him to hurt me, and it's no longer to be forgiven, it's because I want to feel him love me the only way he knows how. "I want you to though," I plead. He slams into me harder and I moan like the little slut he wants me to pretend I am.

"I don't care what you want," he says against my ear, nipping me.

"But you like to hurt me, Ezra." I lock my legs around his waist and pull him deeper inside me. "You want my tears. You want my fear." I rock against him, my fingers digging into the hard muscles of his back.

He grabs the back of my neck and rolls me over, forcing me to straddle him. He guides my hips, his grip tightening to the point of pain as he forces me to grind over him. When he reaches the deepest part of me, I throw my head back.

"I have your tears." He groans and my gaze locks with his. "And you have no fear, Evie."

I want to fuck him. I want to, for one moment, own him. I take his hands and force them away from my hips, working myself over him hard. His hands trails up my body, squeezing my breast before moving over my throat. Every touch, every movement bleeds through me. I no longer feel dirty. I no longer feel the need to find forgiveness because every time he touches me, I am forgiven. There is nothing I can do with Ezra that is not sacred. I can fuck him, I can kill for him, I can love him, and none of its wrong because he rights me in every way. He is my god, and I am his sinner. And when I love him like this, he is my absolution.

His fingers wind into my hair, fisting it with enough force to cause that burn I crave. He wants to own me, he wants to possess me. And I will let him. I will be his little killer. I will be his filthy whore. I will be his saving grace--whatever he wants I will give him. He yanks my body forward, plastering my chest against his. His lips slam over mine. His hold tightens as he thrusts his tongue inside my mouth, claiming me with every stroke. His hips roll, hard and fast, his fingers claw at my waist as he fucks me from beneath. Ezra demands me to meet each of his thrusts as he is both giving and taking power at the same time. I can't help but to stare at him, into those deep, black eyes of his as he takes what he wants from me. And I let him. I let him take every last piece of me.

His teeth sink into my bottom lip, drawing blood. And I moan. He fucks me until all I can feel is him. He consumes me with every thrust, with every kiss he makes me feel pure and righteous and wanted and clean. His grip tightens, and he groans as he pulls my chest back down over him. I'm raw, and I wince at the sudden movement. This is the pain he loves to give me--fucking me until I feel nothing but him. With every breath, every movement, I will feel him.

My eyes flutter closed, a small smile creeping over my lips as my core tightens. Heat washes over me, bathing me in the blissful fog of relief. Ezra stiffens beneath me, his fingers tearing at my hips as he comes. And here I lay, pressed against my own form of heaven and hell, breathless and pleased and forgiven.

His hands fall to his sides and I sit up, staring down at him. He looks so beautiful beneath me, powerful and dangerous in every way. He is like a storm, angry and violent. A force that can make you find power and strength in the ugliest of places. Ezra will scar you with his presence, leave you tasting blood at his memory, and leave you a wreck, a place of utter destruction in his wake. He has forced me to find beauty in my own destruction. I know why I need him, but I can't figure out why he needs me. And I want him to need me.

"Why, Ezra?" I brush my finger over his arm, tracing my finger over his winding tattoos. "Why did you risk the things you did to save me?"

He flattens his palm against my chest, pushing me until I fall back on to bed. And then, he's over me, his bare body pressing between my thighs. He takes my hand in his, lacing my fingers with his as he pushes my arms above my head.

And yes, he is going to hurt me.

His lips brush mine. "Because I love you, little killer."

My breath catches in the back of my throat as I stare at him, my heart pounding in my ears. "Say it again."

He growls, wrapping one hand around my throat as he brings his lips to my ear. "I love you."

And now you own him, Evelyn. Body and soul...

The End.
Forever and Ever. Amen.

THANK you so much for reading Absolution!

If you love super dark, question your soul taboo reads with a little menage, check out The Game. Available HERE and free in Kindle Unlimited.

OR

Wrong, another dark romance with an alpha male. Available HERE and free in Kindle Unlimited.

KEEP UP TO DATE WITH RELEASES

Sign up to receive a text alert about sales and new releases:
Text READ to 77948 to receive new release text alerts
(US only).
Or join our newsletter and stay up to date:
Join the Mailing List

More books by LP Lovell and Stevie J. Cole

Wrong

The Game

No Prince

No Good

Bad

About the Authors:

Lauren Lovell is a ginger from England. She suffers from a total lack of brain to mouth filter and is the friend you have to explain before you introduce her to anyone, and apologise for afterwards.

She's a self-confessed shameless pervert, who may be suffering from slight peen envy.

Facebook: https://www.facebook.com/lplovellauthor

Stevie J. Cole is a secret rock star. Sex, drugs and, oh wait, no, just sex. She's a whore for a British accent and has an unhealthy obsession with Russell Brand. She and LP plan to elope in Vegas and breed the world's most epic child.

Facebook: https://www.facebook.com/authorsteviejcole

Other books by LP Lovell

She Who Dares series:

Besieged #1

Conquered #2

Surrendered #3

Ruined #4

<u>MAFIA WORLD</u>

Kiss of Death Series

Make Me #0.5

Kill Me #1

Kiss Me #2

Collateral Series

Hate Me #1

Hold Me #2

Touch of Death Series

Loathe Me #1

Leave Me #2

Love Me #3

Standalones

Dirty Boss

The Pope

The Saint

Other books by Stevie J. Cole

White Pawn

Darkest Before Dawn

The Sun

Falling In Between

Over You

ExRated

Pandemic Sorrow Series:

Jag

Rush

Roxy

Stone

Made in the USA
Las Vegas, NV
27 July 2021